THE MEDDLESOME GHOST

THE LOVERS OF STEADFORD ABBEY—BOOK II

Also by Sheila Rosalynd Allen
THE RELUCTANT GHOST:
Lovers of Steadford Abbey—Book I

THE MEDDLESOME GHOST

THE LOVERS OF STEADFORD ABBEY — BOOK II

Sheila Rosalynd Allen

Walker and Company
New York

All the characters and events portrayed in this work are fictitious.

First published in the United States of America in 1989 by Walker Publishing
Company, Inc.

Published simultaneously in Canada by Thomas Allen & Son
Canada, Limited, Markham, Ontario.

Library of Congress Cataloging-in-Publication Data
Allen, Sheila Rosalynd.
The meddlesome ghost / Sheila Rosalynd Allen.
p.   cm.—(The lovers of Steadford Abbey ; bk. 2)
ISBN 0-8027-1083-2
I. Title.   II. Series: Allen, Sheila Rosalynd. Lovers of Steadford Abbey ; bk. 2.
PS3551.L425M4   1989
813'.54—dc20   89-5829
CIP

Printed in the United States of America.
10 8 6 4 2 1 3 5 7 9

FANNIE BURNS WAS a sensible woman, the abigail told herself firmly as she finished washing the breakfast dishes. She was not given to missish ways, Fannie reminded herself as she began to put the Bristol porcelain away.

The biggest room in the tiny gatehouse was the sunny kitchen, slate floored with whitewashed walls and sturdy oak cupboards. A breakfast nook rimmed with large many-paned windows looked out towards the gatehouse rose garden.

Fannie felt her eyes misting up again and reached for a handkerchief in her apron pocket as a stout woman made her way past the last of the late-blooming flowers. It was Hetty Mapes, the Steadford Abbey cook, passing the scarlet ramblers and fat pink cabbage roses. Fannie quickly turned away, hiding her tears as she blew her nose and told herself to be sensible.

Hetty Mapes laboured up the gatehouse path hardly noticing the golden autumn day. Beyond her, thick stone walls meandered around the curves of Abbey Hill. Over-grown with ivy, the walls fenced the hill and ended at the Abbey road and the great stone archway.

High up the gentle hillock the Abbey itself stood tall and proud. At the foot of the hill the ancient gate-clock kept silent sentinel in its perch above the Abbey road, the ancient stone walls ending in stables on one side of the archway and the gatehouse and its rose garden on the other.

"Fannie, have you come down with a cold?" Hetty asked as she stepped over the stone doorsill to see the abigail blowing her nose. "You look all red eyed."

"I'm right as rain," Fannie said with more conviction than she felt. She was not going to behave as if she were a chit of a schoolgirl and give herself over to vapours or a fit of the blue sullens. "What's that you've brought?" Fannie asked, changing the subject.

"I was to the village for the Monday shopping and collected the post from the receiving office." Hetty delivered over an envelope along with her words. "There was a letter for Lady Agatha from America. Oh, and I've brought you some turnips and the sugar you asked after. And a bit of good salt pork for your soup. Is it from Lady Jane?"

"Her Grace, she is now."

"Our little Jane a duchess, can you imagine? Who ever would have thought it? And in the New World with heathen Indians and rebels and so far away from her grandmother and the rest of us."

"The American Revolution's been over for almost thirty years, Hetty. Besides, what with Napoleon carrying on across the channel and poor old King George going barmy here at home, we've other things to worry about these days. Our Jane's got a big strapping husband and two wee children to keep her life plenty busy."

"Maybe three," Hetty said hopefully. She looked rather pointedly at the unopened envelope.

"In five years? Good gracious, what a thing to wish on the girl. Do you want a cup of tea while I take this up to her grandmother?"

"I'd dearly love one, but I'd best not. Young Tim's waiting with the cart." The cook cast an eye out the paned window past the last of the drooping summer roses towards Abbey Hill Road and sighed. "I'd best get back before Mrs. Twicks gets testy."

At the mention of the stiff-necked housekeeper Agatha's odious brother Nigel had sent to oversee the empty house,

Fannie pulled a long face and sniffed. "I don't know how you put up with her, I swear I don't."

Hetty Mapes's words took on a tone of long-suffering forbearance. "We do what we must in this life."

"That's all well and good, but I'd not last out a twelve-month if I had to be around that Friday-faced creature day in and day out."

"I misdoubt if I'll last it out much longer, myself," Hetty agreed. "I wouldn't be here still if we didn't all hope and pray that one day Lady Agatha would be back where she belongs, all right and tight in the Abbey instead of down here in the gatehouse."

"There's nary a chance of that, it seems," Fannie replied. "I must admit I thought when that terrible brother of hers died, he might have done better for her in death than he ever did in life, but you see how it is. He's been gone six months and nary a word. Except for his solicitors to send that nasty Mrs. Twicks and not a word about who the Abbey's new owner is to be."

"She's nasty, that's a fact. And I'd best be off before she asks after her midday nuncheon and me not there to have it ready for her."

"I shall come up later and let you know what Jane has to say for herself, shall I?" Fannie asked as the buxom-hipped woman headed for the doorway.

"We'll share a bit of tea and some lovely fresh biscuits. I'll make extras to send down to Lady Agatha."

"I'll tell her," Fannie promised as the cook trudged back towards her duties.

Left alone, Fannie moved swiftly towards the narrow oak stairwell and the second floor of the tiny gatehouse. Before she started up the stairs, she stopped at the gilded mirror that hung over the hall table, making sure no trace of her tears remained. Eyes of an intelligent blue stared back at her. Satisfied no sign of her discomposure remained, the abigail rose towards the lady she had served for over thirty years.

Lady Agatha Steadford-Smyth was a formidable woman. She had survived the loss of her inheritance to pay for her dead husband's gambling debts. She had survived the loss of the Abbey to her conniving brother, her only son in battle, and her only daughter in childbirth.

She had grown stronger and more stern with each of life's onslaughts. And from father to lover to husband to brother to son, she had seen not only the darker side of men's natures but also the careless ease with which they could break one's heart without a backwards glance.

Her animosity towards the other half of the human race had almost cost her granddaughter Jane's happiness and still coloured Agatha's every exchange with the male of the species. The best that could be said was that she tolerated Jane's husband Charles, who had slowly earned Agatha's grudgingly given and still guarded respect.

His wealth, which had recently grown even larger when the young ninth Earl of Warwick succeeded his father and became the fourth Duke of Melton, had convinced Lady Agatha where Jane's love alone could not.

Agatha Steadford-Smyth knew from her own experience how love could lead a young girl astray. The fact that Jane had chosen wisely was something her grandmother still thanked God for in her nightly prayers, but it had not changed her attitude about men in the least whit.

Now in her sixties, Agatha was a handsome woman, her features still aquiline and her dark eyes wideset and clear as they turned towards the bedroom doorway.

"Ah, Fannie, there you are. You see, I was right. I've found that bolt of kerseymere we were looking for. It had never been unpacked." Lady Agatha straightened up from an open brass-bound trunk with the kerseymere cloth in her hands.

"Hetty's baking biscuits for you this afternoon, and she brought the post from the village receiving office." Fannie handed over the paper packet from America.

Agatha's expression softened, her eyes alight as she took

4

the envelope from her serving woman. "It's from Jane." She looked up. "I think I'll have another cup of tea while I read." Agatha studied Fannie as the serving woman turned to go. "What's wrong with your eyes?"

"What?" Fannie asked, startled. "Nothing's wrong with my eyes."

"Are you still all cut up about your birthday? Fannie Burns, I'm ashamed of you, making such a piece of work over nothing."

"I'm sure I don't know what you mean," Fannie replied with a sniff.

"You've been absolutely vapourish for days. I've never seen you like this in all your life. And I also don't scruple to say I've never in my life seen anyone so concerned about a mere birthday."

"Fifty is not a mere birthday," Fannie said in an accusing and long-suffering tone. "It is a turning point in a body's life."

"Nonsense," Lady Agatha said bracingly. "My girl, when you're about to turn sixty-seven, I'll warrant you'll sing a different tune."

The abigail thought of several quelling replies but bit them back before they were spoken. "I'll get the tea ready," was all Fannie said as she turned and left.

Agatha looked down at the welcome packet. She moved to the windowseat and made herself comfortable before breaking the seal and opening the paper within.

Dearest Gram,
I've not received a letter from you since the beginning of summer, and I've told Charles he must remonstrate with the postal authorities, for I'm sure they've lost all the letters you must have sent me.
If you haven't, I must conclude you've forgotten all about your poor granddaughter and great-grandchildren. Charles said I should include him,

too, so please write and tell us we're not forgotten and how well you are and all the village gossip. Are you on speaking terms with Mrs. Merriweather? Has Charlotte Summerville finally married? Tell us all.

As for my little brood, my husband is happily having the whole of the Orleans Territory dug up and planted. Little Charles is beginning to read, and your namesake Agatha is still cutting teeth and having quite a time of it. Would you send me the receipts you mentioned for teething and the salve? Also some James's Powders.

All is well and we've quite settled in. I wish we could persuade you and Fannie to come visit us. It isn't nearly as primitive as it was when first we came, and you could truly have every comfort you might need. We would dearly love to see you, and introduce little Charles and Agatha to their Gram. It will be at least another long year before we might be able to travel back to dear old England. You can't imagine how strange it is to be here surrounded by so many French-speaking peoples whilst England and France are at odds! We get the news so slowly, but I understand that horrible Napoleon is swallowing the entire continent whole. Is it true he has divorced Josephine and married Marie Louise of Austria?

I've enclosed a note from Charles about Abbey business. It seems you are to have company soon, a distant relation I didn't know we had. Did you know about him?

Please, please, please write as ever so fast as you can and let me know you are well and happy and what is happening and how Fannie and Hetty and Homer and Tim and Martha are and all the others. Sit right down and send me all the news so you don't forget one word of it. I look forward to

hearing from you. Your loving granddaughter, Jane.
"Postscript—I've enclosed two receipts for Fannie
from our new cook who is a positive treasure.
Please tell Fannie to never mind they are a bit
Frenchified, just think patriotic thoughts whilst
she cooks them up.

Agatha reread Jane's letter, glanced at the directions for
an oyster escalop and a cream cake and then unfolded the
note from Charles.

Dear Lady Agatha,
As Jane has said, Major Sir Giles Steadford will be
arriving at the Abbey to recover from wounds
received in the Peninsular Wars.
Your brother Nigel's solicitors should be apprising
you of the exact date of your nephew's arrival. It
seems Nigel named him heir. You probably know
much more than I do, so I shall close with best
wishes and the hope all is well. Charles.

Agatha stared down at the parchments she held. Having
been informed of absolutely nothing by Nigel's estate lawyers she was not only irritated, she was also totally con-
fused. Nigel and she had no other siblings. There was no
Steadford nephew.

She read Jane's welcome letter over again before she
went down to join Fannie in the kitchen and hand over the
letter and the receipts.

Fannie wiped her hands on her apron before taking the
papers. "So what has our Jane to say for herself?" Fannie
asked.

"All's well with them, as you can see."

Fannie stared at her employer. "Why such a long face?"

"It seems a Steadford nephew is to take over the Abbey."

"A Steadford nephew? What nephew?" Fannie asked. "I
never heard tell of one."

7

"Nor is there one. Charles talks of a Major Sir Giles Steadford who can't possibly exist," Agatha said crisply.

Fannie's brow wrinkled up in concentration. "Whatever can he mean?"

"Whatever and *whomever*. Since Nigel's solicitors have not seen fit to apprise me of any of this, I haven't a clue. But I can tell you this, you may trust that if my brother had a hand in it, it will be some kind of skullduggery. Even from the grave," Agatha said darkly.

"I've always said you should have accepted the duke's offer and taken the Abbey off his hands when he and Jane left instead of letting it revert to Nigel."

"I have never asked a man a favour in my entire life, let alone accepted such a gift as that. And I never will," she added firmly.

"It was yours to begin with," Fannie reminded her employer.

"I am quite content with the gatehouse," Lady Agatha said flatly. "And you have been, too. It's much better suited to our needs than that huge old Abbey. You yourself have said so."

"I've said it's easier for me to keep up than the Abbey ever was and that's a fact, since all of it would practically fit in your old bedchambers. But it's still not right that you were done out of it, and when Jane's husband was willing to make a present of it to you, you should have accepted."

"Fannie, it's over and done with these five years past."

"And now we shall have to contend with a military man," the abigail said. "That will surely turn Mrs. Twicks topsy-turvy."

Agatha gave a frosty smile. "That thought could almost make a man welcome, whoever he is."

Fannie grinned. "It will give her a fair turn, 'pon my soul. I wonder what he's like?"

"If he's anything near my brother he'll be a tallow-faced, shallow-witted twiddle-pop!" And, with that, Agatha sat down to her tea and toast. "When you go up to the Abbey this afternoon you'd best let them know," Lady Agatha said before dismissing the subject altogether. "The old house certainly isn't ready for a new owner after five years of neglect and six months of that odious Mrs. Twicks."

It was seven days, a sennight, later when a letter finally arrived from Ambruster and Phibes, Solicitors at Law. The executors of Nigel Steadford's estate informed her ladyship that Nigel's heir was the son of Nigel's and Agatha's long-dead cousin Frederick.

"They say that Major Sir Giles Steadford, having distinguished himself in the Peninsular Wars and having been wounded on the famous march to Talavera has sold out his cavalry commission and will be making his home at the Abbey at least until he recovers his health," Lady Agatha told Fannie as they sat in the gatehouse parlour, mending hems.

"He's to arrive before the month is out," she continued.

"And what's this about staying until his health is better?" Fannie asked.

"It seems they've not talked directly. They don't know if he intends to keep or to sell the property. After all, he's inherited a great deal more than the Abbey."

"And so he's to sell and some strangers are moving in?" Fannie asked.

"We'll just have to wait and see."

"And isn't that nice? Are we to try to curry favour with this upstart rather than be thrown out on our ears, then? Is that what it has all come to?"

"We've nothing to fear," her employer said. "Thanks to Charles," she added unwillingly. "The duke insisted on giving me clear title to the gatehouse when he sold back the rest of the land to Nigel. So this great-nephew I never heard of can keep to himself and not bother with our comings and goings."

"Mayhap he'll not be so bad," Fannie said.

"Mayhap he'll be just like the man who chose him, a

narrow-minded idiot who probably has his military title because Nigel bought him his pair of colours."

"Lord help us," Fannie replied.

"The Lord will do as He pleases. Whilst He does, you'd best let Twicks know her new master will be arriving any day."

"I suppose I shall have to tell her," Fannie said in a fatalistic tone. "Though I can think of nothing I should like less."

= 2 =

THE GOLDEN AUTUMN sun was high in the clear afternoon sky as Fannie trudged up the Abbey road towards the building which was built when Henry the Eighth ruled England.

The hill fell away behind her gently, towards the home farms in the near distance. Farther away, the northern moors were lost from view behind a forest of elms and chestnuts and ancient oaks. Nearer by copper beeches lined the driveway Fannie followed as she rose through woodland violets towards the wide porticoe that housed the Abbey's huge front doors.

Large oriel windows supported by sturdy stone corbels were set to each side of the entrance which sat above wide, shallow steps. Fannie walked around the side of the three-storey house to the kitchen entrance, the sound of muffled voices growing louder as she neared the side door.

"I demand it stops at once!" Fannie heard Mrs. Twicks say, the housekeeper's voice even more strident than usual.

The answer she received was too low for Fannie to hear as she opened the kitchen door. The smell of baking cinnamon filled the warm air inside the massive room, the voices coming from the pantry beyond.

"I don't care what you say!" Mrs. Twicks's words were raspy, as if she had been yelling for a very long time.

"But, Mrs. Twicks, I swear, I don't know anything about—"

"I don't want to hear it. Do you hear me? I won't put up

with such treatment a moment longer."

The young houseboy Tim slipped into the kitchen from the door to the backstairs. Seeing Fannie, he put his finger to his lips, silencing her until he came near enough to whisper.

"Mrs. Twicks be in rare form, Miss Fannie. Best not to disturb her."

"What's happened?"

The lad took on an innocent expression, looking more like twelve than his actual eighteen years of age. "I'm sure I couldn't say, Miss Fannie."

Fannie's blue eyes twinkled. "Couldn't say I can believe. What have you been up to?"

"It's not me," he replied. "It's the Ghost."

Before Fannie could reply the pantry door burst open, a gaunt-looking woman hurtling herself forwards. She braked just before she ran into Fannie Burns.

"You," she rasped. "I know you're part of it, too!"

"I don't know what you're talking about," Fannie said, nettled. The taller woman was only inches from Fannie's face and looked ready to fight.

"Oh, you don't, don't you? I'm talking about tricks! My sewing basket upended, my lamps doused, my windows unlocked in the dead of the night. I could have died of a chill and none of you would have cared. I can't even play Patience without my cards flying off the table!"

"Well, you certainly can't blame me for that," Fannie told the woman.

"I don't know which of you is doing what, but I don't believe in ghosts and I won't be treated in such a vicious, underhanded fashion. I shall leave," she ended dramatically.

"Would you want me to get the cart for you, Mrs. Twicks?" young Tim asked hopefully.

Fannie gave the young man a quelling glance. "She can't leave now. The new master's on his way."

Tim looked towards Hetty Mapes for support, but Mrs. Twicks was already moving towards the front hall.

"I can and I shall," Mrs. Twicks was saying. "You think you'll send me to Bedlam but you won't. I'll have the last word, just you wait and see. I shall inform the solicitors of your behaviour. All of you."

"Now wait just a minute, there," Fannie began, but Mrs. Twicks was already slamming the green baise door.

"Don't, Fannie," the cook said. "Don't try to stop her. It's better this way."

"And what's to be done about the new master?" Fannie asked.

"We can take care of things," Tim put in. "Lady Agatha can come back and make things right."

Before Fannie could reply, Tim turned on his heels and headed outside, fairly racing to get the Abbey cart hitched up.

"This is a terrible state of affairs," Fannie said without much conviction.

"Perhaps you could convince Lady Agatha?" Hetty asked hopefully.

"I'm sure I couldn't do any such thing. She'll be aghast. She'll be . . ." The abigail trailed off, trying to imagine her employer's reaction to this turn of events. "She'll disapprove of all of you."

"But it's Mrs. Twicks who's gone off and left us in the lurch," the cook replied. "You heard it with your own two ears."

Fannie hesitated, watching the hopeful expression on her old friend's face. "If I tell her what the woman said, Lady Agatha will think her demented."

Hetty smiled. And, slowly, so did Fannie.

Within the hour, Mrs. Twicks had thrown her belongings helter-skelter into her large valise and dragged it down the stairs towards the wide front door.

Tim sprang towards her when he saw her come through the door, reaching for the bag and helping her heft it into the back of the cart.

In another moment the steady clip-clop of a horse's hoofs started down the Abbey road, as the stable man Homer drove Mrs. Twicks away. Watched by Fannie, Tim, the cook on the steps, and the maid Martha hiding in the open doorway, the carriage reached the curve of the road under the Abbey gateway and disappeared from view.

Fannie stared at the empty road. "What on earth brought all this on?"

"She said we were playing tricks on her," Hetty replied. "But none were."

"It was the Ghost," Tim put in.

"Ghost?" Fannie glared at the boy. "If you want to keep your head on top of your neck, you'll not mention such things around Lady Agatha. She doesn't believe in ghosts and gets very upset when the subject is brought up."

"I think it was just one ghost," Hetty put in.

"Not *a* ghost. The *Abbey* Ghost," Tim corrected the cook. "She's quite done up about it, poor thing." His sympathy would have sounded more genuine if it had not been accompanied by a wide grin. "I can't imagine why."

Hetty Mapes tried to stifle the laughter that gurgled up inside and threatened to spill over. She pulled her apron to her mouth and pressed it there, her small brown eyes alight with mischief as her pudgy hands held the apron high.

"Wherever does the woman think she is going?" Fannie asked. "Running off from a job with no references. She won't get very far."

"She's going as far as her two legs will carry her. At least that's what she said, and we're taking her at her word," Tim replied, still grinning.

"You had a hand in this, Timothy," Fannie said as the three of them walked back inside the huge house and towards the Abbey kitchens.

"She got all done up about a wee bit of spookery." Tim's eyes grew large and innocent. "Made her take to the blue ruin, it did. I can't imagine why. And then, tippled, she nearly killed herself on the stairwell last night. I guess her cards flying today were the last straw."

"I'm sure I don't care how much gin she drank, and I'm sure I didn't like her, nor did I approve of cardplaying in the middle of the day, but I don't hold with trying to kill people either. No matter who they are."

"We never!" Hetty and Timothy both burst out almost in the same breath.

"And she knew her job," Fannie continued relentlessly. "Whether we liked how she did it or not. Thanks to all this tomfoolery she may have the last laugh yet."

Hetty and Tom stopped walking as they neared the green baise door to the kitchens and stared at Lady Agatha's abigail.

Hetty slowly dropped her apron. "What's wrong then, Fannie? What are you saying? Are you going to tell Lady Agatha and have us put off for driving her away?"

"As if I ever would," Fannie scoffed.

"Because we didn't do all that," Hetty said. "She must have been drunk as a lord to imagine some of the things she imagined happening. It's good riddance to bad rubbish, if any want my opinion. You yourself told me she followed you around when you came up to the Abbey as if you were going to steal the silver, and this having been your lifelong home and her barely here a year."

"I've not said I feel the least particle of sympathy for her. It's you all I'm worried about," Fannie replied. She pushed the green baise door open and walked down the narrow hall to the wide, spacious kitchens.

"We was just having a bit of fun," Tim defended as he and Hetty followed Lady Agatha's servant. "Keeping her awake at night with stories about the Ghost and noises and all. If she took them to heart and started imagining things, it's not all our fault."

"That's all well and good," Fannie said. "But now who will ready the house for the new owner?"

Hetty stared at her companion. "Have you heard when he's to come?"

"That's what I was coming to tell you. He's to arrive any day," Fannie told the cook and the footman.

Tim stared back with rounded eyes. "The new owner, he's a military man, isn't he?" he asked, his voice full of worship.

"Any day!" Hetty Mapes gave young Tim a push. "Go quick and saddle up. You've got to stop Homer before he reaches the post road, or Mrs. Twicks will be gone for good."

"But we wanted her gone," Tim complained.

"Yes, but now we need her back double-quick."

"Why?" Tim asked. He turned towards Fannie. "Why can't you and Lady Agatha see to the house? You've done it for years past remembering."

"It's no longer our concern," Fannie told the boy. "It was sold out from under us, and that's that."

"But couldn't you help?"

Fannie looked at the boy and then at the cook. If truth were told, she hadn't minded seeing the back of the house-keeper who had been foisted upon them to ensure that Nigel Steadford's holdings were not interfered with by his sister. His holdings that he'd stolen right out from under that sister and all knew it.

"I could ask her," Fannie said slowly. She was rewarded by wide smiles. "Not that you can count on it, mind. She just may wash her hands of the whole affair."

"It's her house and always has been, no matter who says what," Hetty Mapes replied. "And she'll not want it looking poorly when the nephew arrives. Speaking of the nephew, didn't you say she hadn't any? Who is this new owner?"

"He's not her nephew. There was only Nigel and herself after all. This is her cousin Frederick's son, not a nephew at all."

"What's he like?" Tim asked, his eyes alight with questions.

"Since she never knew he existed, I'm sure I've no idea," Fannie replied tartly. "He's a major and a sir and was with the Cavalry, wounded in Portugal. That's all I know."

"The poor man, how was he wounded?" Hetty asked.

"Poor man," Tim scoffed. "He's a right and proper soldier, that's what he is!"

"I don't know anything about his wounds, and I don't know anything about his being right and proper. What I do know is he's to arrive any day, and,"—she gave young Tim a long look—"being a military man, he shall probably expect discipline and obedience in his household." Fannie let her words sink in before she continued to Hetty. "I'd best get back and inform her ladyship of what's what."

"You've no cause to blame us," Tim said. "Mrs. Twicks complained about all kinds of things we didn't do. We just helped her along a little."

"All kinds of things you didn't do," Fannie said disparagingly.

"Well, we didn't," Tim defended himself and the rest of the staff. "Like the terrible drafts she complained about. We all know it's the chinks in the windows, but she kept saying there was something unnatural about them, as if the house were after her or something."

"How silly," Hetty Mapes interjected.

As the words hit the air, a terrible draft poured through the overheated kitchen. The cook, the abigail, and the footman shivered, staring at each other.

"Did you feel something?" Tim asked.

"No," Fannie replied. "Did you hear something?"

Hetty shivered. "No. I mean, I didn't . . . did you?"

"Of course not," Fannie rejoined crisply, her hands still rubbing her arms. "I'd best get back to Lady Agatha," she told them.

"Put in a good word about helping, then," Hetty called out as Fannie started away.

Young Tim watched the abigail. "Things are going to be different around here with a military man in charge," he said, his face alight with hero worship.

"No doubt they are, and you'd best watch he doesn't find out what a lazy layabout you are, Timothy Jones, or you'll be the next to show his backside to the Abbey walls."

"I never!" Tim replied hotly.

"That's exactly my point," Hetty Mapes told him. "You never." With that, she left the youth standing on the wide front porch, going back to her duties, as Lady Agatha's abigail disappeared down the Abbey road.

Two weeks later yet another letter for Lady Agatha was brought up to the Abbey where she and Fannie were overseeing the readying of the Abbey for its new owner. Surprised to receive another letter from the solicitors for her brother's estate, she broke the seal and began to read. Her expression turned grim.

"I'm to be compensated," Agatha Steadford-Smyth voiced the words in ringing tones that spoke of both wrath and shock. "Compensated!" Her scorn rose to higher limits as she turned to confront her abigail. "Since Mrs. Twicks tendered her resignation at such an awkward moment, Nigel's solicitors propose that I see to putting the Abbey in order and to the new owner's comfort until a new house-keeper can be procured. They say I will be fairly compen-sated." Lady Agatha's eyes blazed.

"They wouldn't dare say such a thing," Fannie defended stoutly.

Lady Agatha waved the lawyers' parchment towards her abigail. "They could, they would, and they do. As if I would neglect my duty unless some stranger offered me money, and so they propose to pay me. I've never been so insulted in my life."

Fannie sniffed. "Londoners," she said, as if the one word explained all bad manners. "You should wash your hands of all of this."

"My duty is still my duty, no matter what my feelings are in the matter," her employer said practically. "Aside from which we've been seeing to getting the Abbey ready ever since Mrs. Twicks left so precipitously." Agatha shook her head a little, the lace on her white silk cap moving against her thick chestnut hair. "For the life of me I still don't understand what made the woman run off like that. I own I didn't like her, but I never thought her to be flighty."

Fannie kept a prudent silence on the subject of Mrs. Twicks's departure. Lady Agatha would not approve of the servants playing tricks on a housekeeper, and she would like talk of the Abbey Ghost even less.

Fannie was saved from answering by Martha's arrival with an armload of bed linens.

"Lady Agatha, I can't find even one that hasn't been mended already or isn't in need of it," the maid told the Abbey's former owner.

"We've pinched pennies for years and that's a fact," Fannie put in.

"We'll sort them into piles," Agatha said. "The ones with the least mending will be for the major's bed. You must make sure to make up the beds with the mending at the foot, Martha, not at the top."

"Mayhap the new master will be rich and buy all new," Martha said hopefully.

"If he's anything near my late brother, his wealth won't be put to use in house repairs but gambling and other foolish male occupations."

As she spoke, Lady Agatha walked towards the small blue parlour, Martha and Fannie following. Behind them the hall widened into the large entryway, light streaming down into it from above.

Up above the oak stairwell tall, square, mullioned windows lined the Long Gallery, letting in the autumn sunlight that warmed the wide oak stairs and poured down onto the stone floor below.

In the fingers of light that brightened the dark hall a form shimmered just on the edge of visibility. The voices of the three women came back along the hallway from the open door to the blue parlour.

"Get the rest of the pillowcases, too," Agatha said as Martha came out of the parlour and started towards the stairs. The maid walked straight through the almost visible apparition, never seeing a thing.

"I believe the words 'excuse me' are still in the English vocabulary," Harry said, his form growing more luminous in the dark hall as he moved towards the open doorway. "I don't know why I bother to talk, since none of you have the wit to hear me."

Dressed in tattered pantaloons and an antique velvet jacket that had also seen better days, Sir Harry was not in the finest of form as he headed towards the blue parlour.

Inside Fannie was helping Lady Agatha sort the linens. The Ghost drew near unobserved and peered at the work they were doing.

"The old house seems like itself again with you back in it, Aggie." He rubbed what used to be his hands together. "It's taken you too long to decide to move back in."

"Is the master's suite ready?" Agatha asked her servant.

"Martha says young June from the village is finishing up the polishing and all's been aired and the carpets beaten. She says the girl hopes you'll keep her on once the new owner arrives."

"New owner?" Harry straightened up. "What's all this about a new owner? I haven't heard anything about a new owner."

"That will be his decision to make," Lady Agatha said.

"If some rattlepate thinks he can come here and take over, he'll have me to contend with," Harry promised, his brow beetling into angry lines. "I got rid of that miserable excuse for a woman, Twicks, and I'll get rid of any others that move into Aggie's house."

"I wonder what the major's like?" Fannie said as she folded another mended sheet.

"Much too much like Nigel probably."

"Nigel!" Harry's voice rose and so did his frustration as none heard him. "I thought he died."

"Lord, that's all we need around here," said Fannie. "I'll take these up then and see where Martha's gotten to."

"Have Hetty set out some tea while you're about it,"

Agatha replied, bending over her task.

"Aggie, I won't stand for it. I won't have any more outsiders here," Harry declared.

Lady Agatha straightened up and turned, her brow furrowing. She gazed straight towards Harry, her look took his breath away.

"Aggie, girl, can you finally see me?" he asked hopefully.

Harry watched her eyes narrow.

"Lady Agatha." The footman Tim stood in the doorway.

She shook her head and turned away from the apparition.

"Drat the young pup," Harry roared silently. "She almost saw me, I'd swear it."

"Lady Agatha, Homer says you're to look at the washstand he's brought down from the attics to see if it's the one you wanted."

"I'll be there directly," she told Tim. Agatha picked up the sorted linens and started out into the hall, Tim ahead of her and Harry trailing behind, still voicing dire threats that none could hear.

"I won't have it," he declared at the foot of the steps, watching her start up towards the second floor. "I'll have you here or I'll have none. And it has to be Steadfords who live here or I'll *never* be free of this cursed condition!"

As they reached the second floor young June passed Lady Agatha and Fannie, coming down the stairs carrying a pile of blankets that almost reached her nose.

As she neared the bottom step she slowed. Standing at the foot of the stairs was a giant of a man, a man she'd never seen before. Dressed in odd clothes, his face angry, the outlines of his body seemed to grow larger and larger as he thundered at her. "I won't have any here but Aggie!"

June's eyes widened as her knees weakened. Her arms went numb, the blankets falling to the floor as she cried out. "Dear Lord, it's the Abbey Ghost!"

Harry, taken aback by the girls seeing him, shrank out of sight as she watched. She began to scream for her mother as she pulled her apron up in front of her face and ducked her head, running towards the green baise door and other humans.

Upstairs Agatha looked back down the hall. "What was that?" she asked.

"It's probably just another new maid seeing the Ghost," Tim said in a practical tone of voice.

"What on earth are you talking about?" Lady Agatha asked.

"The boy doesn't know what he's saying," Fannie said quickly.

"He's got the right of it, nonetheless," Homer said. "The new ones every once in a while see a curtain move or some such and remember the tales told in the village."

Lady Agatha clucked her tongue. "Is that old nonsense still being bandied about?"

Young Tim stared at her. "Have you never seen him then?"

Agatha Steadford-Smyth hesitated for just a fraction of a second, remembering the moment in the parlour below when she'd thought something was with her. Fleeting thoughts of other times long ago came to mind, but she dismissed them. She knew there was no such thing as a ghost.

"There's no such thing, and I've no time to discuss such nonsense," Lady Agatha told her servants flatly. "Fannie, go see what all that noise was about. And if it was some silly ninnyhammer scaring herself because a breeze bestirred, give her a good talking to. I won't have any of that behaviour around the new owner. Nor talk of nonsense such as ghosts. Tim, you help Homer bring this to the master's suite," she said. "Come along now, we've got more than enough work to keep everyone busy."

Lady Agatha led the way down the upper hallway, passing directly in front of the invisible Harry.

"Don't you worrit your head about his new owner, Aggie, my dear. I'll take care of the likes of him," Harry promised. "He'll be sorry he ever stepped foot in Steadford Abbey."

=== 3 ===

THE ARRIVAL OF Major Sir Giles Steadford, late of the First Cavalry, sent the long-unused Abbey into a whirlwind of activity.

For three weeks before his coach-and-four drove up the Abbey hill, Lady Agatha saw to the hiring of more help and the cleaning, polishing, and refurbishing of every inch of the ancient house.

The Holland covers that had protected chairs and divans for almost five years were taken off. The floors in the downstairs public rooms were polished to a shine. The carpets in the bedrooms aired and beaten, the worn drugget in the upstairs hallway replaced with money forwarded by the lawyers.

The house smelled of soap, beeswax, and turpentine. The curtains and drapes had been taken down and cleaned and aired, and sunlight poured into all the parlours and lounges and bedchambers and sitting-rooms.

Homer was the first to see the coach coming up the Abbey hill. He came running into the house to inform Lady Agatha so that the staff could be assembled to greet the new owner.

She hurried the servants into position in the entrance hall, arranging them in order of importance. With a butler yet to be hired, the cook took precedence over the maids, undermaids, stable men, and footmen who prepared to bow low to the new master of Steadford Abbey.

Fannie stood at the head of the line of servants but behind

Lady Agatha, apart from the household help. The sounds of the coach-and-four echoed through the entrance hall as it came to a stop at the foot of the wide, shallow steps. Lady Agatha nodded towards young Tim. He leapt forwards and opened the heavy brass-hinged front door in time to see the coachman leap from his seat to the ground.

The man leaned down to lower the coach steps as Tim watched, his young and innocent eyes round with hope and expectation. Behind him, he could feel the entire staff straining forwards to get a first glimpse at the man who would make or break their careers.

Tim saw a tall, slim man descend the few short steps and motion to the coachman. At first Tim thought this thin patrician was the new owner, but a moment's reflexion brought other thoughts. The man seemed whole, no wounds afflicting his narrow form. And that narrow form was encased in plain black garments which bespoke a servant. Not a military officer, let alone a wounded one who had left the glory of the Peninsular Wars to come to such a backwater as these Dorset hills.

As Timothy watched, his questions were answered by a loud voice which suddenly barked from the innards of the huge coach, startling the listeners in the Abbey hall.

"Jack? Jack! Where are you, man? How long am I to be kept waiting by your bungling incompetence?"

His voice carried inside, sobering the faces of the waiting servants. Fannie made a disapproving sound and was immediately reprimanded by one quelling look from Lady Agatha.

Fannie, however, was undeterred by her employer's gaze. "I feel sorry for us all," she said.

"You'll feel sorrier," Agatha told her tartly, "if you don't learn to govern your tongue."

"Just listen to him," Fannie replied, voicing what the others were thinking.

Outside, at the bottom of the wide stone steps, the thin man in black glanced towards young Tim who still held the door open.

"You'd best help," the man said as Tim bounded down the steps. "You can take his feet and guide us to his bed."

Tim did as he was bid, standing by the bottom of the coach steps and peering inside, curious about the man who was at the moment cursing loudly and continually inside the closed coach.

"Be careful there, blast you, I'm not a side of beef! Pull up my cape, imbecile, you'll step on it and send us all careening. Damn and blast! Be careful with that leg. What the devil do you think you're about?"

As the deep voice continued to bellow instructions and abuse, the owner's body appeared from the interior of the coach. Jack emerged first, holding the bottom of the hammock carrier very like a sailor's berth aboard ship.

Tim backed up the Abbey steps, Jack following Tim's lead. The coachman, holding the top of the hammoc contraption, was nearest to the source of the vituperation which still issued from the lips of the man who lay prone on the hammock.

"Watch what you're doing, you've nearly slammed my arm into the doorway, you dolt. Jack! Jack!"

"I'm here, Sir Giles," Jack replied.

"And where else would you be?" Giles asked pettishly. "I'm well aware of where you are, how could I not be? I can't move an inch without your help, damn and blast your miserable hide."

As Major Sir Giles Steadford bespoke himself, he was being carried aloft up the Abbey steps and into the wide, echoing entrance hall, filling it with the sound of the new master's petulant anger.

The expectant looks and smiles evaporated from the waiting servants' faces. Their eyes dropped as the man on the litter was carried, complaining, into the house.

"Take care what you're about," he snapped, "I am not a sack of potatoes."

Lady Agatha stepped forwards. "Major Steadford, I am Agatha Steadford-Smyth. Welcome to Steadford Abbey."

Dark blue eyes turned to rake across the older woman's patrician face. Pain lines edged the soldier's eyes, grooving his forehead and thinning the line of his lips.

"I wasn't aware I had to suffer through any relatives," he said ungraciously.

Unseen and unheard, Harry shimmered in one of the tall, mullioned windows. "How *dare* you speak to your betters in such a fashion, you ungracious upstart."

"I was told I had the Abbey to myself," Sir Giles continued curtly.

"As you do," Agatha said crisply.

"We'll just see about that," Harry said darkly.

"I was asked to put the house in order for your arrival," Lady Agatha continued.

"The young pup ain't worth his salt," Harry told one and all, but none heard him. "Aggie, I won't have him here, I won't, and that's flat."

"I have done as my late brothers' solicitors required, and I have waited only for you to arrive and approve of your staff before I leave."

"How the deuce can I approve of them? I don't know just how bad they are yet. But I'm sure I shall soon find out," he said waspishly.

Harry drifted down from the ceiling, enraged at the man's tone. "Bad? I'll show you bad, you addlepated twit. If this is the kind of ungracious whelp our soldiers have become, I shudder for the entire Kingdom."

Lady Agatha showed no sign of the quick anger that had risen within her at Sir Giles's words. "I assure you, you will find your staff to be the most competent in the entire county."

"Which probably doesn't signify much," the wounded soldier said even more ungraciously. "Jack, see me to my rooms."

"Yes, Sir Giles, the boy was just about to show the way." The obviously long-suffering Jack motioned to young Tim.

"Well, be quick about it," Giles said irritably. "This confounded contraption is breaking my back."

Fannie watched the coachman and Jack manoeuver the testy man's litter up the wide stairwell. Tim reached to help as Sir Giles gave curt instructions to each of them.

"Watch what you're about, Jack. You'll have me on the floor. You, there, hold my head higher, I can't see the stairs."

"He's worse than Sir Nigel," Fannie told Aggie as the men disappeared up the oak stairwell. "I didn't think it possible."

"Men." Lady Agatha dismissed the entire subject, her expression and tone of voice carrying the weight of a lifetime's disappointments with the male of the species.

"You'd best get back to your work," Lady Agatha told the staff. "I'm sure you'll be meeting Sir Giles as the days continue."

"As if we want to," Homer said sourly, voicing reactions of the others as he stomped out of the house. "Good thing the stables are far enough away not to hear him bellowing, that's all I can say."

Harry drifted down closer to Agatha. "I won't allow this, Aggie. I'm sorry, for he's a Steadford and your relative and all, but I won't have him here. I'm to do penance to Steadfords but not *that* much penance." Harry followed the unhearing Agatha as she walked through the green baise door behind Hetty. "Besides, I couldn't help him if I tried. None can help the likes of him, and well you can see it. There's no hope for this one." Harry watched Hetty pour tea from a brown-glazed pot. "I don't know how I can help *anyone*," he said fretfully. "If you can't even hear me, how am I supposed to help, and if I can't help, what's to become of me? Forced to wander these halls forever, that's what I'll be. It's almost as if Nigel planned all this just to foil me from his grave."

While Harry carried on his solitary litany of grievances, Lady Agatha accepted a cup of tea from the cook.

"I'll never stay, Lady Agatha. You know how much I think of you, but I'll never be able to work for that man."

"I don't blame you," Fannie told Hetty Mapes.

"Fannie," Agatha said repressively, "this is not your concern."

"Living in the gatehouse is going to be living too close to the likes of him, if you ask me," Fannie said flatly.

"None *are* asking you," Lady Agatha told her serving woman tartly. She turned her attention to the cook. "Hetty, the man is wounded and has just completed a long and arduous journey. It's not fair to judge upon such short acquaintance."

"But you can see how he treats his own man," Hetty retorted. "He'll not be better with the rest of us."

"I was asked to ensure the household was in order for the major," Agatha told the cook. "As I'm sure you are aware I was asked to help because Mrs. Twicks left. And I am perfectly sure you realise the poor woman was practically driven from these walls." Agatha watched Hetty's round cheeks stain red.

"It wasn't only me," Hetty defended herself.

"Nevertheless, I was asked to put the Abbey staff in order, and if you leave upon such short notice I will not have carried out my duty."

The cook hesitated, torn between her instant dislike of the new owner and her loyalty to Lady Agatha.

"I suppose I can manage until he settles in," Hetty replied fatalistically. "For you, Lady Agatha. Not for any else would I do it."

"Thank you, Hetty."

The cook watched the aging matriarch start away. "I can't promise how long I'll be able to stay," she warned Lady Agatha's back as the Abbey's former owner walked towards the front of the house.

Fannie added before she followed her mistress, "If I were you, Hetty Mapes, and I own I'm glad I'm not, I'd stay to my kitchens and never give the man a chance to see more than my backside moving away from him."

"Fannie?" Lady Agatha's imperious voice called out from the hallway beyond, and Fannie hurried to catch up.

Hetty Mapes was left alone in the kitchen. She poured herself a cup of tea and sat down at the bare kitchen table, reaching for sugar and an earthenware jug of fresh cream. Filling the chipped porcelain cup to the brim with cream and sugar, the rotund woman stirred the tea, her expression glum.

The Abbey had been her home for almost two decades, long before Nigel Steadford stole it out from under his only sister. It was a shame, that's what it was. The whole thing was a terrible shame and more than a person should be expected to stand. Hetty wondered how Lady Agatha was able to be so calm about it all.

While the cook drank her tea in the kitchen far below, young Tim was being ushered out of the master's suite along with the coachman.

"You'd best go to stables and see to the horses," Jack told the driver. "The major is very particular about his cattle."

"He's a mite too particular about a mort of things, if you ask me," the coachman said in a low tone.

"Did you say something?" Jack asked the man.

"My dad's the best stable man in the county," Tim put in.

"Jack," the major's voice barked out from the bedroom beyond.

"He'll want his tea in an hour," Jack told Tim. "Buttered toast and sausage or ham should do it, along with some brandy."

"Jack, where are you, have you gone deaf?"

"I'll be there directly, Sir Giles," Jack called out. He closed the hall door on young Tim and the coachman before walking back into the master bedroom.

The master's suite consisted of a good-sized sitting-room, a large bedroom, and three smaller rooms—one a dressing room, one the valet's bedroom, and the other a private bath installed by Lady Agatha's father, Sir Ambrose Steadford.

The suite was wainscotted in oak and papered with a dark blue design flecked with tiny golden crescents. Richly appointed with Chippendale cherrywood furniture and a huge carved walnut clothespress, the bedroom faced the west lawns and a stand of ancient oaks far across the grounds. Beyond the oaks, glimpses of the River Stour could be seen glittering in the early September sunlight.

Giles Steadford was propped up in the huge carved walnut bed, staring out the windows at the lands that slipped away down the hillside and towards the distant river and the village beyond.

"Are you ready to bathe, Sir Giles?" Jack asked as he came into the bedroom.

"Are they gone?" Giles asked back.

"Yes, sir, we're alone."

"Good." He waved his man back as Jack came near the bed. "I haven't the strength to do anything more than lie here. Damn and blast the miserable Frenchies."

"I've sent for tea in an hour. Perhaps you'd rather have it earlier?"

"Let me try to sleep," Giles said. "Tell them two hours, and wake me when it arrives."

"Of course, Sir Giles."

Jack picked up the major's discarded clothes and boots, Giles making a sound under his breath when he stared at the highly polished boots. "Useless," he said.

"I beg your pardon, sir?"

"Useless boots for useless feet," Giles said. He watched the perfect equanimity of his manservant's expression, his own mouth twisting into a lopsided smile. "I suppose all of them below-stairs are already cursing my arrival and vowing to stay well away from me."

Jack looked his employer in the eye. "I would rather imagine they are, sir. Wasn't that your plan?"

Giles lost his smile. "You know me too well," was all he replied.

He closed his eyes, his head resting on fat down pillows, his body stretching the length of the overlong bed. His forehead remained creased with the visible stamp of the pain that wracked his limbs as he drifted off into an uneasy sleep.

$==4==$

A WEEK AFTER Major Sir Giles Steadford arrived at Steadford Abbey, the nights turned cold as autumn touched the Dorset hills and coloured the landscape. The cooling weather was no colder than the uneasy situation between master and servants in the huge old house.

The word which came down the hill to the Abbey gate-house was brought by disgruntled servants who informed Fannie in ringing terms, and Lady Agatha in more subdued ones, that the only thing keeping them from walking out altogether was loyalty to their former mistress.

Lady Agatha thanked each of them quietly, but her words were firm and to the point. They had a duty to perform their tasks well, no matter their personal feelings for the man. He was not only their master. He was also a soldier wounded in performance of his duties for King and country. He had been fearfully wounded while protecting England's interests abroad, and he had earned the right to respect and respectful service from his employees.

Fannie had fewer and less kind words for Lady Agatha's unlikable relative but grudgingly admitted they must live up to their responsibilities and do their duty like good English people always had and always would. And so, a week to the day from when he arrived, Major Sir Giles had not yet driven any of Lady Agatha's old retainers from the Abbey. Although there were dark hints he soon might.

That Friday night a late September chill frosted the

branches of the large oak that leaned over the gatehouse eaves, brushing against the roof. The moon was a sliver of white surrounded by a vast ink-black sky, the countryside shrouded in shadows.

The silence around the gatehouse was disturbed here and there by small sounds: a dog's faraway bark, the restlessness of a stabled horse, Fannie's light snoring in the small bedroom at the end of the upstairs hall.

The pounding which suddenly began against the gatehouse door resonated through the small house, forcing its two inhabitants awake. Fannie awoke with a start, her heart pounding along with the fist on the front door. Lady Agatha came to sleepy consciousness, her hearing bad enough that she was aware of only an echo of the urgent rapping.

"Fannie? What is that?" Lady Agatha called out.

Fannie opened Lady Agatha's bedroom door. "Someone must have lost their minds," she said tartly. "Bothering people at this hour of the night."

"You'd best see who it is."

"I'll not only see them, I'll give them a piece of my mind," Fannie replied. "If it's that young scamp Timothy all upset about another foaling mare, I'll give him a proper melting."

Agatha sat up in bed, her nightcap askew. Long tendrils of silver grey escaped their cotton lace confines and hung about her shoulders as she turned up the bedside oil lamp and reached for a nightrobe on the oak rocker beside her bed.

Downstairs, Fannie finished belting her warm wool flannel robe as she reached the front door. "Stop that noise," she hollered.

"Lady Agatha?"

"Who's that?" she asked suspiciously.

"This is Jack Fence. For God's sake, open up. My master is ill, and I must talk to Lady Agatha."

Lady Agatha had reached the bottom of the narrow stairwell. "Open the door, Fannie."

"It sounds as if we've a crazed Bedlamite out there," Fannie protested. But she obeyed Lady Agatha's instructions and unlatched the door.

Major Steadford's valet pushed past Fannie, a nightrobe over his white sleeping gown. "Lady Agatha, they said you'd know who to call. My master's ill." He stopped just below the first step to the upper floor where Lady Agatha still stood.

"What are his symptoms?" she asked.

"He's bad. I think it's the wound in his back again. He's feverish, and I can't get the fever down. He doesn't know who I am or where he is. We've got to get help!"

"Calm yourself," Agatha told the man sternly. "You were a soldier, weren't you?"

Jack Fence stared at the woman, then slowly took a deep breath, and another. "It's different in the field," he told her. "There's danger all around and not a lot of time to think about it. You just do what you're told."

Agatha looked past the agitated man. "Fannie, rouse up young Tim and send him for Dr. Sayles in Stoneybridge. Tell him to take the fastest horse and tell the doctor we've a wounded and delirious soldier here." Agatha Steadford-Smyth looked at the thin man before her.

Pale, dishevelled from lack of sleep, his face was sober, his eyes honest.

"Your Major must not be quite the ogre one might think at first meeting, for you to care so much about him."

Jack's expression flickered between concern and a flash of wry humour. "His bark is far worse than his bite, as they say, Lady Agatha."

"I'm glad to hear it," she told him briskly. "You should get back to the major. I shall dress and follow directly."

"My master will thank you," Jack told her.

"Whether he does or not, you'd best hurry."

The bedroom of the Abbey master's suite had the disarrayed look of a sickroom, bottles of medicines and piles of fresh towels and used cloths covering the tops of the bedside table and the chests of drawers.

A porcelain basin, with tiny pink buds painted against an ivory background, sat on the floor beside the huge carved bed. A cloth soaked in the wide shallow bowl.

Lady Agatha was shown up the stairs by a sleepy Martha as the first thin threads of dawn began to lighten the eastern horizon.

"Is he dying?" the maid asked.

"Don't be such a goose," Lady Agatha reprimanded the young woman.

"Will you be coming back to the Abbey if he dies, Lady Agatha? Now that your brother's dead and all?"

"No," Lady Agatha said.

A chill swept through the hallway, making both women shiver.

Behind them the vague outlines of a large man materialised. "How can you say that? You're a cruel woman, Aggie, and you always were."

"Did you hear something?" Martha asked Agatha.

"I hear the wind," Lady Agatha replied.

Inside the master's suite, Jack led Lady Agatha towards the bedroom. As they neared the doorway he slowed.

"I don't know if you should go inside, Lady Agatha. He's in a terrible state."

"Nonsense," Agatha dismissed the man's hesitation. "I am a sister, a widow, a mother, and a grandmother twice over. I have seen my share of your sex, in sickness and in health. There's naught that will shock me at my age, nor much I haven't seen."

But even the redoubtable Agatha was taken aback by the sight of the large man who filled the bed that had once belonged to her husband.

The man was writhing, asleep but not peaceful. His gaunt face was pale except for where his growing beard stubbled his chin with dark shadows. His forehead shone with perspiration, his chiselled lips chapped and dry.

It had been many long years since Agatha had tended to a man's illness. Looking at him, her thoughts fled backwards in time to when her husband lay dying in this very same room, in this very same bed.

"Lady Agatha, are you unwell?"

Agatha shook her head a little, glancing at Jack before moving towards the bed. "Have more liquids brought up. Weak tea and chicken broth and whatever fruit juice is handy. And a jug of plain water." She felt the major's forehead, her thin, patrician fingers cool against the younger man's hot skin. "Tell Martha to get help and ready a tub of cold water."

The man left to do as she bid. Agatha leaned down to wring out the soaking towel. She placed it against the soldier's hot forehead and sat beside him, bringing the covers up to his chin before reaching for another cloth and swirling it in the water in the porcelain basin beside her chair.

"Over the hill . . . over the hill . . ."

Giles spoke in his sleep, the words mumbled and urgent. His arm thrashed out, nearly hitting Agatha. She ducked back as he moved again, the bedding wrapped around his body, restraining movement except for his one arm.

"Major, it's all right. Let me help you," Agatha said.

Unconsciously, he fought the restraints, lashing out in his troubled sleep.

Agatha was not equal physically to the young soldier. Fortunately, the bedding kept all but his one arm imprisoned. She reached to capture that arm. Standing beside the bed, Agatha Steadford-Smyth used all her strength to keep the arm quiet against the bed.

"Major Steadford, you must stop," she told the delirious man, trying to reach through to where he could hear her.

"Lady Agatha!" Martha's horrified tones came from the doorway. She ran towards Lady Steadford-Smyth. "What is he doing to you?"

"Help me keep him down," Agatha commanded the maid.

"He's not attacking me, girl. He's delirious with fever."

Martha had started forwards and stopped, her eyes rounded with fright. "What's wrong with him?"

"I don't know. The doctor is coming, but we need to keep him quiet and get his fever down."

"You want me to touch him?" Martha asked in horrified accents.

Behind Martha, Fannie arrived in the room.

"Tim's on the way," Fannie told her mistress.

"Good. Come help me," Agatha said. "And send this girl back to bed and out of the way."

Before Fannie could speak, Martha dropped a quick curtsey and fled the room. Fannie reached the major's bedside and tried to help Agatha untangle the bedding.

They were still wrestling with the unconscious and fretful Giles when Jack came back into the bedchamber.

"I've readied the cold bath," he said.

"Help me to untangle these," Agatha commanded. "Fannie, stop that girl and tell her to run for Homer. We'll need his help before this night is out."

"What are you planning to do?" Jack asked as Fannie hurried out.

"First we need more blankets and we must keep them on him. Then you must help undress him and carry him to the tub," she replied.

Jack stared at her. "Are you intending to put him into the cold water?"

"Yes."

"But, he'll chill. You need to keep him warm."

"Our first hope is in forcing liquids into him and making him perspire enough to break the fever. If that fails and he is worse before the doctor arrives, we must immerse him in the coldest water possible."

"He'll catch pneumonia," Jack objected.

"If the fever rises, he will die," Agatha told the valet. "It affects the brain."

Jack was subdued as he helped her pile more blankets on

the major. "You are quite knowledgeable about medical matters for a . . ." His words trailed off.

"For a woman?" Her quick gaze raked across his face and then went back to the cold wet cloths she was soaking for her cousin's forehead.

"For a civilian," Jack ended. He stared at his master. "If he wakes, he won't like it above half. He'll be a terrour to deal with."

"As a soldier he must have bathed in cold water before this," she said practically.

"Oh, the cold won't upset him, but having a woman taking care of him will. Even if she is a relative."

Agatha grimaced. "I assure you, I understand completely. But in some circumstances we must suffer in order to survive."

"I'm not all that sure he wants to survive," Jack said quietly.

Agatha's gaze was penetrating as she studied the valet. "Why do you say that?"

Jack shrugged. "It's hard for a man, a strong man, a soldier in his prime, when he has to lie about and do nothing. And the pain."

"Is there no hope he'll regain the use of his legs?" Agatha asked.

"They don't know," Jack told her. "I think the hope is what keeps him hanging on. That and his youth."

She bent back to the basin to wring out another cloth and replace the one on the major's forehead, while Jack helped her hold Giles down.

"It's a pity," Agatha said quietly, watching the young soldier.

"Yes," Jack agreed.

It was another hour before sounds from below marked the doctor's arrival. A pale sun was high in the cloudy blue sky outside as the Abbey household stirred to its morning tasks. Martha led the way up the stairs and left as soon as she'd shown him the doorway.

Inside he found Agatha Steadford-Smyth standing beside the bed with Fannie hovering nearby. Homer and a tall, thin man were lifting a man from the bed into a bathtub. By now Sir Giles was naked except for his long underwear.

"That clothing will have to come off, too," the physician told them. "Agatha, you and Fannie can leave him to me now."

"Yes, of course." She turned to leave and then looked back. "We shall be in the kitchens if you need us."

"Why don't you go back home and get some rest? I'll stop by before I leave."

"If you're sure you won't need us . . ."

"I'm quite sure," the doctor told Lady Agatha. He could see the dark tired circles that lined her eyes. "There's no need to provide me another patient to deal with."

She gave him a mechanical little smile. "Never fear. I'm hale and hearty and will outlive you all."

"I'm sure of it," Agatha Steadford-Smyth was told. "But think of poor Fannie."

Fannie's eyes darted fearfully towards the doctor. "Do I look unwell?"

"Fannie, come away," her employer insisted. "There's nothing wrong with you that sleep won't cure."

The doctor turned his attention to his patient as the two women left the room.

"It's my age," Fannie told Agatha as she followed the older woman into the hall beyond the sitting-room. "I knew it, I could see it in my mirror. It's only been three weeks and I've already changed."

"Fannie Burns, you can be odiously provoking at times. I don't know why I put up with you."

"You put up with me because I put up with you," Fannie said with the familiarity of long and close association.

"I should box your ears," Agatha replied.

"I'd like to see anyone try," Fannie retorted.

"Aggie?" Harry came through the hallway wall, floating

ahead of them in the Long Gallery that ringed the wide oak stairwell. "Ah, Aggie, what's happening here?"

Fannie yawned, and Harry's invisible form floated upwards in frustration.

"I don't know what the world is coming to. And none to hear or see me, what am I supposed to do about all this? What's wrong with the blasted man? He's as queer in the attic as Dick's hatband, and I can't rouse him at all no matter what I try."

Since none could hear him, none answered. Peeved beyond mortal or ghostly endurance he slammed off through the walls towards the master bedchamber.

"If I don't make someone hear me soon, I can't vouch for what I'll do," Harry threatened the unhearing humans. "Years going by and none to talk to, none to see me except screeching females who run and blither and blubber. I tell you, it's more than a ghost should be asked to bear."

It was after the normal hour for the noon meal when Doctor Sayles arrived at the gatehouse to share tea and chicken stew with Agatha and Fannie.

"He's come through the crisis, but he's a very sick man, Agatha. He suffers from a malady he must have caught in Portugal when he was wounded. The infection has to work out its course."

"When it does, will he be able to walk?" she asked.

Doctor Sayles accepted a thick slice of homemade bread from Fannie as he replied. "He may never be able to walk, depending upon how much damage was done to his spine from the sabre wound. The first order of business is to get him well. Then we can worry about the rest of it."

"His man, Jack, said he has given up the will to live without the use of his legs," Agatha told the doctor.

"Then it will be even harder to help him through this. I shall send a woman out to care for him."

"I beg your pardon?"

Doctor Sayles smiled at her shocked expression. "Yes. A woman."

"I don't understand."

"The servants won't know how to deal with his illness nor his convalescence. Nor will they want to, since they fear catching it and I can't guarantee they won't, given long enough association with the sickroom. There is a woman who was trained by the nursing sisters and who has dedicated her life to helping the suffering. She has helped me before, and I recommend her highly."

"But—a woman! She'll not have the strength, nor is it proper—"

"There's nothing improper possible with a gravely ill and paralysed man. She'll have his man, Jack, to help her, and she has the knowledge to bring your young cousin through this. There have been nursing nuns for generations, and well you know it."

"Is she a nun then?" Lady Agatha asked dubiously.

"No, but she was trained by them and is excellent at her profession. Surely you want to give him the best chance possible."

"Of course," she replied doubtfully. "But—"

"Good," the doctor pronounced briskly. "Now, let's talk of other things. Fannie, did I hear you complaining of ill health last night?"

"Don't get her started," Agatha warned. "She is in a tizzy because she has had a birthday."

"I've not had a birthday," Fannie defended herself. "I've turned fifty years of age. One half of a century. That's a far different thing than just another birthday."

"Why?" the doctor asked.

"Why?" she replied.

He smiled, his small eyes nearly disappearing in the lined flesh that surrounded them. "I'm not sure I remember my fiftieth birthday. Do you Agatha?"

"What a question to ask a woman. Really, Doctor, your manners become more atrocious with every passing year."

"That's the truth. What's more, with every passing year I care less about manners and decorum and all such nonsense. I'm surprised you don't agree."

"Well, I don't," she replied tartly. "And I would be ashamed to voice such sentiments if I were you. Far from being nonsense, I think manners and decorum are absolutely necessary to the smooth running of society," Agatha pronounced.

"Well, I'm not ashamed, but I won't argue with you if you think I should be," he replied mildly.

"I do. And I also say that sensible spinster women have no need to go nattering on about age and birthdays."

Fannie sniffed as she poured them each more tea. "I'm sure I don't mean to provoke anyone."

"Then don't," Agatha said with considerable asperity.

The meal was finished with more silence than conversation, none of them quite happy with the others.

=== 5 ===

DR. SAYLES ARRIVED the next day accompanied by a dark-haired young woman, dressed in modest clothes of a dark blue colour. Her name, he informed the valet, was Elizabeth Wallace, and she was to nurse the major until the doctor deemed him well.

"She's not a nun, not a sister, at all," young Tim told the curious household staff below-stairs. "She's a rare one, she is," Tim enthused. "The prettiest dark curls and the bluest eyes I ever saw."

"How old is she?" Fannie sat down as she spoke. She began to help Martha peel carrots and potatoes.

"Oh, she's old, I think," Tim replied. "She's at least five and twenty, I'll bet."

"That's not old," Martha objected. "I'm four and twenty myself."

"it's old for quality and still unmarried and she's quality. She's a swell, I can tell," Tim countered. "Besides, you're always going on about Charlotte Summerville not being married yet and she's only two and twenty."

Fannie's face dropped into unhappy lines as she listened to the words around her. "Lady Agatha doesn't like any of this above half," she said. "I mean this young woman coming to nurse the major."

The cook's round bulbous nose wrinkled up as she sniffed with a ladylike delicacy. "I'm sure she doesn't, and nor do I. But my guess is the major is going to like it least of all.

42

And he'll have something to say about it, you can be sure."

While the staff discussed the newcomer below-stairs, up in the master's suite, Elizabeth Wallace was facing a truculent Jack Fence.

"It's not right," the valet declared.

"Now, see here," Dr. Sayles replied reasonably. "There is nothing unseemly about it. There are many nursing sisters."

"She's not a religious," Jack declared.

"And is that what makes the difference?" the doctor snapped. "I thought the subject here was to heal a critically ill patient."

"It is, but—," Jack began and then stopped. "It's just not right," he repeated. "He won't like it. He won't like it at all."

"Suppose we wait, and when he's well we can ask him," the young woman said, the smallest hint of defiance in her voice. "In the meantime, if my conduct lacks any propriety you will, of course, inform the doctor. Until then, I suggest we get to the business at hand." She delivered her words with every sign of reasonableness and then turned towards the patient, paying no further heed to jack Fence's presence in the sickroom.

"He's a soldier," Jack said as if that explained all.

"He was a soldier," Dr. Sayles corrected. "Now he is merely an ill man in need of medical care. Elizabeth, since Mr. Fence is here, you can show him what to do to help."

"He can help me make the bed," she replied.

"You're not strong enough," the valet told her. "It takes two to lift him right or it pains him something fierce."

"There's no need to lift him."

"You can't make the bed with him in it," Jack scoffed.

"Yes," she replied, "I can. Furthermore, if you intend to stay, you might as well begin to help. You may bring some fresh bedding, and I will show you how we do it."

The valet hesitated. He watched the doctor and nurse bending over his master's feverish body and finally turned away, going in search of the bedding.

Dr. Sayles gave Elizabeth a sideways glance as he cut away bandages. "You've got quite a job cut out for you, my girl."

Elizabeth spread medicinal salve on fresh bandage linen and handed it to the doctor. "They can get as tongue-valient as they like. I shall reward your help and trust by doing my job properly. No matter what," the slim young woman added firmly.

By the time Jack arrived back in the major's bedchamber the doctor was gone, a row of medicines and a list of instructions for Elizabeth left behind.

"You may bring the bedding here," Elizabeth told the valet.

"I don't know how you think you'll manage," Jack said.

"First we take off the covers, like so. Then, I shall undo one side of the bedding and roll it towards the major, like so. Now if you'll please hand me a fresh sheet—thank you."

Jack watched Elizabeth unfold the sheet lengthwise and tuck it in.

"Now," she continued, "If you will help me roll Sir Giles onto his side. Towards me, please."

She continued to move as she talked. Jack reached unwillingly to do as she bade.

"I shall hold him while you pull the old sheet off, like so," she demonstrated. "Yes, that's it. Now you tuck the new one in as I did on this side."

She watched Jack work, encouraging him and then allowing him to help tuck in the top sheet and blankets.

"Very good," she told him when they were done. "Now you may leave."

The man stared at her. Elizabeth considered him for a moment, then sat down in a tall, narrow chair beside the bed and picked up a slim volume from the bed table.

Jack stood where he was, watching her for an uncomfortable moment before moving towards the door to the sitting-room. "I shall be right outside," he warned.

"Fine," the nurse replied. She went back to her reading,

ignoring the valet as he reluctantly left the room.

Two days later, the sun was a high, pale light in the cloudy afternoon sky outside the master bedroom window. Elizabeth Wallace was dressed in a high-waisted gown of pomona green, with long, narrow sleeves and a tiny frill of ivory lace at collar and cuffs, as she leaned over the medical book she was perusing.

A brass clock ticked away atop the black marble mantel across the room, and distant voices from the household below drifted upwards through the house as the staff readied for the evening meal. The major's heavy breathing was the only other sound Elizabeth heard until he began to stir.

The nurse put down her book and leaned forwards. She put the palm of her hand on his forehead feeling for more fever. He was warm to the touch but no longer feverish.

Major Sir Giles Steadford came awake slowly. His eyes still closed, he felt a coolness against his forehead. A touch as soft as an angel's wing against his skin. It calmed him in a way he would have found hard to explain.

Giles opened his eyes and tried to make sense out of his surroundings and the beautiful dark-haired angel who stood above him.

His first thought was that heaven was very much like England. The rooms were familiar English rooms. Even the angels looked like proper English girls—pretty and sensible and kind, so kind they stroked one's forehead.

His next thought was that the room looked vaguely familiar, and his next brought him fully awake.

"What the devil is going on?" Giles asked, his voice croaking over the words. "And who the blue blazes are you?"

His voice startled Elizabeth. She dropped her hand from his forehead. "Major," she remonstrated, "there is no need to shout at me, nor to curse."

"Who the devil are you?" Giles demanded.

"Major Steadford, I am not in the habit of being sworn

at," she told the soldier firmly.

"Jack? Jack!" Giles roared. "Where the hell are you?"

Jack Fence had kept a lonely and unneeded vigil in the master's suite sitting-room for the past two days. Except for the times Elizabeth needed help changing the bedding, or sent for fresh basins of clean water to bathe the major's wound and change his bandages, he had felt totally useless. And, he had to admit, the woman seemed to know what she was doing. She had a rare spunk, that one, Jack told Homer over a late supper the night of her arrival. She could look torn and unhealing flesh in the eye and not flinch. Which was more than you could say for most—male or female.

By the middle of the second day, Jack had tired of sitting about and feeling useless. He went below-stairs, and asked Hetty if there was something he could do.

He had polished all the major's unused boots, shined up all his brass buckles and insignias, cleaned and put away ever bit of the major's possessions, and still found himself at loose ends. Hetty sent the valet to the stables, where Homer asked what the man knew about horses. Finding out that Jack had been the major's batman all through his illustrious military career, Homer unbent so far as to offer the newcomer the free run of the stables. Since the old stable man guarded his horseflesh religiously, this was a high honour.

And so it was that Jack was in the stables when his master awoke and bellowed out the valet's name, along with an imaginative assortment of swear words.

"I said I will not tolerate that sort of language," Elizabeth said crisply. "No matter how ill you may be, there is no need for—"

"Who *are* you?" Giles bellowed. His ringing tones brought Harry through the far wall to stare at the human as if he were demented.

"What's going on?" Harry demanded, neither Giles nor Elizabeth noticing.

"Blast you, woman, I want my man!" Giles roared. "I won't be coddled and I won't be pitied."

"Pitied? How could you possibly be pitied?" Elizabeth Wallace stared at the man as if he were demented. "You should count yourself lucky even to be *liked* if this is your normal attitude."

Giles grabbed a glass of water from the bedside table and threw it against the wall.

As the crystal missile sailed across the room it whizzed past the invisible Harry. Harry recoiled instinctively before he reminded himself the material world could no longer hurt him.

"God's teeth, you people, there's no reason for such shouting. One can't hear oneself think."

The glass hit the wall and would have fallen to the thick burgundy and navy carpeting if not for Harry. His body may have very nearly evaporated when his life ended—the life that others thought of as human, that is—but many powers had remained. Why he wasn't quite sure.

However, when certain earthly emotions emerged, Harry found himself feeling as human as he ever had. Which was why Harry willed the glass back at its thrower, then was almost as surprised as Giles and Elizabeth when the glass actually hit the wall and boomeranged back at the army man.

"What the Goddamn hell?" Giles expostulated as he ducked away from the flying crystal.

It hit the wall behind his pillow and bounced to the hard wooden floor, missing the thick carpeting and shattering into a hundred pieces.

"Major," Elizabeth Wallace spoke sharply, her eyes sparkling with anger. "I shall return when you come to your senses."

After she had gone, Giles stared across what he thought was an empty bedchamber. "Good riddance to bad rubbish!" The words sounded hollow even to his own ears.

Harry contemplated the bedridden soldier. "I wouldn't

let her hear you, if I were you. She sounds as if she can give as good as she gets . . . No answer? I should have known you'd not be able to hear me. Addlepated humans." Beetling what used to be his brows together, Harry clasped his hands behind his back and stomped off through the dressing-room wall.

Giles Steadford looked across the room towards the dressing-room beyond. "Jack? Is that you?" he called out, but the steps were gone and he heard no more.

= 6 =

THE AUTUMN AIR nipped at the tip of Elizabeth Wallace's nose as she walked across the Abbey grounds in the waning afternoon. She buried her hands deeper in the pockets of her grey woollen cloak, watching her footsteps and thinking about the impossible patient she'd just left.

Ahead of her a figure bent to retrieve something from amongst the thick, gnarled roots of an ancient oak. As Elizabeth came closer Agatha Steadford straightened up, depositing her find in a small basket as the younger woman approached through the stand of trees. Lady Agatha had been searching through the undergrowth for wood mushrooms and had already half filled the basket she was carrying.

"May I help you?" Lady Agatha asked.

"I'm sorry, I didn't mean to startle you. I am Elizabeth Wallace. I am working at the Abbey."

Lady Agatha gave the young woman an attentive gaze. She was young, with large eyes of the deepest blue and true English skin of peaches and cream. "I am Agatha Steadford-Smyth."

"Oh." Elizabeth's eyes lit up. "I didn't realise there were any Steadfords here—except for Major Steadford, of course."

Agatha heard the change in Elizabeth's voice when she spoke his name. "You are the nurse Dr. Sayles sent up."

"Yes," the younger woman admitted.

Something about the young woman reminded Agatha of

her granddaughter Jane. It wasn't her colouring, which was quite different from Jane's fair hair and grey eyes. It was the calm, direct gaze that met Lady Agatha's penetrating one. "I am told Dr. Sayles holds you in the highest regard," Agatha told the nurse.

"I am glad to hear it."

"Some say he can sometimes be too kind."

"I have never found him so," Elizabeth answered honestly, taking no umbrage. "I have taken any compliments from him gladly, as he has given out so few."

She was rewarded by an appraising look and then a smile from the older woman.

"If the truth be told," Agatha replied, "I confess I've never heard him give many compliments either. I assume your patient is feeling better, since you are out and about."

Elizabeth looked down. She bit her lip as she replied: "He is awake, and he has ordered me out of his sight. As to whether he is better, I am not sure—unless a prodigious amount of swearing signifies health in the male of the species."

Lady Agatha smiled in spite of herself. "I assure you, swearing in a man is what vanity is in a woman—the first sign of regaining health."

There was a moment of deep silence.

"Forgive me, Lady Agatha, but I sense that none here is glad of my arrival. There seems to be a general lack of enthusiasm which, I fear, extends to include yourself."

"I admire your honesty and directness," Agatha answered slowly. "It is nothing to do with you, precisely. However, it is an improper situation for a single female to nurse a bachelor. The good doctor felt our fears were groundless, but I must tell you I find his sense of propriety woefully lacking. Not to put too fine a point on it, I feel his attitudes much too modern and, in fact, deplorable."

"Because of me?" Elizabeth asked.

"Because of many things. You are merely the current issue. I do not mean to offend you, Miss Wallace, but I speak my mind."

"And I take no offence, believe me. I much prefer plain unvarnished honesty."

"Then, whilst you are here, we should deal quite tolerably with each other."

Elizabeth's mouth curved into a gentle smile that lit her eyes. "You make it sound as if that shan't be for long duration."

Lady Agatha was too polite to shrug. "You have just said your patient refuses to accept your help. And Major Steadford is, after all, a military man. He is used to being obeyed."

"I intend to stay on until Dr. Sayles is satisfied with the major's improvement."

"Aren't you concerned about what people will think?"

"About what?" Elizabeth asked.

"You are a spinster and he is a bachelor," Agatha clarified.

"Oh, that," the younger woman replied, shocking Lady Agatha. "I do not hold with the old-fashioned view that a man and a woman cannot be left alone in a room without getting themselves involved in some sort of romantic intrigue. I assure you, there is nothing the least romantic about the major's current condition."

"I may be old-fashioned, but I have known deep grief to come from not paying attention to the proprieties. Society can be cruel."

"Throughout history there have been female nurses," Elizabeth defended herself. "In the years and decades to come I am convinced we will be as plentiful on the battlefields as in hospitals and homes."

"Good grief," Agatha said, thoroughly shocked. "On the battlefield? Never. Nor would any sane woman want to be."

"No sane man should want to be on a battlefield, either, but it's never seemed to stop them from going out and killing one another."

"But that's so different," Agatha protested.

"Is it?"

"Yes. Soldiers are protecting society, protecting our very way of life."

"Then should they not receive the very best care we can give them?" Elizabeth continued before Agatha could summon words. "As we all know, women have a gentler touch and much more patience with illness and disease than does the male of the species."

"Certainly. I myself have nursed my husband and my children in days long past. But that is an entirely different matter. Nursing one's own is not the same as nursing strangers."

"Not necessarily," Elizabeth replied.

"You are taking your thinking from the nursing sisters, possibly. But you do not appear to be a member of a religious order."

"I am not, but I do not think good deeds should only be allowed the good sisters who trained me. I was trained by the Sisters of Charity and I am positive, Lady Agatha, that one day women will be at the very forefront of the nursing profession."

"Society will have to change drastically for such things to occur. In the meantime your immediate concern is the major, and it seems he wants nothing to do with female nursing. Nor does he seem to be adjusting himself to living out the rest of his life with useless legs. I warrant I can understand his feelings. I think such a fate might be something any of us would fight, let alone one as young and as energetic as Sir Giles."

"But I can help," Elizabeth burst in.

"Help him regain the use of his legs?" Agatha asked. Her expression told of her disbelief.

"It is possible to try," Elizabeth said, warming to her subject. "There are new ideas, modern methods and exercises, all kinds of discoveries I've been trained in that may help if only the patient can be convinced to let me try. Perhaps someone close to him could help."

Lady Agatha observed the younger woman's hopeful expression. "I can see where you are aiming, young lady, and I admit I admire your persistence and dedication.

However, if you are counting on my assistance, I must disabuse you of that hope."

"But he might listen to you," Elizabeth coaxed.

"I hardly see why," Agatha replied.

"You are family."

"Miss Wallace, until shortly before the major arrived at the Abbey I did not even know he existed. And I am persuaded he knew as little about me. Thus, let me assure you, I have little knowledge of him and less influence *over* him."

"But if you might mention that I could help him—"

"I doubt that I will," Agatha cut in. "As I said, I myself am not persuaded your presence is required. Or is even in the best of taste."

"But if you do come to feel that I can offer him help," Elizabeth persisted.

"Young lady, I will not be badgered." The chagrinned expression on the young woman's pretty oval face made the older woman relent a little. "I am not against you, child. However, I do not trust the male of the species, bedridden or no. Nor should you. I bid you good-day." With that, Lady Agatha turned back towards the gatehouse.

Elizabeth Wallace watched Agatha Steadford-Smyth's proud carriage as she walked away. "You might think about it," she called out but received no reply. The younger woman gazed up at the old grey stones of the Abbey walls. "I shall succeed," she promised the wind that nipped at her nose and the tips of her ears. "Somehow," she added, a little less optimistically.

The Abbey halls were almost as chilly as the darkening evening outside as Elizabeth entered the house and ran quickly up the stairs towards the master's suite. Jack Fence looked up from stoking the fire as she entered the sitting-room.

"Miss Wallace," he called out in an urgent whisper, "he's just fallen asleep."

Elizabeth slowed her step and walked to the fireplace, holding her hands out to its warmth.

"It has turned quite cold."

Jack Fence agreed with her but added nothing more to her attempt at conversation.

"I hope you will see your way clear to help me persuade the major so that I may nurse him back to health."

Jack's answer came slowly. "Miss Wallace, I honestly don't think he'll put up with you—or any female nurse, as far as that goes. I'm not sure he wants any nurse at all."

Elizabeth frowned. "What are you saying?"

"I'm saying the major is not very interested in his future at this point."

"Because he is ill?"

"Because he'll never be able to walk again," the valet corrected.

"What if I could help him regain the use of his limbs?" she asked.

Jack stared at her. "You can't."

"But if I can, then what?" she persisted.

"He would probably give you his entire fortune if you could give him back the use of his legs. But there isn't a crueler thing you could do than to give him false hope," Jack said flatly.

"Hope is not false," the nurse countered. "And if his irritability stems from being bedridden, then we shall have to get him out of bed."

"Begging your pardon, miss, but sitting in a chair or lying in a bed, he's still not able to get around."

Elizabeth gave him a bemused look. " . . . Not able to get around . . . ," she repeated. "You're absolutely right," she exclaimed. "Absolutely. Mr. Fence, you are brilliant."

"I am?" Jack asked.

"Excuse me, I'll be right back."

The valet watched her abrupt departure. Her steps were swift and purposeful as she headed out into the hall. Elizabeth Wallace looked like a young woman who had reached an important decision.

Curious, Jack followed her out into the upper hallway. He could hear her voice rise from the entrance hall below as she sent a young maid to fetch young Tim. He must come straight to the Abbey and collect a note which was to be taken to Dr. Sayles's surgery immediately, Jack heard the nurse say.

The valet was still looking down the stairwell when Elizabeth climbed back towards him in the Long Gallery beside the upper landing.

"I shall need paper and pen," she informed him. "Jack Fence, there may be a way out of this coil yet."

A doubtful look was his only answer.

7

THE NEXT DAYS were tortuous for the entire Abbey household. Sir Giles insisted that only Jack touch him or his bandages, let alone see his naked form or bathe him. Jack made a valiant attempt to comply, but the mixture of salves, ointments, and medicines which were to be applied in specific amounts and in a certain order baffled him.

Afraid to make a mistake, Jack begged off; but the major still would not let Elizabeth near him until Jack saw the wound worsening once again.

From that point on, Sir Giles accused Jack of being a thankless turncoat. Helpless to stop Elizabeth, short of physically assaulting her, Giles at first resorted to throwing every dish within his reach and then to blasphemies that would have done the devil proud. The sounds of crashing pottery and glassware punctuated the swearing that was teaching the entire household an entirely new vocabulary.

"I swear, Fannie," the cook told her old friend over tea at the gatehouse, "Homer himself doesn't understand some of it."

If they could have heard Sir Harry's ghost, they would have learned yet a few more unusual words. However, Harry himself was becoming intrigued with the interloper who now thought he owned the Abbey. Balanced on the back of a tall wing chair, Harry's feet were planted on the seat of navy blue velvet as firmly as almost visible feet could be. Leaning forwards, his chin in one hand, he studied the man on the bed across the room.

"I must say, you've got quite a vocabulary," Harry the ghost told Giles Steadford. "If you weren't so blasted dense and so blasted loud about everything, I might be able to tolerate you for a while. Or if you had the wit to see. You might at least have the good manners or the decency to be able to hear me occasionally."

"What?" Giles moved against his pillows, using his elbows to sit up higher. "Who's there?" he asked.

"You're looking in the wrong direction," the Ghost told Giles. Harry's expression turned sour. "I suppose I shall have to resort to rattling chains and that sort of fuss and bother, but I hardly think it worth the effort. After all, being a soldier, you must have got used to loud noises on the battlefield. Of course," Harry continued pragmatically, "loud noises in the midst of battle are different from loud noises in the midst of sleep."

"Jack? Is that you in there?"

"No one's in the bloody dressing-room, you cork-brained fool." As Harry spoke Elizabeth walked into the bedroom, carrying a tray of broth and juice. "I don't know why I bother," Harry said.

Elizabeth was staring towards the chair and directly at Harry. Her eyes were rounded with surprise.

"What on earth?" she asked in a low tone.

"Nothing," Giles answered irritably. "I was calling for Jack, not you."

"She doesn't mean you," Harry said with glee. "You heard me, didn't you?" Harry's hopes were quickly dashed as Elizabeth shook her head as if clearing it.

"I thought I—nothing," she told Giles. "I must be more tired than I realised."

"You've no need to complain to me about your tiredness," the major said ungraciously.

"I'm not," she replied. "I'm merely making conversation."

"Well, don't. I have no need of it. Or of you."

She was putting the tray on the bedside table. "If you

want to get well, you need me," she told him.

"Ha! I'll never be well again and you know it."

"That's not true," Elizabeth said.

Sir Giles studied her face from under hooded eyes. "You don't know what you're talking about," he ventured.

"I know that if you don't eat, you won't gain strength, and there will be no hope of health," she told him tartly.

"Get out of my sight," he barked.

Nettled, Elizabeth stood beside the table, glaring down at the impossible man. "Why? Are you planning on throwing more childish tantrums?" she asked sweetly.

She was rewarded by a derisive snort. He was about to utter another of the rough snubs with which he was attempting to drive the woman away when movement caught the corner of his eye.

He glanced towards the velvet wing chair with a quizzical expression. "Miss Wallace."

Elizabeth stopped in the doorway and turned back. "If you intend to throw something at—"

"Look there," he said, pointing towards the chair. "I heard something earlier and now, I swear, I saw something move."

"You swear entirely too much, if you ask me," she told him. "I assume that whatever you saw was not something you threw?"

"Damn and blast you, I haven't thrown anything," Giles said peevishly.

"Lately," she corrected. She was glancing at the blue velvet chair that sat near the windows. "It's a trick of light. When I came in I thought for a moment I saw something there, too. But it's nothing."

"I'm not nothing, you imbeciles. You did see something." Harry's impatience won out over his curiousity. "I'm washing my hands of both of you," he said as he faded back through the walls and headed for the old schoolroom at the top of the third floor. It was one of the few places in the entire Abbey where Giles's bellowing could not be heard.

Jack Fence came up the stairs two at a time. "Miss Wallace, this state of affairs can't go on. I have never heard him this bad. The entire staff is threatening to quit the premises," he told her. "And I, not far behind. There's only so much abuse a body can be expected to stand."

"Tell them it will soon be over," the nurse replied.

"That's all well and good, but *how* soon?" he persisted.

"Very soon," she promised. "Very soon indeed."

"It had better be," Jack said darkly.

That very night, Giles woke from an uneasy sleep to find Elizabeth bathing him with Jack's help. Giles began roaring into the night's silence around them. "Get away from me, both of you."

"Hush up, Major," Elizabeth said. "We have to bring your fever down."

"I said, get away from me," he bellowed.

"That's the outside of enough," Elizabeth declared. "*One* more word from you and I shall be forced to dunk you bodily into that tub."

Giles glared at her, never looking towards the bathtub Sir Ambrose Steadford had installed in the tiny chamber next to the master bedroom. "You wouldn't dare," he told her. "Nor would you be able to," he added.

"I will have help," Elizabeth promised quietly.

White with rage, Giles Steadford stared at her. "If you think this jackanapes can manhandle me about, with or without your help, you are going to be sorely disappointed. And I shall sack him if he tries."

Elizabeth Wallace smiled, angering Giles further. "The help I'm referring to is not Jack. It is the entire household, who are so intent on quitting the premises that your threats to fire them will have no avail."

"They can all go to Hell itself for all I care," he declared.

Elizabeth's elegant brow rose slightly. "You are, of course, so self-sufficient that you can cook, feed, clean, and clothe yourself with no help whatsoever."

The major was shocked into momentary silence. Even

Jack Fence was stunned by the young woman's direct attack on the major's invalided condition.

"Well?" she continued. "Are you a soldier or a runaway?"

"*Runaway*? How dare you?" Giles roared.

"A soldier sees his duty and does it," Elizabeth declared. "And you duty is to get well and stop being a trial to everyone around you."

Major Sir Giles Steadford flushed. Then, the oddest expression crossed his face as he watched the outspoken nurse. For the first time in weeks Jack Fence could almost have sworn the major was near smiling. The smile, however, never came. Nor did more expletives.

Elizabeth Wallace did not question her luck. She simply bent back to the bandages she had been changing. Giles Steadford watched her tired movements, seeing the dark half-moons that smudged the skin beneath her eyes. His eyes wandered to the clock across the room, taking in the lateness of the hour.

As she worked, his eyes closed. Giles let himself drift off into a troubled sleep, weary of fighting her attempts to get him well.

He woke later to find himself alone, the room alive with flickering shadows from the oil lamp on the bedside table. The huge house was silent except for small, creaking night noises and the brush of wind against the shuttered windows. Giles Steadford sighed, resigning himself to another long and wakeful night of pain. Using his powerful arms for leverage, he hoisted himself higher against the pillows piled beneath his head, cursing silently at his useless legs.

He settled back against the smooth linen cases that covered the thick feather pillows. His eyes closed for a moment against the pain, then opened, staring towards the dying embers in the fireplace across the room. Someone was sitting in the wing chair nearest the fire. Giles blinked, trying to make out the form better.

"Jack?" he called out. "What the devil do you think you're

doing, staying up all night. I don't need a keeper."

An unfamiliar voice answered. "I'd say you're in bad need of a keeper. Or a cell in Bedlam."

Giles came fully awake. "What did you say? How dare you, sir?"

The ghost of Sir Henry Aldworth leaned forwards in the chair and turned to stare back at the man on the bed. "I say, can you actually hear me?"

"Of course I can hear you, I'm not deaf, man. What I want to know is who you are and why you're in my chambers."

Harry leapt to his feet, his smile widening as he answered. "By God, there must be some justice left in the Universe after all. I am Sir Henry Daniel George Aldworth, Bart." Harry sketched a bow. "Or at least I used to be. You may call me Harry."

"What do you mean, you used to be," Giles began, but the words trailed off into silence. His brow furrowed as he continued to stare at the stranger. "I can see through you," Giles said, his tone disbelieving. "I can see the fire and the logs right—through you."

Harry shrugged. "At least you can see me. And you can hear me, too," he continued warming to his subject. "I can't tell you how long I've waited for someone to be able to hear me again."

"I don't understand," Giles replied.

"Yes, well, you mustn't tax yourself. I don't mind telling you, I'd given up on you altogether."

"Given up on me," Giles repeated blankly. If he had been more awake he would have been more argumentative. As it was, he merely said, "Who are you?"

Harry came closer. "I already told you."

"I know what you told me. But who *are* you? How did you come to be here? And what are you doing in my rooms in the middle of the night? Who let you in?"

"Let me in? No one let me in. Why would anybody have to let me in? I live here," Harry replied.

"Live here where?"

"Anywhere I want," Harry declared.

"I don't understand. And stay where I can see you," he added irritably.

Harry stopped a few feet from the huge walnut bed. "It's not my fault if your eyesight's bad."

"You fade in and out unless the light is behind you," Giles objected. He thought about what he had just said. "I am going mad. Or I'm delirious. Or dreaming. That's it, I must be dreaming."

"You humans have so little imagination," Harry told the bedridden soldier.

"Humans?" Giles caught hold of the part of Harry's words that didn't make sense.

Harry allowed himself a prodigious sigh. "If you've no more sense than to repeat what I say, how can we ever hold a decent conversation?"

"I'm dreaming," Giles repeated.

"You won't think so when I force you from this house," Harry promised.

"You may hold title, Major Steadford, but it is I who own this house. None can long stay within its walls unless I allow it."

Harry spoke in such a definite tone it took Giles aback for a moment. When the soldier rallied, he glared at the half-seen man. "You are a figment of my imagination, and I can banish you with a snap of my fingers."

Giles matched action to words, snapping his fingers smartly. But Harry still remained. Giles snapped again, and yet again, as Harry wafted closer to the bedside.

"If I were you," Harry told the younger man, "I would keep a more civil tongue in my head when talking to my elders and betters."

Giles stared at the apparition which, before his eyes, faded into invisibility. Giles blinked, staring at the empty air Harry had just vacated. "I'm dreaming," Giles repeated softly to himself.

"That's what you think," Harry's voice echoed back through

the empty room. Harry laughed, the sound ringing in the bedchamber long after he himself had disappeared.

His entire life long, Giles Steadford had been able to depend upon his large, powerful frame. Until his wounds on the battlefield felled the strong body, he had always taken that physical power for granted.

Now, lying in the master's bed of Steadford Abbey, Giles's inability even to stand coloured his thoughts and dreams. He was as defenceless as a baby in its cradle. That defenceless-ness was causing him to hallucinate, he told himself. There was no other explanation.

The echoes of ghostly laughter chilled the young man who lay upon the huge, ornately carved bed.

Later he was to tell himself none of it happened. It was all a dream. But, for the moment, he buried his head in the thick pillows and quilts that surrounded him, determined not to hear the fading sounds of ghostly mirth.

=== 8 ===

IN THE EARLY morning hours of a raw October day, a commercial coach came bowling up the Abbey road. Gusting winds sent fallen leaves dancing across the roadway. The horses' hoofs trampled some underfoot, the rest escaping to skitter across the browning landscape.

Major Steadford's nurse was called to the front hall upon the arrival of the foreign coachman. The driver doffed his cap and proffered a bill of lading, which she was to sign. As she did, the man informed Elizabeth it would take more than just himself to pull down the equipment from the top of the coach.

Young Tim was sent for to help Jack and the coach driver as Elizabeth called out advice. Finally, a very strange contraption sat upon the Abbey's wide stone porch. Young Tim took off his woollen cap and scratched his head as the commercial coach turned and headed back down the Abbey road.

"What is it?" Tim asked. His wondering eyes glanced towards the dark-haired nurse who had directed their efforts.

Elizabeth gave the young man a wide, happy smile. "It is the future."

Tim's eyes widened.

"It is also the means by which we shall bring peace back to this household," Elizabeth continued.

Tim took another look at the ungainly contraption before

replacing his cap upon his head. "Well, miss, the way I see it, it may be something and it may not. But it don't look like the future, and it surely don't look like something that can bring peace."

"Wait and see," she told the young man. Elizabeth turned to Jack Fence. "Now, we must get your master down here."

Jack looked dubious. "What am I to tell him?"

"Tell him the first step to recovery of the use of his limbs is at hand."

Jack was prepared to argue with the nurse but found himself at a total loss for words. No one could be cruel enough to send such a message to the suffering major unless there was truth in it. Still, how there *could* be truth in it was beyond Jack.

Elizabeth watched Jack wrestle with his reactions to what she had told him. When he turned to do as she asked, she told herself she was perfectly capable of handling what was to come next. But while she waited for Jack to bring the major below-stairs, her confidence wavered and her fears grew.

The major's voice carried down the stairwell and out the open front door. Hearing it, young Tim backed away from Elizabeth Wallace and the contraption beside her.

Elizabeth noted the boy's retreat. "He doesn't sound very enthusiastic," she said.

"No, miss," Tim edged farther away. "I think I'd best get back to the stables."

"Wait, please," the nurse said in firm tones. "We may need your help."

"That's what I'm afraid of, miss," Tim replied unhappily.

"Loud noises are nothing to fear," Elizabeth assured the boy. "I have found his bark to be much worse than his bite."

Tim didn't look convinced. He was ready to run when Jack and Homer arrived outside, carrying the major, dressed in his nightrobe with slippers on his feet and invectives on his tongue.

"What the devil do you think you are doing now?" Sir

Giles demanded of Elizabeth as soon as he saw her. "I am in no condition to be manhandled like this. What's that?"

"That is the first step to getting you back on your feet."

Giles Steadford was startled into momentary silence.

Elizabeth smiled encouragingly. "You sit in it," she said.

"I know what to do with a chair," he replied irritably. "And I want no part of it."

"Please put him down," she told Jack and Homer. To Sir Giles she said, "You are a large man, Major. There is no reason to strain these poor men any longer than necessary. Gentlemen—," she concluded, waiting for them to do as they were told.

Before the major had the chance to disagree, he found himself deposited in the large, wheeled chair.

"It is called a Bath chair," Elizabeth was saying as they deposited him. "It was developed for the invalids who came to take the waters at Bath."

"Just what do you think you're accomplishing, bringing this thing all the way here? I don't intend to pay for its cartage—nor for you, for that matter. You're an irritation and a nuisance." Giles glared at her.

"I haven't asked you for money, Sir Giles. Dr. Sayles takes care of my fees."

"Out of money I'll end up paying him," Giles shot back.

"If you're afraid, we'll understand."

"Afraid?" Rising anger flushed his face.

"I realise it will be a tiring, not to mention hurtful, process to regain the use of your legs. If you feel you're not up to the work or the pain, we shall all understand," she said again.

"Not up—" Giles was at a loss for words foul enough to throw at the woman who stood before him. "No man has ever been able to say I ran from a battle. Any battle. I won't have some *woman* dare to malign my courage."

"Have I done that?" she asked with large innocent eyes. "Oh, dear."

"Woman, get out of my sight," he roared.

"Of course, I will. I realise you won't want any of us to witness your fear of failure."

He spoke from between gritted teeth. "If you don't get her away from me, I won't be responsible for what I do or say."

"Don't blame yourself, Major," Elizabeth said consolingly. "The task would be daunting to many other men, too, I'm sure."

Giles gripped the arms of the unwieldy Bath chair, his entire body rigid with anger.

"Sir—," Jack began as Elizabeth disappeared inside the Abbey.

"Leave me," Giles demanded. "All of you. Leave me," he repeated in a tone that brooked no argument.

Homer gazed at the valet behind the major's back, shaking his head before he moved off, heading back towards the stables.

Jack took a step but stopped. "Sir Giles, don't you want me to help you inside?"

"Confound it, man, can't you understand English? I said I want to be alone and I *mean* I want to be alone."

"Yes, sir," Jack responded unwillingly, then walked inside, leaving his master alone on the wide stone porch.

Elizabeth was just inside the door, her finger going to her lips in quick supplication as Jack started to speak. He frowned, and then looked back towards the major.

What he saw was the wheeled chair sitting in the middle of the porch with the autumn landscape spreading out beyond. The sun was high and far away in the cloudy blue sky. North winds washed down across the faraway hills.

"I'll get him a cloak," Jack said quietly. "He's barely over the fever. He shouldn't get a chill."

"Yes, good," Elizabeth replied just as quietly.

Jack Fence stared at the nurse. "I hope you know what you're doing."

Elizabeth turned worried eyes towards him. "I hope I do, too," she said sincerely, her gaze straying back towards the man on the porch as the valet went in search of a warm woollen cloak.

She heard a scraping sound from outside and waited until she saw the major's hands on the side of the chair, reaching for the overlarge wheels. The chair moved an inch, then another, forward towards the wide, shallow steps that led to the gravel roadside.

Elizabeth took an involuntary step, ready to grab the bar that ran across the back of the large movable chair. She checked her progress as the chair inched along, moving backwards for a moment, then forwards again, faster.

"No!" Elizabeth called out. She ran to grab the chair before it careened down the steps and overturned.

"I'm all right," he snapped. "Let go of me."

"I'm not holding you, I'm holding the chair," Elizabeth countered.

"Well, let go of it."

"Why?"

"Because I said so."

Elizabeth released the chair. Giles felt the small movement and used his hands on the oversized wheels, propelling himself forward towards the steps.

Elizabeth walked behind the Bath chair, keeping her hands near the back bar, ready to steady it. He headed straight for the steps, yelling at her to stay away. He took the wheels in hand and bumped down the wide, shallow steps towards the gravel drive.

Behind him, Elizabeth righted the chair as it tilted on the last step, one wheel edging over before the other.

"Be careful," she shouted at him.

"Let go," he shouted back, his hands wheeling faster as he propelled himself down the slightly sloping drive.

Elizabeth ran along behind, letting him race forward in the wheeled Bath chair.

Giles felt the wind whip at his hair and cheeks. He heard Jack shouting about a cloak behind him as he thrust the chair forward, his hands gripping the oversized wheels and propelling them 'round and 'round, faster and faster.

At the bottom of the drive, Fannie was helping Lady Agatha clip dead blooms from the massed rose bushes that surrounded the gatehouse walkway.

"My Lord, would you look at that," Fannie exclaimed.

Agatha Steadford-Smyth glanced towards the drive and then snapped upright to stare. Coming towards her was a small horseless sort of covered two-wheel buggy with a man inside. Behind the strange contraption the new nurse, Elizabeth Wallace, was running down the drive after the machine. Farther behind, the valet was gaining ground, shouting something Agatha couldn't hear as he held a bundle to his chest and ran.

"It's out of control," Agatha gasped and started towards the roadway.

"What *is* it?" Fannie asked, coming behind her mistress. None answered.

Giles saw Lady Agatha coming out of her gate towards him. "Stand back," he shouted.

"Nonsense," Agatha called back sharply. "Stop at once."

Giles tried to swerve to avoid hitting the woman, the downhill slope of the roadway still propelling him forwards.

"I said stop that thing," Agatha demanded.

Elizabeth, out of breath, reached for the back bar, breaking the chair's speed as Jack Fence came nearer. The change in speed thrust Giles forwards in the chair. Fannie shouted to warn them, "He's going to fall out!"

Elizabeth wrenched the back bar, swivelling the chair, which angled off the roadway, towards Agatha and the gatehouse rose garden. The ground was more level here, but so bumpy it jostled Giles up and down, the top of his head hitting the roof of the Bath chair.

Jack caught up, and Elizabeth pulled on the back bar with all her might as Fannie and Agatha and Jack converged in front and to the sides, reaching out to stop the careening chair.

"Is he all right?" Fannie asked, breathless from running.

"Why'd you stop me?" Giles demanded of them all.

"Are you all right?" Elizabeth asked.

"What did you think you were doing?" Lady Agatha demanded severely, looking from Giles to Elizabeth to Jack.

"None of your business," Giles said baldly and was rewarded by a withering glance from his second cousin and dead silence from all around him. He grimaced, pulling a long face and continuing unwillingly. "I beg your pardon. That was rather bad manners."

"I should say so," Agatha replied in clipped tones.

Giles was flushed from his exertion and the October winds which still whipped around him. Jack thrust a dark brown woollen cloak towards his master, but Giles brushed it aside.

"I don't need that," he said.

"Put it on," Agatha told him. "We have all had quite enough upset over your health. If you have no concern for yourself, please have some for the rest of us."

"I beg your pardon?" Giles said.

"And well you should," Agatha replied. "You'd best come inside and get warm and have some tea before going back."

"I don't want to go inside, and I don't want any tea."

"Major Steadford, I must tell you that illness can be used to excuse bad manners only so long, after which one must assume a detestable nature to be the cause. At best. Fannie, please pour tea for the major and for Miss Wallace."

Fannie turned back towards the rose garden.

"There's no need—," Giles began.

"There's every need," Elizabeth said firmly. "And I for one shall be glad of a cup of tea."

"I want to go about more," Giles said, suddenly hungry for the movement he had been so long denied. Even sitting in a strange contraption, he was still moving again.

"You shall. After your tea." Agatha turned in the direction of the gatehouse as Elizabeth looked towards Giles.

The major glared first at her and then at Jack. "All right,

give that thing to me," he said. He took the cloak from his valet and held it on his lap.

Jack reached behind the Bath chair, propelling it through the gate and into the rose garden as Elizabeth walked ahead, following Lady Agatha.

"Lady Agatha," Giles called to her. "Please, may I have the tea out here, in your garden?" She turned back towards him, her dark eyes appraising. "It's been so long since I've been able to be outside. To enjoy any movement at all."

A faint smile curved Agatha's thin lips. "That's the first sensible thing I've heard you say, Major. Yes, of course, you may have tea in the garden. But I suggest you put that cloak on. The weather is changeable today."

Agatha went inside. Elizabeth followed her, leaving Jack to help Giles shrug into the cloak and wrap it around himself.

The gatehouse kitchen was snug and warm. Fannie was pouring boiling hot water from a large kettle into a smaller Bristol porcelain teapot. Agatha moved to ready milk and sugar as she entered.

"Thank you," Elizabeth said to them both. "This is very kind of you."

Fannie looked towards the young woman who hovered near the doorway, keeping an eye on her charge outside. "What did he think he was doing?"

"Running away, I should suppose," Elizabeth answered.

Agatha gave the younger woman a questioning glance. "And you think that is a good sign?"

"I think it an independent sign. And yes, perhaps, even good, concerning the circumstances."

Fannie shook her head. "I hope you and the doctor know what you're doing."

Agatha said, "I doubt the doctor knows very much about this."

Elizabeth smiled a little sheepishly. "Are you always right in your guesses?"

Fannie made a snorting sound. "She's uncanny, is what she is."

"However much I might like the topic of myself and my extraordinary powers," Agatha told the two of them, "we have people waiting for us. Fannie, bring the tea."

Impatiently, Giles allowed the women to feed him a biscuit along with one cup of tea. "That's fine. That's enough," he told them.

Agatha spoke mildly. "And is Miss Wallace through with hers?"

"She can stay, for all I care," Giles replied.

With great effort he turned the chair around, forcing Jack away and saying he wanted no help, by God, from any of them.

Jack turned to Elizabeth as Giles forced the Bath chair up the walk and out the small gate. "Shouldn't someone stay with him?"

"He'll not get far," Elizabeth told the valet. "It's all uphill. Soon he'll be asking for help."

She was, however, wrong. Giles Steadford did not ask for help. Nor did he call out to any of them. He laboured more than a third of the way up the Abbey grounds before he found himself too tired to continue. He waited there until Jack and Elizabeth caught up with him.

"Would you care for some assistance, Sir Giles?" Elizabeth asked sweetly.

His dark eyes studied her carefully. "Thank you," he finally replied.

"You are welcome," she said.

Jack walked behind the chair, pushing it up the incline towards the Abbey which stood sentinel at the top of the gentle hill. The winds had heightened as the afternoon lengthened. They whipped around the Abbey's stone walls and through the oaks and copper beeches which lined the road as Jack and Elizabeth trudged upwards with the wheeled chair.

None spoke until they reached the Abbey steps. As Jack tipped the chair, both Elizabeth and Giles helped steer it up the three flat steps.

Giles finally spoke. "I shall want to go out first thing tomorrow morning."

"As you wish," Elizabeth said with every sign of humble agreement.

"Don't pitch it too rum, Miss Wallace," Giles warned her. "Winning a battle is far different from winning a war."

"Yes, Major. I'm quite sure it is," she replied.

= 9 =

THE WINDS BLEW harder as the sun fell from the sky. Homer and Tim closed the stable doors and portioned out extra hay to their charges in preparation for a cold and stormy night.

Inside the gatehouse, Fannie brought more logs to the bin near the parlour fireplace. She reached for the irons and gave the burning logs a prod before glancing towards where Lady Agatha sat writing. Not wanting to disturb her mistress's thoughts, Fannie wiped her hands on her checked cotton apron and returned to the kitchen's cosy warmth.

Lady Agatha finished writing a long letter to her granddaughter, Jane, a quill pen pensively at her lips as she reread her last words. "As for the new owner, he is indeed a Steadford, though a most distant relation at best. His father and your great-grandfather Ambrose were cousins, which makes him your second cousin twice-removed. He seems to have been on the battlefields a very great deal too long. His manners are distressing at best, from what I have seen at this early juncture, although, to his credit, he was wounded in the service of the King. I can think of no more of what you call delicious gossip—I call it prattle—except we hear that our poor good Farmer George is ailing again. There is talk about that the Price of Wales is to be made Regent of the Kingdom soon. I rather fancy that is like taking the hen coop away from the farmer and giving it to the fox. I'm enclosing a new receipt for a Dutch sauce that Fannie wants you to have. She says it's best with fish, and a very good stomach remedy. If you're eating all that Frenchified food, Fannie is sure you will be needing it. Our love comes with this for you all. Your grandmother, Agatha, this 12 October, 1810."

The daylight was quite ended when Agatha finally put away her writing material and stood up.

At the top of the hill the winds were more fierce, flying at the ancient stones of the Abbey and rattling the windows, from the third storey attics and classroom to the silent public rooms far below.

Elizabeth had been ordered out of the master's suite until the major was finished bathing and changing for the evening. She wandered along the upper hallway and followed the curve of the stairwell railing as it made an ell at the front of the second floor, forming the inner side of the Long Gallery. Looking down she could see the stone-floored front hall and the huge oak doorway.

Elizabeth glanced towards the empty front hall below, then turned her attention back to the Long Gallery itself.

Portraits marched the length of the area, thick Turkey carpeting below Elizabeth's feet, faraway panelled ceilings of Spanish chestnut high above her head. The Steadfords had once been a prolific family, judging by the swarms of children posed around many of the former owner's portraits. Then, as the clothing and hair styles became more modern, there were smaller family groups, or single, sober pictures of Steadford men.

Elizabeth studied the most recent portrait. A lovely young woman with pale golden curls piled atop her head stood next to a very tall, dark-haired man. The gentle curves of her cheeks and body counterpointed the man's angular face and body. Large grey eyes looked up into smiling blue-green ones, the couple very obviously in love. Elizabeth looked at the small brass plaque attached to the bottom of the portrait frame. It read, Lady Jane Steadford, Duchess of Melton, and Charles, 4th Duke of Melton.

Next to the portrait of Jane and Charles a whey-faced man with side-whiskers, a powdered wig, and the most fantastic assortment of fobs, seals, and paraphernalia across his narrow chest, stared rather defiantly back at Elizabeth as she looked in amazement from him to Jane. They bore no family resemblance at all, rather luckily for the pale blonde beauty, Elizabeth decided. The man's name was Sir Nigel Steadford.

Next in line was a portrait Elizabeth recognised immediately as being of Lady Agatha. On some long-ago day in her youth, Agatha's beauty had forever been captured on canvas. She wore a daringly low-cut dress of deep red velvet and a smile that must have won many hearts. Beside her and slightly behind stood a man of rather nondescript appearance, dressed in military fashion. Lady Agatha Steadford-Smyth and Homer Smyth, Esquire, the plaque read.

Elizabeth stared at the picture for quite a long time. Something about Lady Agatha's dark eyes was decidedly sad beneath the radiance of her smile. She seemed to be unconnected with the man behind her, almost as if they'd posed at different times for different pictures and the artist had put them together later.

Beyond the disturbing portrait of young Lady Agatha a man glared out from the next painting, looking rather like a larger version of Nigel Steadford. Sir Ambrose Steadford, the plaque read. Elizabeth glanced beyond and saw another family dressed in even more dated garments. There was no family portrait of Sir Ambrose, his wife, and children. The children, Nigel and Agatha, had their own paintings, but their mother was unknown to these walls.

Elizabeth paced slowly back along the row of portraits, not realising until she reached the very first picture that Sir Ambrose Steadford had been the one to break with tradition. All of the portraits before him were of family groups. His was the first solitary pose.

Elizabeth searched the painting just ahead of Ambrose's portrait, trying to pick out a young Ambrose from the two boys who stood beside their parents while a third, younger son, was dandled on his father's knee.

"He never was much to look at," Harry declared behind her.

Startled, Elizabeth turned. She saw none.

"I'm up here," Harry told her.

Elizabeth stood peering behind her. Finally, she turned around again, her eyes on the thick carpeting at her feet. She gazed higher at the air in front of her and then, almost against her will, even higher towards the most distant portraits and the mullioned windows above.

She saw him then, and the back of her hand went to her mouth, stifling a small scream as her heart began to pound with painful severity against her rib cage.

"What—are—you?" she asked in a strangled tone when she regained the use of her voice.

"I'm a ghost. What do I look like I am?" Harry asked back.

"A . . . ghost?"

"If you're going to dissolve into palpitations or some such, you might as well get it over with."

"How dare you, sir," Elizabeth mustered considerable asperity as she found her voice. "I may have suffered a horrible shock, but I am not a fainting female. I am a nurse and accustomed to shocking circumstances."

"I don't suppose you're accustomed to meeting ghosts," Harry replied.

Elizabeth's expression was resolute, but her large eyes still widened with shock. "I cannot say that I am. However, I—almost—saw you before."

"I thought you did," he replied complacently. "But like most humans confronted with something you don't understand, you simply dismissed it from possibility and pretended it wasn't there."

"In his bedchamber," Elizabeth continued, trying to appear calm while still attempting to slow her heartbeats.

"Take a deep breath," Harry advised. "I've found that helps."

"Thank you, I know that," she replied. But she did as the Ghost bid all the same.

"Better?" he asked.

"Thank you, yes. A little."

"As I was saying, Ambrose Steadford never was much good to look at, young or old," Harry declared.

"I take it, then, you knew him," Elizabeth said, telling herself she could not possibly be having a conversation with a ghost.

"Yes, I knew him, and his personality was as slumgudgeon as his looks."

She stared at the handsome ghost. He looked to be a youngish man of not more than five and thirty. Actually, he looked quite normal, except that his purple velvet clothing was rather tattered and out of style. Of course, being able to see straight through his body, clothing and all, was difficult to ascribe as exactly normal and unexceptional—as was the fact that he had perched himself on a narrow windowsill a full twenty feet above the gallery floor and somehow seemed quite comfortable.

"Did you know him quite well? Sir Ambrose?" Elizabeth asked, trying to make polite conversation. She wasn't quite sure what the proper form of address or inquiry might be when speaking to a ghost.

"Did I know him well? Too dashed well. He's the reason I'm in this infernal mess," Harry declared in dark tones. As he spoke he floated off his perch, coming nearer.

Elizabeth did not precisely shrink from him. She did, however, take an involuntary step backwards at his approach.

"I don't bite," Harry told her. "I might, if I could, but I can't. So there you are." He gave the young woman an appraising look from her curly dark hair to the tip of her flat navy velvet shoes. "I must say, if that's the newest style, it's excessively plain."

"Thank you," she said crisply.

Harry stared at her. She didn't look to be much more than

a girl. "I suppose my manners are atrocious."

"Perfectly odious," she responded.

"Well, damn and blast, so would yours be if you'd been slumbering for almost half a decade," he defended himself. "If you think it's easy being a ghost, you've got the wrong end of it all 'round." Harry delivered himself of his defence in aggrieved tones and was rewarded by seeing Elizabeth's brow screw up into perplexed lines.

"Do ghosts sleep?" she asked. "I cannot feature why you would have to."

"Boredom, mostly," Harry groused. "Nothing for me to do for years on end so nothing for it but to snooze."

"Then you must be quite happy to have the Abbey so occupied and busy these days."

"Pleased?" He looked at her as if she had turned suddenly demented. "The house has gone mad. First that man who has the audacity to think he's the new owner no more than crosses the threshold, but he begins ranting and raving at the top of his lungs for days on end. And now, when he's got tired of flying into passions from sunrise to sunset, he pays workmen to come make the house sound like Bedlam itself."

"Have you any personal knowledge of Bedlam?" Elizabeth asked, edging a little away.

"No, I haven't," Harry answered peevishly. "Just because I'm a ghost doesn't mean I'm demented. The county would be more inclined to say you were the demented one, wandering about talking to ghosts."

"I don't wander about talking to ghosts," she told him flatly. "This, I assure you, is an exceptional happenstance."

"Thank you," he replied.

Elizabeth wasn't quite sure why he assumed that to be a compliment, but before she could ask he moved again, a little away this time, making himself comfortable by perching on the two-inch-wide stairwell railing. Behind him were the stairs and thirty feet below, the stone-floored entrance hall.

"Be careful," Elizabeth said automatically, then lapsed into silence, feeling suddenly foolish.

"I appreciate your concern," he said dryly. "But I can't very well get hurt much more than I already have been. After all, I'm dead."

"I suppose you must be," she replied. "But I would much rather you weren't."

"I've wished the same myself many's the time."

"You couldn't possibly be a dependent relative who's a little touched, could you? Given to flights of fancy and pranks, that sort of thing?" she asked hopefully.

"I'm not cracked in the noggin."

"I see. Or rather, I really don't see. I mean, if you're dead, why are you here, still walking around, as it were?"

"Long nights have I wrestled with that very problem," Harry told her. "It came as quite a shock, I can tell you."

"It must have," Elizabeth replied truthfully.

"After all," Harry said, warming to his subject, "you may think it upsetting to turn around and see me, but imagine how you would feel if you woke up one morning and *were* me?"

"I would be terribly upset."

"Precisely," he agreed. "Not to mention, I must say, that the afterlife isn't run in any better fashion than life itself is. At least not as far as I can see. Here I was with no preparation, none to tell me what the rules were, or precisely how I was to go about my new occupation. I can tell you, it wasn't easy."

"I don't know what I'd do," she said honestly.

"You would do as I did, and muddle through like any good Englishman," he said bracingly. "Mind you, it won't be easy, if you ever have to go through it. But at least you'll have my example to fall back on. I had none."

"Pardon me if this sounds impertinent, but how does one become a ghost exactly? How did you get into this predicament? I mean, I believe you mentioned Sir Ambrose Steadford, but I don't quite see how he could—do this to one."

"I didn't say he did it. I said it was his fault. I had a rather sudden, not to say untimely, departure from the prime of life and no chance to right a wrong I'd done—a wrong I hadn't intended doing. But, damn and blast the man, because of Sir Ambrose it turned out about as wrong as wrong can be. So I must stay here at Steadford Abbey until I've made things right again."

"How?"

Harry warmed to his topic. "Now, that's exactly my problem. I know what I am to do, but the how of it, I must tell you, is a mystery I keep banging smack up against. You see, I have to bring Steadfords together with their true loves, but I never know which Steadfords let alone who their true loves may be. Not until they can see and hear me, that is. And even then, I'm finding that it can still be a rather impossible task, given the thickness of human skulls, not to mention their downright orneryness—which I think is one of the problems we're going to have with Giles in there."

"Giles?" she said and stopped. Staring at the Ghost, her forehead bunched up into a concentrated confusion. "We?" she finally asked.

"From what I've seen of the man so far, he's none to easy to get along with—as well you know—and he doesn't listen above half to anybody. Then there's the chip on his shoulder over his legs and all. I must say you've chosen a rather sad rattle to fall in love with."

"Fall in love?" she said in a shocked tone. "I've done no such thing!"

"Defend him all you want, but he certainly needs some getting used to."

"I'm not defending him," Elizabeth declared in ringing tones. "I'm not in love with him!"

"Of course you are," Harry replied.

Before Elizabeth could muster a stinging enough retort, the master's suite door opened. Jack Fence stood in the doorway, looking towards her.

"I thought I heard you speaking to someone," the valet said.

Elizabeth stared at the man. "Do you see anyone here for me to be speaking to?"

"No."

Elizabeth allowed herself to glance back towards where Harry had been perched. He was no longer there. "Nor do I," she told the major's servant.

"Sir Giles wished me to convey an invitation for you to join him for the evening meal in his sitting-room."

Elizabeth was surprised. "Why, thank you. I mean, please thank him."

"In an hour, if that meets with your approval."

The pretty young nurse nodded. "That will be fine."

The valet closed the door again. Elizabeth hesitated before she went towards her room, looking around as if hoping to see the Ghost still nearby.

She thought about calling out, but realised she did not even know how to call him or if he could hear her wherever he was. *If* he was, she told herself sharply, trying to persuade herself she could have imagined what just transpired. Still, deep within her, she knew that whatever else the Ghost was or was not, he existed in this house and not in her head.

She walked back along the wide chilly hall to the room she had been given at the back of the upper floor. Her room was as arctic as the hall had been, no fire laid in the grate. Elizabeth bent to the task of lighting the kindling, trying to dismiss the chill before changing for dinner.

Her thoughts ran back to the Ghost's comment about her clothing. Just like a man to assume women must dress in fancy styles and furbelows, she told herself, then realised she was speaking of a ghost. Not a man, at all, or at least not still so.

When she straightened up, her reflexion in the narrow pier-glass stopped her in her tracks to stare at her own serious face. Her simple hairstyle of short curls was stuffed mostly under a navy muslin cap. Only a few dark tendrils drifted towards her forehead and peaked out from the nape of her neck. Her dress was of sensible country woollen, its colour a navy blue, its design almost as plain as the habits of the nursing Sisters of Charity with whom she had studied. Her own dark blue eyes told the truth. She looked very like a poor orphan who had been thrown upon the parish for her sustenance and clothing.

In the back of her mind a tiny seed of a question tried to make itself heard but she would not listen. There was no need for her to castigate herself about her sudden awareness of the effect of her dress and physical appearance. There was nothing unusual about occasionally taking stock of how one presented oneself. It has absolutely nothing whatsoever to do with how Major Sir Giles Steadford might view her, she would have told herself firmly if she had allowed the tiny voice to grow louder. Absolutely nothing at all.

=== 10 ===

A COLD-WEATHER MEAL of mutton with haricot beans and soup was served by Jack himself to Sir Giles Steadford and Elizabeth Wallace, the nurse he had fought against from first sight. Rain had begun to pour down outside the thick stone walls. The watery sounds were pleasantly soothing as they filtered into the warm, dry room.

A leaping fire under the black marble mantel lit the room with dancing lights which glimmered in Elizabeth's dark curls and made the tiny gold crescents in the dark blue wallpaper gleam into brilliance here and there as the flickering lights of fire and candle illuminated them. Branches of candles flickered atop the cherrywood table where patient and nurse sat before blue and white Wedgewood plates.

"I don't know quite how to say this," he was telling her diffidently as Jack withdrew from the room. "I suppose the best way is always the most direct."

Echoes of her conversation with the Abbey Ghost made Elizabeth's heart lurch and stop for a moment until she heard his next words.

"What I'm trying to say is something I never thought to hear myself say. But, the truth is, I'm glad you were insubordinate."

She tried to read his expression. His eyes were darkest brown and seemed to shroud his thoughts rather than to illuminate them. "I beg your pardon?" she said finally.

"I'm expressing this badly," he told her. "What I'm trying

to say is that you were right and I was wrong. That Bath chair was a good idea."

"Thank you," Elizabeth said warmly. "I was hoping you would come to appreciate it."

"I do. And I appreciate your thinking of it," he added.

Elizabeth looked down at her plate, avoiding his gaze as she felt herself blushing.

He continued to speak as he poured more claret into their goblets, the ruby colour of the wine and the ruby colour of the cut glass blending into each other. "Jack has been telling me we could change the gearing mechanism on the wheels and add a steering stick which would help me manoeuver better. I've been thinking of ways to remodel some of the doorways so that I could get around inside the house by using the chair, or possibly another like it, but a little smaller and without the roofing."

"I suppose it could be done," Elizabeth replied. "But—"

He interrupted her, not seeming to notice her words. "The only real problem to be solved is the stairs."

Elizabeth gave him a quick smile. "You seemed to deal with them quite well this afternoon."

"Not those stairs. The ones here," he said, earning a startled look from his nurse.

"You can't ride that chair down the stairwell," she told him. "It's not possible."

"Not without some kind of platform for it and some sort of a funicular pulley system."

"I beg your pardon?"

He smiled. "Sorry. Some sort of rope system, amongst other things—brakes and such."

"I was thinking of something else. A different approach," Elizabeth told the major.

"A smaller chair? I bethought of that myself," Giles said.

"No. Something entirely different."

His brow furrowed. "Really? For the stairwell?"

"Yes. Amongst other things," she added, repeating his phrase.

He leaned forwards, his elbows on the white linen table-cloth. "Tell me."

"I was thinking of your own good legs."

There was a long pause while Giles Steadford considered the woman's words. "I don't understand," he said finally.

"It is possible, just possible—with much work, with exercise and massage—that the use of your legs could be strengthened."

Giles stared at her, his dark eyes haunted. When he spoke, his words seemed devoid of all emotion, belying the sudden churning of hope and fear that filled him. "Are you telling me I will walk again?"

"I am telling you it is possible, with enough hard work."

He took a deep breath. From long years on the battlefield he had learned to mask his own worries, his own fears, from his subordinates. A leader was not allowed such luxuries. Long habit made him contain all sign of softer emotions.

"Yours, or mine?" he asked finally with an ironic smile. "The hard work," he clarified.

"Both," she answered forthrightly.

Jack Fence walked back into a room thick with silence, and Giles glanced towards him. "Bring some cognac, the best that's in the cellars."

"Yes, sir." Jack reached for their plates before he left the room in search of the brandy.

Giles Steadford never took his eyes off Elizabeth. He had dressed for dinner for the first time since he had arrived at the Abbey. His thick dark hair was brushed in the Brutus style, short, curly, and almost windblown in its casualness. A finely tailored Venetian waistcoat covered his creamy white shirt. He wore the palest of fawn pantaloons and a dark blue coat.

"I've not seen that dress," he told her and was rewarded with a quick flush that stained her cheeks a deep rose red. "Then again, I've not bothered to change for dinner before either."

"My mother always said one should mark all the niceties

of convention, because in following them one helped ensure society's standards would never lower."

He watched her. "And what would happen if society's standards did lower?"

"Why, one step down a stairwell leads to another and another until society would hit rock bottom and civilisation itself would disappear," she said earnestly.

He studied the Empire-styled, high-waisted dress she wore this evening. It was made of a demure sprigged muslin, white with tiny green sprigs embroidered all over it, high necked and long sleeved. "I am sure you will help ensure civilisation is kept safe," he said.

"I would hope so," Elizabeth told him.

"Do you then change every night for dinner?" he asked. "In the interests of civilisation, I mean."

Elizabeth dimpled prettily. "I confess, since I have entered the Abbey walls, I have been continually remiss. But I intend to mend my ways."

"Capital." Giles smiled, his straight, even features crinkling into warmer lines.

Elizabeth Wallace's heart skipped a beat as she smiled back at the face she realised was the most handsome she had ever seen.

Jack Fence knocked on the door before opening it. He entered carrying a silver tray laden with cognac and brandy glasses.

Giles spoke to the valet as he poured. "Miss Wallace thinks she knows how to bring the use of my legs back. What do you think about that, Jack?"

The valet placed one cut crystal brandy glass in front of the nurse and the other before his master.

"I wouldn't know, sir."

"Wouldn't know what?" Giles asked.

"Wouldn't know if it was possible, sir," Jack clarified.

Giles grimaced. "No, you wouldn't. But the real question is whether Miss Wallace knows if it's possible."

"I do," she replied succinctly. "And it is. It is not a positive thing, you understand. The amount of strength you regain has much to do with how hard you work for it. And, of course, how you heal."

"The healing I cannot control. That is in your hands and the doctor's and God's own. But the amount of work I do, that I can control. If my work will make the difference I will move Heaven, Earth, and the whole of England anywhere and for as long as you say."

Elizabeth cast him a positively roguish smile. "If you will do all that, I have no doubt we shall succeed famously. But we must start with a few less Herculean tasks."

"Such as?" he challenged, disbelieving but wanting to believe.

"I will help you do some exercises until you can do them on your own," she told him.

Giles gauged her for a long silent moment. He picked up his brandy snifter, rolling the glass back and forth between his palms, warming the golden liquid. Leaning forwards, he extended his glass towards her, making his decision.

"When do we begin?" he asked.

Elizabeth reached her own snifter forwards, touching his. "As soon as you wish." She took her first sip, coughing as the brandy burned her unaccustomed throat.

"Are you all right?" Giles asked her.

She reached for the ruby-coloured wineglass which still held most of its contents and took a long sip before answering him. "I'm fine, really." She smiled, blinking back unexpected tears. "We could begin tonight. Right now."

"Good," he replied. "What do we do? Shall I ring for Jack?"

"No, we can begin with you sitting where you are."

Elizabeth stood up. She reached for the small table and tugged at it. Giles saw what she was doing and helped push it away from his chair.

"What do you intend to do?" he asked.

The nurse went to the fireside and retrieved a footstool from in front of a wide, leather-covered easy chair. Bringing the footstool towards Giles, she placed it on the floor near his feet. Adjusting the skirt of her muslin gown, she smoothed it beneath her and sat down on the footstool.

"Your gown—," Giles Steadford objected as she reached to pick up his leg and place it across her lap.

"My gown will be fine," she told him.

She took off the soft velvet slipper that encased his left foot and looked up to see him watching her intently. She gave him an encouraging smile.

"I put my hand behind your knee, thus, and my other hand here, under your foot, you see. Now, I bend"—she suited action to words—"and straighten it as you would normally, if you could move it. You see?" She didn't wait for him to reply. "I repeat the movement over and over, and then we do it with the other leg."

"I hardly see anything Herculean for me to do," Giles said. "Assuming I could do what you are, which I can't."

"You will soon be surprised at how tired you will become from this. That is when your work begins, for we must do it until you are tired and long after in some cases. However, you may curse freely, if you care to."

"Thank you," he said dryly. "I had rather thought you disapproved of my swearing over the past few weeks."

"Oh, I did, but this is different," Elizabeth Wallace told her patient.

"I'm not sure I understand the difference."

"Your swearing at this point will keep you awake and working. Before it was merely petulance."

"Petulance," he exclaimed loudly.

"Such as a small boy's temper tantrums," the nurse added smugly.

Her head was bent to her task, and she did not see the play of quizzical emotions that crossed the major's handsome face. He looked down at her as she worked and wondered what this could possibly accomplish. He felt nothing, but soon he realised his back was beginning to ache with tiredness. He said nothing, then something in the stiffening of his posture made Elizabeth look up.

"Why are you stopping?" he asked.

"I've gone too long to begin with," she replied. "In the morning we start with the other leg and do half as much so both are worked equally."

"Then you must continue with the right leg now."

"You will grow too tired," she told him.

Giles Steadford grimaced. "Miss Wallace, you began your work earlier. I am just beginning mine at this moment. Please continue."

She hesitated. Then, rising to her feet, she moved the footstool to his right side and sat down again. Gingerly, she raised his right leg and began bending it as she had the left one, over and over, in the same movements.

Elizabeth cast frequent sidelong glances up at the soldier's tense face, gauging just how far she could go. She stopped after ten minutes but he urged her onwards.

"Do not stop yet," he told her.

"I must."

"It is not as long as you moved the other one," he told her.

"If we tire you too much we shall cause more harm than good. This is something that will take long, steady work over many weeks, perhaps months. There is no quick solution, Major." She stopped her lecture when she saw his clenched jaw. Quick remorse filled her eyes and her voice. "I'm sorry, I've already tired you far too much. Here, this will help." As she spoke she began to massage his right calf, kneading the long-unused muscles. He leaned back in the wing chair, a sigh escaping him as his eyes closed.

Elizabeth also massaged the left calf for long minutes, then around his knee where it connected with his thigh. She was massaging his left knee when she felt him shift in the chair. Looking up to gauge his discomfort, she saw that he was staring at her, his dark eyes looking deep into hers.

A slight tremour attacked her fingers. Sudden awareness of the familiarity with which she was handling this man's limbs washed through her. In that moment he was no longer a sexless patient. He was a full-blooded handsome man in his prime who was staring at her in a way that no man had ever before done. His eyes made her tremble with a soft *frisson* which warmed her blood and weakened her limbs. She couldn't look away.

Slowly, she relaxed her hands, withdrawing them from his knee. She hesitated, his eyes still holding hers in thrall, and then, very deliberately, she began to massage his right knee and thigh.

Giles, for his part, looked down at the nurse who had been manhandling his limbs and suddenly realised she was an attractive woman whose hands were upon his thigh. As he stared into the blue depths of her eyes he saw her confusion. And, as he recognised her awareness of his flesh, he shocked himself by becoming aroused.

The air in the room was suddenly charged with an electrical current that magnetised them to each other; and, in that moment, Jack Fence knocked and walked into the room.

The valet stopped in midstride, shocked at the scene before his eyes. The nurse was at the major's feet, her hands upon his knees.

"Sir," Jack exclaimed, his disapproval apparent.

Elizabeth pulled back sharply and Giles stiffened, both of them looking as guilty as they felt.

Giles glared at the valet. "Well, what is it?" he asked irritably.

"I—nothing. That is, I mean, it is the time you usually get ready to retire," Jack said and stopped, feeling as if he had intruded upon a very private situation.

Elizabeth rose to her feet. "Yes, we are quite through for the day."

Giles said nothing. He watched her move swiftly to the hall door. As she opened it, she looked back towards him.

"Good-night," she said softly.

He nodded slightly. "Good-night." He watched her close

the door behind herself and found himself still staring at the panels of the closed door.

A log crackled in the fireplace, part of it breaking off and falling through the grate. The valet went to the fireplace, replenishing the fire before he turned towards his master.

"Do you wish to ready yourself for bed, sir?" Jack asked.

His words interrupted Giles's thoughts. "What?" Giles looked towards the man. "Oh, yes . . . of course."

Jack Fence approached the chair, ready to lift his master and carry him to the bed in the adjoining room. He hesitated for a moment as Giles looked down at his legs, then stared at his feet, willing himself to lift them. Nothing happened.

"Sir?" Jack said.

Giles was still staring at his feet. "Look at my feet," he commanded.

The valet stared at Giles's stocking'd feet. "Yes, sir?"

"My right big toe," the major said.

Both men watched the major's right foot. His right big toe bent slightly and straightened. Giles stopped and looked up into his valet's face.

"Do you see that?" Giles asked the man.

"Yes, sir. You are moving your toe."

Giles Steadford sighed. "Good. I was afraid I was imagining it. I seem to be imagining a lot of things these days."

"Sir?"

"Nothing. Let's get me to bed."

"Yes, sir."

Jack Fence hoisted the young soldier and carried him the few steps to the large walnut bed in the next room.

Giles sat on the bed, helping Jack disrobe him. Then, Giles stretched out, closing his eyes as Jack lowered the bedside lamp.

"Do you want the door closed, sir?" Jack asked.

"No, leave it open."

Jack did as the major bade, then crossed the outer room and let himself out as Giles Steadford stared up at the shadowy corniced ceiling far above his head. Down the hall

Elizabeth Wallace was also disrobing and readying herself for bed. The thought gave Giles great pleasure.

= 11 =

FOR THE NEXT few weeks, the entire countryside talked of little else but the comings and goings up at Steadford Abbey; but none was as upset as the Abbey Ghost. The first morning Harry awoke from what he called his sleep—which was really a rather stationary floating doze—to the sounds of Bedlam itself let loose within the Abbey walls, he fell to his knees.

His first thought was that somehow he had escaped Ghostdom. His next was that somehow he had tried the good Lord's patience just one inch too far and had now sunk even lower in His esteem, and had been sent to some hellish underlife.

"I didn't do it," he said, his chin on his chest and his knees on the bare planks of the long-unused third storey school-room. "Whatever it is, I haven't done it. I promise you, Dear Lord of Us All. I've done bad and I've done worse, but I surely woke with a start when you put me here, and I've not done a blasted thing—pardon me—not a thing lately. Please don't sentence me to Eternal Perdition."

He received no immediate reply. Neither did he feel the plank boards open up to expose eternal flames below. In fact the schoolroom planks seemed as solid as ever.

Judiciously, one at a time, Harry opened his eyes. What met his frightened gaze were the dust motes which played in the sunlight streaming in the schoolroom windows. Everything seemed normal—except for the god-awful din that had awakened him to visions of Bedlam and worse.

He got to his feet in one quick, startled movement. The hellish racket that had awakened him slowly resolved itself into the separate, distinct, and loud sounds of hammering and sawing.

Harry's first reaction was to flee to the topmost attic rafters, but the sounds carried right through the walls, echoing up the stairwells.

By the third day of incessant din he ventured outside the walls, pacing the spinney and railing at the Fates for allowing such heresies to be committed upon the Abbey. It was Lady Agatha's by rights, and none else should have a say in what happened to it—let alone subject it to these indignities.

The thought of Aggie sent Harry farther down the hill, trepidatiously, it's true, to the gatehouse rose garden. The erstwhile Sir Harry hesitated at the doorway to the small stone building, wondering exactly where the Abbey walls ended and if the gatehouse counted as part of the walls or a separate entity. Unsure, he hovered outside, peering in the windows, trying to see Agatha. All he saw was Fannie, bustling about the kitchen baking bread.

Harry tried again the next day and the next, finally rewarded by Agatha's coming outside and walking amongst the bare-branched rose bushes.

Fannie stood in the doorway. "I'm making up a list for Hetty to take to market. Is there anything in particular you fancy?"

"No."

"You'd best come in, it's cold out there," Fannie said.

Harry made an unseen face at her. "Stay out of this. It's none of your business," the Ghost told the serving woman tartly. Unfortunately, since she could not hear him, his words did little good.

"I shall be in directly," Agatha informed Fannie. "I just want to make sure the bushes are covered properly. It will soon be cold enough to freeze their roots at night."

"Yes," Fannie agreed. "Well, don't freeze your own roots, Aggie. You stay out there and you're liable to catch your own death."

"Aggie, you'll not catch your death," Harry's unheard voice said. He looked concerned as he appraised Agatha's colour. "You're not feeling peaked, or some such, are you? You can't up and die on me while I'm in a state like this. You've got to take care of yourself and stay here as long as I have to."

As he spoke Lady Agatha walked back inside, oblivious to his presence.

Sadness engulfed the Ghost as he turned back towards the Abbey. Seeing Agatha, being near her, always seemed to sadden him even while he warmed himself with her presence. He wanted to reach out and touch her. She was the only one he really wanted to have near him, and she seemed to be the only one who never did. Perhaps never would.

These unhappy thoughts accompanied Harry back to the Abbey. Other thoughts intruded once he passed easily through the ancient stones and the workmen's din accosted his ghostly ears.

"By Jupiter, of all the things I have to put up with, this infernal racket ain't among them," he thundered impressively.

Unfortunately, he was thundering to himself.

From that afternoon on, the Abbey's legend grew quickly, as Harry did his best to dissuade the workers from continuing with their noisy repairs and remodeling. The next few days found tools misplaced, full tins of paint suddenly emptied, sometimes in the unlikeliest of places. Workers began to blame each other for the mess and confusion, and tempers flared higher as the work went slower.

Late one afternoon two of the local workmen were arguing about the replacement of the library door. The original door had been hinged on the outside right when it should have been hinged on the inside left. The workman who was responsible for marking, repairing, and replacing the bearing walls during the remodeling told the carpenter he was not only wrong, he was out and out crazy.

As they argued, two painters pushed past them, yelling about who had spilled whose paint on whom.

"It was you and I saw you," the shorter one declaimed, only to be withered with a glance from the taller, skinnier one. "You did it before and now you've done it again."

"Go away with you, you're daft."

"Daft is it? Well, the paint's on the floor and there'll be hell to pay, I can tell you that, for I shall tell them who did what."

"What kind of knock in the cradle do you take me for? You think you can upset my work and then blame me? It's you that's playing tricks, and that's what I shall say."

"Stubble it," the short man yelled, "or I'll deal you a facer straight in the noggin."

"Go milk a pigeon!" the other man shouted back.

The rest of their argument was lost as they stormed past the carpenters and headed towards the morning room where the new owner of the house sat pouring over architectural plans of the Abbey. The carpenter turned his back on his workmate, pulling a handful of three-penny nails from a pocket of his leather apron. Ignoring his companion, he began to pound the nails into the doorframe with energetic ferocity.

As he pounded the third iron nail, the first popped back out, almost falling to the floor. The carpenter slammed his hammer into the wide head of the first nail once again forcing it back into the wall. As he slammed the first one back in, the second and third ones popped almost all the way out.

"Ezra Bartholomew, you'd best stop this humdudgeon this very minute or I'll be forced to give you a what-for the likes of which you've never had in your entire misspent life," the carpenter shouted at his companion.

Ezra turned from measuring the next doorway.

"What are you yelling about now, Jim Frey?" Ezra asked.

"Stop fooling with my nails," Jim Frey demanded.

"Have you gone daft?" Ezra replied. "What would I want with your nails? I've got my own."

"You're punching mine back out of the doorjamb."

"What nails?" Ezra stared at the doorway he was measuring. "There's no nails here."

"Not that one, *this* one."

"Jim Frey, have you gone queer in the attic? Look at yourself, man. How can I be fooling about with your nails over there when I'm standing all the way over here."

Jim Frey stared at Ezra Bartholomew. Then he stared back at the doorjamb and the nails that wouldn't stay put. He pulled off his cap, scratched the back of his head, and then turned back towards his companion. "Come over here, then," Jim said.

Ezra left his work. "You want me to do your pounding for you, Jim?"

"Go ahead," Jim said. "You think you're so smart."

Ezra grinned. He reached for the hammer. "I'll show you how, never you fear, Jim Frey."

Ezra pounded one of the three-penny nails flush with the wall. He turned towards Jim. "Want another lesson?"

"Look again, if you're so confounded smart," Jim taunted.

Ezra glanced back over his shoulder. "Don't try to hoax me, I—" He stopped talking. "What the bloody hell—"

"I told you," Jim Frey said smugly. He lost his smug expression as he stared at his friend. "What's going on around here."

"You hit one while I hit another," Ezra commanded.

Jim reached to pound the bottom nail, Ezra the one above it. The minute they took their hammers off the nailheads, the nails popped back out of the doorjamb.

Ezra spoke slowly. "Have you heard about the Abbey having ghosts?"

"What's the matter? You think we've both gone queer in the attic?" Jim asked.

"It's my belief you were *born* with rats in your upper storey, Jim Frey, but what I'm talking about here is something I'm seeing with both my own eyes. And what I'm seeing doesn't make sense."

"There's no such thing as ghosts," Jim said flatly, his attention going back to the doorjamb.

His companion started to reply as he turned back to his own work, but the words got stuck in his throat. Ahead of him, farther down the wide cold hallway, something large and black loomed. "Jim—Jim," Ezra repeated, his voice sounding strange.

"What's the—" Jim Frey stared at the looming figure coming towards them. "Dub my mummer," he said, backing away from the apparition. "I'm getting out of here."

Ezra was backing up towards Jim, his eyes on the thing that was approaching. "What is it?" he finally managed to ask.

"I don't know and I'm not waiting to be introduced." Jim turned as he spoke and moved so quickly down the hall he very nearly slammed into Elizabeth Wallace.

The nurse was emerging from a parlour doorway with Jack Fence just behind her.

"Good grief," she exclaimed, startled. "Is there a problem?"

"Problem?" Jim Frey stared wide eyed at the nurse. "Look behind me."

"Jack?" Giles Steadford called from within the room.

Jack turned back towards Giles and the interior of the room as Elizabeth gasped, her hand going to her mouth.

Giles grabbed the wheels of the Bath chair and propelled it towards the parlour's wide double doors where Elizabeth stood transfixed by what she saw. Beyond Elizabeth the two workmen ran towards the front hall and escaped from the Abbey, as Jack Fence helped Giles manoeuver past Elizabeth and into the hallway.

Behind the wheeled chair, Jack peered out to see better down the hall. "What the devil—"

Giles grasped the arms of his chair. "What are you doing?" he demanded.

The dark apparition stopped where it was and seemed to hesitate.

"Is that you?" Giles demanded.

The apparition shrank into smaller proportions, resolving into the semblance of a man, and then disappeared into thin air as nurse, valet, and soldier watched.

Jack Fence found his voice. "What—what was that?"

"The Abbey Ghost," Giles replied.

Elizabeth turned her attention towards her patient. "He really exists," she said.

Giles rewarded her with a quizzical look. "You don't seem too surprised."

She swallowed. "I saw him in the Long Gallery."

"I don't believe it," Jack Fence said.

"Oh, but I did," Elizabeth assured the valet.

Jack stared at her. "No, I mean, I don't believe in ghosts. There's no such thing."

Giles answered, "Perhaps you would tell us what other explanation exists. I should be most happy to be proven wrong, I assure you."

"But, sir—," Jack began and stopped. "I don't know," he said finally, shaking his head.

Giles sat back against the chair cushion. "While you're thinking about it, I think you'd best send someone to the gatehouse. I would like a personal interview with Lady Agatha at her earliest convenience."

Elizabeth dragged her eyes from the empty air that had so recently held the vision. When she returned her gaze to Giles in the chair beside her, her eyes were large and round.

"I think he's upset," she said in a small voice.

"He's not the only one," Giles said and gave her a frosty smile. "Help me back inside."

Elizabeth did as the major bade.

A few minutes later, Jack Fence pushed through the green baise door to the kitchens, earning Hetty Mapes's amazement.

"You saw what?" she asked the valet.

"I'm not daft and I'm not alone," Jack Fence declared stoutly. "The workmen ran off, and the master and Miss Elizabeth all saw it. It's the master who wants Lady Agatha sent for."

Hetty looked towards her assistant who had stopped shelling peas to listen to their conversation. "Martha, you go about your work. This doesn't concern you."

"But he says he's seen the Ghost," Martha protested.

Hetty glared at the younger woman. "You get back to shelling those peas and let me worry about Abbey ghosts. If any ghost dares to set foot in my kitchen, he'll soon learn to stay out, I can tell you that."

"Maybe it's a she-ghost," Martha said fearfully as she picked up another pea pod.

"He-ghost, she-ghost, or she-devil—you've naught to fear as long as you stay here in the kitchen with me," Hetty said firmly. The cook turned her attention back to the major's valet. "Timothy is down at the stables, Mr. Fence, and June is in the dairy, but I can spare her for a bit. You can send her, if you like."

"I'd better go myself," he told the cook.

"If you're going yourself, a word to the wise," the cook volunteered. "You'd be best served by giving your message to Fannie and letting her tell Lady Agatha."

"I don't understand," Jack replied.

"Lady Agatha doesn't care for talk of a ghost. She can get quite put out about it. You've not seen Lady Agatha when she's in a state."

The valet nodded his thanks before he closed the door.

"What do you suppose Lady Agatha can do?" Martha asked.

"I'm sure I don't know. And I'm sure it's none of my business. Nor is it yours," Hetty informed Martha as she moved back to the long oak table and sank gratefully to a wide-bottomed wooden chair.

After a minute the cook began to help with the peas, keeping her thoughts to herself as she worked.

== 12 ==

GILES WAS STILL in the small side parlour with Elizabeth when Jack Fence returned with Lady Agatha. Fannie had come along also, talking as fast as she could, trying to calm Lady Agatha's ire.

"I'm through with these for today," Sir Giles was saying, handing a sheaf of architectural drawings towards Elizabeth.

She took the plans as an indignant Lady Agatha entered the room and Fannie hovered near the threshold, looking worried. Jack Fence went to stand near his master.

Lady Agatha glared at Sir Giles. "What's all this nonsense about a ghost?" she asked.

Sir Giles took his time answering. "Actually, that was precisely the question I wanted to ask you."

"There are no ghosts," Agatha declared, looking from one to the next as if daring them to dispute her.

"That gives us a difficulty," Giles replied.

"And why does it?" Agatha asked him.

"Because two workmen, my valet, my nurse, and my very own eyes, have seen him."

"My stars, are you saying you've all seen the Ghost?" Fannie blurted out, then fell silent at Lady Agatha's look.

"All," Sir Giles pronounced in firm tones. He studied Lady Agatha's disbelieving face. "Now how do you propose we explain that?"

"I don't have to propose anything at all," Agatha replied tartly. "It wasn't my eyes playing tricks."

"Five pair of eyes all playing tricks at the same time?" Giles sounded unconvinced.

"Are you going to tell me, Major, that you, an Army man, believe in hobgoblins and ghosties?" Agatha's tone left no doubt as to her own feelings on the subject.

"I believe in very little other than what I can see with my own two eyes," he told her.

"Back to our eyes, are we?" Agatha gave him a frosty smile. "I would suggest you can't always believe what you see either, Sir Giles."

"What about believing what *you* see?" Giles countered.

"I have never seen a ghost," Agatha declared.

"Never?" The word slipped out before Elizabeth could stop it.

"Never," Agatha replied emphatically.

"How odd," Elizabeth said quietly, a peculiar expression in her dark sapphire eyes.

"What's odd is that any of *you* have," Agatha told the nurse crisply.

"I quite agree," Giles put in. "Nevertheless, there it is."

"There what is?" Agatha asked. "I fail to see why you summoned me up here, Sir Giles."

"I hope my man was more polite than that, Lady Agatha. I asked him to extend an invitation to you for tea and conversation."

"Ghostly conversation, I take it," she said dryly.

"I sincerely hope our conversation will not be only real but also entirely forthright and honest."

"If you are suggesting that I am being anything but entirely forthcoming on this topic, you are misleading yourself, Major."

A small smile played across the major's face. "I am assured you would tell us anything you knew about such an—awkward occupant."

"There's been talk for years," Fannie said. She was rewarded with a withering glance from her employer. Fannie's straight jaw set a little firmer, but she was not silenced. "None of it's been anything other than maid's whimseys."

Lady Agatha awarded her abigail with a brief smile. "As Fannie says, there have been unfounded stories for years."

They were still discussing the apparition when tea was served.

"I imagine a play of light in the hall seemed to make movement or some such," Agatha said as she stirred her tea. "And with stories of a ghost bandied about by the servants, it's no wonder if people think they see things. I'll warrant if no ghost stories had ever been told, each of you would have seen the truth of it at once."

"The truth," Elizabeth repeated.

"A play of light," Giles added.

"Yes."

Elizabeth hesitated over her words. "But what if one could talk to him?"

"Talk to? And here I thought you were a sensible sort of girl," Agatha said.

"Why don't you stay the night, Lady Agatha, and disprove the entire episode?" Giles waited for her reply.

Agatha was surprised. She looked at Fannie, who sat near the fire. "I assure you, having spent all the nights of over sixty years in this house, and having never seen hide nor hair of any strange beings, I should hardly be likely to see one this night."

"Would you care to stay this particular night and find out one way or another?" Giles asked again.

"You make it sound like a challenge," Agatha told him. When he did not reply, she gauged him. "Are you saying if I myself do not have a visitation from this figment of your imaginations, you will put the matter to rest?"

"If you stay the night and the Ghost does not dare to put in an appearance before you, I shall assume you are correct. That we are all hysterics and Bedlamites and you the only sane one amongst us," Giles pronounced.

Agatha Steadford-Smyth considered the young soldier

before her, then the young woman across the room, Fannie beyond by the fire. "I suppose I shall have to say yes in order to end this nonsense once and for ever."

"I sincerely hope you shall," Giles returned. "Accept the invitation and end the—nonsense."

Agatha spoke to Fannie. "You'd best have the man take you down to the gatehouse to collect what few things we may need for overnight."

Fannie moved with alacrity. "I'll be off right away then, shall I?"

"Don't look so pleased," Agatha told the woman crossly.

Elizabeth stood up and walked towards the fire, extending her hands towards its warmth. She thought about telling them of her own conversation with the Ghost, but kept biting back the words. Agatha would definitely think her demented, and Giles might think her so, too."

"You're very quiet, Miss Wallace," Agatha said behind her.

Elizabeth turned back towards Sir Giles and Lady Agatha. "I'm sorry, I seem to be the very worst of conversationalists this evening." She found Giles watching her intently and coloured a little.

"You're not frightened, are you?" he asked her.

"Frightened? No, not at all." Elizabeth gave him a small smile.

Agatha considered the young woman who stood across the room in her sensible blue dress. "I'm sure Miss Wallace has seen much more distressing things in her career of nursing duties than dark shadows in a hallway."

"Yes, I have," Elizabeth said firmly.

They had finished a second cup of tea before they heard Fannie arriving back at the Abbey. Her footsteps echoed towards the small parlour as she traversed the hallway. She appeared in the wide doorway with a small valise.

"Ah, Fannie, there you are." Agatha stood up. "I suppose we should see to freshening up and changing for the evening." She looked rather quizzically at the small case. "I wonder how you've managed to pack all we need into that?"

"I didn't. The large case is at the stairwell. I wasn't sure where to take it," Fannie informed the room.

Elizabeth came forwards. "Let me help you with your things." She looked back at the major. "Then we can get to your exercises."

Giles hesitated, his expression enigmatic. "You'd best ask Jack to get hold of Tim, then, to get me upstairs."

Elizabeth waited for Agatha, who had turned back towards the seated man. "Would you prefer I use guest rooms?" she asked.

"Whyever should you?" he asked back.

"My former rooms adjoin the master's suite," Agatha said.

"I assure you, Lady Agatha, I do not snore. At least not loudly enough to disturb you in your own rooms," he replied with a trace of a smile.

Her small smile was more a grimace. "I was thinking about propriety, not proximity."

"Then you must lock your side of our connecting doors," he told her merrily. "And I shall trust you to keep them locked."

"Major!" Agatha said scandalised, but an unexpected laugh accompanied the lone word. "Come along, Fannie, this man is the outside of enough. First hobgoblins and now suggestive behaviour. Miss Wallace, I fear for your safety in this house alone with such a gentleman."

Agatha was speaking lightly and so was quite surprised at the sudden crimson which flushed the young nurse's cheeks.

Elizabeth ducked her head and preceded the two other women down the hall towards the grand stairway to the upper regions of the ancient Abbey.

Two hours later a formal dinner was served in the dining-room for the first time since the new owner had arrived at the Abbey.

Hetty Mapes prepared broiled rump steaks with oyster sauce for the occasion—yeast dumplings and carrots and potatoes to go with it, pea soup before, and raspberry tarts to follow.

"My Lord, I'm quite stuffed," Giles told the others. He smiled down the table to where Agatha sat at the opposite end.

"Hetty has outdone herself," Agatha agreed.

Elizabeth Wallace sat to Sir Giles's right, halfway down the long mahogany table between Giles at one end and Lady Agatha at the other. She picked at her meal, a shyness that was new to her keeping her mostly silent.

While the two cousins made conversation about various relatives they had in common, Elizabeth castigated herself for being such a ninnyhammer, for feeling so shy and out of place. There was no need, there was no reason, and there was no excuse she could find for her emotions to be tumbling about within her and confusing her so—except that she was acutely aware of the physical presence of the man at the head of the table.

She told herself she had been totally professional in conducting his physical therapy an hour earlier. She told herself she was not affected in the least by his handsomeness which she could not deny. She told herself to stop thinking about him.

"Are you quite all right, Miss Wallace?" Agatha was asking.

Elizabeth looked up, flashing the older woman a brilliant smile. "Oh yes, thank you, I've enjoyed the meal immensely." Silence met her words. "The food was excellent."

Agatha gave the girl a searching look. "Yes, I agree. Hetty is to be applauded."

"Yes, quite," Elizabeth replied.

Giles spoke then. "You didn't eat much, for having liked it so excessively."

"I've truly outdone myself," Elizabeth countered. "I've eaten twice what I usually do."

Fannie came through the green baise door across the

room behind Giles's chair. She carried coffee and cream.

Giles stopped her before she began to serve. "Lady Agatha, what do you say to having coffee and sherry in the library?"

"Thank you," Lady Agatha said. "Shall we?"

In the library Jack had already laid a fresh fire. They settled to a quiet evening, Fannie with her knitting, Agatha idly watching the chess game between Elizabeth and the major. Each engaged in desultory conversation about the Abbey, the village, and the world at large.

"You're sure you don't want to play, Lady Agatha?" Elizabeth had asked when they first sat down. Agatha disabused the girl of that notion immediately, saying she was totally unwilling to tax her tired brain and wanted nothing more than to enjoy the fire and the company until it was time for bed.

"You're sure you're not saving your strength for an encounter?" Giles teased as he moved a black knight in response to Elizabeth's white bishop.

Lady Agatha allowed him a small smile. "I hardly think I shall be worn out chasing ghosts this night, Sir Giles."

"Perhaps not. But since we are cousins I think we should allow ourselves more familiarity. I confess I am quite uncomfortable being called Sir Giles continually. I hope you'll call me simply by my name and I shall do likewise, if you do not object. I find Agatha a lovely name and much less formal than Lady Agatha."

"As you wish, Giles," Agatha replied. She did not seem displeased by his request.

The evening stretched quietly before them, the only sounds those of the fire in the grate and the quiet conversation in the room.

When Jack Fence brought a nightcap tray of brandy, Giles breathed a prodigious sigh. He smiled at his second cousin and shook his head a little woefully.

"I was hoping for some grand sort of disturbance this evening to prove to you that we have not lost our reason, but I fear the Ghost is not going to oblige me."

Agatha made a face. "Giles Steadford, if you are joshing about a ghost, you are using very poor taste and will find it harder and harder to get and keep servants if you keep up this nonsense. On the other hand, if you are truly suggesting that such an entity might actually exist, then I must tell you I do indeed fear for your reason. I know of no mental aberrations in the Steadford line, but there could always be a first."

Don't give up on me, Agatha," Giles told her, grinning. "I've not gone quite 'round the bend yet."

"I'm glad to hear it," she told him. "Fannie, I think it's time we retired."

"I'm sure I'm not keeping you up," Fannie replied. She finished off a line of stitches and put her knitting away.

"What are you making?" Giles asked, curious.

"A shawl, I think," Fannie replied. "Or a muffler."

"That's a very lovely colour of green," Elizabeth said.

"Yes, I think so, too," Fannie agreed. "Pomona green, they call it."

Agatha was standing. "Is there any help you need?" she asked Giles. "Should I call for Homer to help your man take you upstairs?"

"Thank you, no," Giles replied. "Not just yet. I think I'll enjoy my brandy down here for a bit."

"We shall leave you then," Agatha said, then hesitated, glancing a little uncertainly towards Elizabeth. "Is your game completed?" Agatha asked. "I can wait if you like."

"There's no need, I've already lost abysmally," Elizabeth replied. She prepared to stand up, but Giles spoke, stopping her.

"Miss Wallace, I'd like a private word if you don't mind."

Elizabeth settled back once more against the tapestry-covered gilt chair. Agatha hesitated a moment more, then led Fannie from the room.

As they traversed the cold hallway, Fannie spoke. "There's naught the two of them can get up to alone, Aggie. He's in no shape to be a danger to her virtue."

"Yet," Agatha replied. "Something's going on between the two of them though."

"What?" Fannie asked.

"I don't know," Agatha said.

"If you ask me, there's blessed little that could be going on. And borrowing trouble's a worthless occupation. You just don't trust men."

"I've never seen them to be worth trusting. As a gender, they are wholly deplorable."

"What about Charles?" Fannie asked, reminding Agatha of her granddaughter's husband.

"One exception simply proves a rule," Agatha said as they climbed the stairs towards their beds.

"I like the major," Fannie continued after a minute.

"Until this evening, he's given us precious little reason to. His arrival was not designed to make him popular with his people."

"He's in some little pain most of the time, I think. That's why he was so cussed. He even looked a little peaked tonight, if you ask me."

"I didn't," Agatha pointed out, ending the conversation.

Meanwhile, in the library Giles was offering brandy to Elizabeth, who refused it.

"Perhaps some sherry?" he persisted.

"Nothing, thank you. "I'm quite full. Unless there's something further, I really would like to retire."

"Why?" he asked quietly, his gaze never leaving her eyes.

His inspection made her uncomfortable. "I—I beg your pardon?"

"You seem to be distracted this evening," Giles said.

"I'm not," she defended a little too quickly. "That is, I have a little headache, that's all."

He leaned forwards, concerned. "I'm sorry, I didn't realise."

"If there's nothing else—," she persisted, eager to be away.

The expectant, almost hopeful, expression left his eyes which clouded over as he nodded absently. "Yes, please let Jack know I'll be turning in shortly. He'll need to find Homer." Giles turned his gaze towards the fire, brandy glass in hand, and apparently ignored her quick departure.

Hours later, as the Abbey stood sentinel at the top of its hill, the moon floated high above in the far-off reaches of the dark night sky, heading slowly towards the horizon. The countryside had frosted over with the midnight winds chilling the silent landscape.

Inside the huge stone house, master, servants, and guests were all tucked safely into their beds, the only sounds those of light snoring and the winds that buffetted the outer walls and rattled the shutters and windowpanes. Of all the household, only the Ghost walked the halls, restless and forlorn.

Harry paced the third-storey schoolroom, glumly considering the signal lack of success his best efforts had, thus far, produced. With ghostly hands clasped behind his nearly nonexistent back, Harry considered alternatives with very little enthusiasm.

He was so distracted he didn't notice the walls he passed through until he saw the stairs ahead of him. Morose, he continued on that path, allowing himself to float down to the second floor and landing in the Long Gallery, where Ambrose Steadford's dour face stared blankly back at Harry.

"Go on and look at me with your supercilious expression," Harry the ghost told the oil painting. "What care should I have what you think of me?" Harry's countenance turned woefully sad. "I am reduced to speaking to paintings."

The oil painting did not answer. Harry took this omission as a sign of his current disfavour with the Almighty and lapsed into fretful silence as he turned away.

The Ghost paced the Long Gallery, muttering to himself about the disgraceful turn of events that had led the Abbey to such a sad state of affairs, with strangers running amok throughout the premises, changing the old building beyond all recognition, and none to make them stop—at least none they could see or hear.

"What is all this noise?" Agatha's voice startled Harry into invisibility. His heart seemed to hit his throat and his body jumped, the top of his head grazing the ceiling before he calmed down and descended back towards the second floor.

"Aggie, you're here!" Harry cried out, his eyes lighting up with pleasure. "Can you finally see me?"

"Whoever's pacing about out here must stop, this instant," Agatha Steadford-Smyth said in a loud whisper. "It's enough to wake the dead, let alone those merely asleep. I won't have it."

"I'm sorry, Aggie, I didn't mean to disturb you," Harry said, thoroughly chastened. "I've been hiding in the upper attics, trying to figure a plan to get all these strangers out of the house. I didn't know you'd come back, or I'd have been quiet, I swear it."

"I won't tolerate tricks, Giles," Agatha was saying as Harry spoke. She was peering into the Long Gallery directly towards where Harry stood.

"It's not Giles, Aggie. Can't you see me?" Harry asked.

Agatha came a few steps closer, searching the shadows for a shape. "I know someone is out here," she said.

"I'm right here," Harry told her.

For the first time since the subject of the Ghost had come up earlier, Agatha hesitated. Something glowed a few feet ahead of her, near her father's portrait. She blinked at the ghostly light in the Long Gallery. The moon's reflexion, she told herself, but she did not look up towards the mullioned windows.

Harry took a step closer and was rewarded by Agatha taking an involuntary step backwards. Hope brought Harry another step closer. "Aggie, can you see me at least a little?"

"Stay where you are," Agatha was saying over Harry's own words. "You're just a trick of light, it's true, but stay put, all the same."

"I'm not a trick of light," he told her offended.

"Ghosts don't exist," she said firmly, hearing nothing but her own words. "Someone's playing tricks, and it's going to stop as of now. If ghosts did exist, I would explain in no uncertain terms that this household has no need of one."

"That's what you think," Harry groused.

"And I want this noise to stop. People are trying to sleep."

Harry watched her turn away. "I must say your disposition isn't getting better with the passing years, my girl."

Agatha hesitated on the threshold, as if listening. She seemed about to turn, then shaking her head, she opened the door and went through without looking back.

"I could follow you, you know," Harry told the empty air. "But I won't. What's the use if you can't see or hear me? For all the good I'm accomplishing, I might as well do away with myself right here and now," he said as he dissolved into unhappy invisibility.

== 13 ==

THE NEXT MORNING Elizabeth was up early. She dressed quickly in the cold back bedroom, bundling into a warm cloak before hurrying down the kitchen stairs and out into the chill morning air.

October had brought north winds hurtling through Dorset and the smell of snow in the air. Elizabeth watched the uneven ground beneath her half-boots as she hurried away from the Abbey walls and the dreams that had kept her wakeful throughout the long night.

Biting her lip, she headed towards the spinney, her thoughts upon the Ghost. She should have told them of her own encounter with him. She should have been brave instead of silent. Lady Agatha might deny him all she wished, but Elizabeth had seen him with her own eyes—and not just a vague dark form in a hallway. She had talked to him.

In the crisp morning air, the entire episode sounded unreal and silly. Elizabeth Wallace picked her way amongst the oak trees' gnarled roots, her eyes to the ground, her thoughts poring over the events of the past few weeks. Which was why she didn't see Harry until she almost walked through him.

"Oh, no!" She brought herself up with a start, her eyes growing large as the subject of her thoughts appeared directly ahead of her. "It's you," she said.

Harry glowered at her. "I must say you humans seem to

be losing what few manners you once had. How would you like to be greeted by 'Oh, no, it's you'?"

"I'm sorry," Elizabeth replied, feeling foolish. "You startled me."

"Well, you startled me, but I wasn't impolite about it. Now you can leave me my last moments alone, if you please. I don't wish to share them."

The nurse started to turn away and then stopped. "I beg your pardon?"

"Can't a ghost have a little privacy around here?" he asked.

"You were complaining about too much privacy at our last conversation," she replied.

"Yes, well, it's all one to me now. I'm doing away with myself."

Elizabeth considered his words. "Are you sure?"

"What the devil do you mean, am I sure?"

"It's just that I can still see you," she pointed out. "And others have, too. I mean, that was you in the hall yesterday, scaring the workmen, wasn't it?"

"For all the good it did. That's part of the reason I've given up. She doesn't want me around, so that's that."

"I beg your pardon?"

"And well you should," Harry told the girl. "All of you should, but there's no way to make amends. Now leave me to end it all."

"How does one go about doing away with itself?"

He eyed her. "A curious little baggage, aren't you? If you must know, I'm not allowed to leave the Abbey walls. Upon pain of horrible happenings."

"Such as?"

Harry glowered. "I don't know yet. I imagine I'll end up in limbo or fall through to some fiery domain, and that'll be the end of it."

"Are you quite sure you've got it right?" she asked. "Nothing seems to be happening to you yet."

"You're in a hurry to see the last of me, no doubt, just

like she is. Well, Sir Harry Aldworth's never stayed a place he wasn't wanted."

"Sir Harry Aldworth?"

He glowered at the girl. And then, rather ungraciously, sketched a rather slight bow. "My manners are atrocious these years, but that's how it is. Now, if you'll go, I'll get on with it."

"Are you sure you want to?"

"Of course I'm sure," he thundered. Gratified when she took an involuntary step backwards, he spoke next in a more mollified tone. "Actually, if you must know, I'm building up the courage to take the next step. I have to pass past the Abbey's outer walls. I'm sorry I can't stay around long enough to get you and Giles together, you'll just have to handle it yourself."

Elizabeth blushed. "I don't know what you're talking about."

"You love him."

"That's ridiculous," Elizabeth told Harry.

"Ridiculous or not, it's the truth. And he's supposed to fall in love with you."

"You can't know that."

"Of course I can. That's why I'm here. Or why I've been here, at any rate," Harry amended.

"You're crazed," she told the Ghost. "Love is the farthest thought from our minds."

"You can see and hear me, therefore you love a Steadford. And he can see and hear me, but is determined I am nothing but a bad dream."

"I rather hoped to use that excuse, too," Elizabeth said. "You see, I really do feel I should say something about you to Lady Agatha."

"She won't believe me, I doubt she'll believe you," Harry replied. "The fact that you're human might be a point in your favour. If you could persuade her." Harry sounded almost hopeful.

Elizabeth, however, was pursuing another question. "Sir

117

Harry, you said when last we met that you were here to bring Steadfords together with their loved ones."

"Ay, and with that clan, it's no easy task, I'll tell you."

"But why should you have been charged with such a fate?" Elizabeth asked.

Harry glowered. "To earn forgiveness from Steadfords."

"But why?" she repeated.

"Why, why, why, is that all you can say?" he asked peevishly. "It's a long story. I'm to help Steadfords find their true loves until I've earned out my freedom."

"Then what?" Elizabeth asked.

"I'm not quite sure. Except that I can rest finally."

"And if you go outside the Abbey walls, what then?" she persisted.

"I'm doomed to dangle for ever, never free, never at peace, with never another chance to make things right."

Elizabeth considered the almost transparent figure who leaned against one of the large oaks, his face a study in unhappiness as he considered his fate.

"If leaving the grounds dooms you for ever, I don't understand why you want to go."

"Because she said she doesn't want any ghosts here," Harry said, for all the world looking as if he were pouting.

"She?"

"Aggie."

"Aggie? Lady Agatha? Has she seen you?"

"No," he told the girl. "If she could see me, do you think I'd be here, ready to throw myself away for ever? She heard me walking about and she told me to stop. Actually she told Sir Giles to stop—she thought at first it was him. Then she wasn't so sure and she said if there was a ghost, which she was sure there wasn't, that she wanted him up and gone and that was flat."

"If she could see you, what then?"

Harry considered the girl. "If she could see me, if she knew it was me, she'd not send me away."

"I take it, she knows you? I mean, knew you?"

Harry nodded. "Once upon a time, she did."

"Then I think you'd best stay," Elizabeth told him.

He eyed her curiously. "What good will that do?"

"I shall tell her myself," Elizabeth promised.

Harry stared at the girl. "What?"

"I promise you, she shall know it's you. That's what you want, isn't it?"

"Yes, but—" Harry lapsed into thoughtful silence. "I doubt you can make her believe it."

"But if I can?"

Harry thought about that. He said finally, "If she knew I was here, mayhap she'd be able to see me, or hear me, or both."

"Well, now, isn't that a better alternative to being doomed for ever? After all, you've been here quite a while, haven't you?"

"I should say so. I've put a great deal of effort into getting her to notice me."

Elizabeth nodded. "If you quit now, all that work will have been for nothing."

"I am not a quitter," he told the young woman in no uncertain terms.

"Good. Then, that's settled."

The nurse turned back towards the Abbey with a resolute step, leaving Harry behind to sort out what had just transpired. He had the feeling he had somehow been managed quite successfully by this human. His hand went to his head, scratching it a little as he drifted back towards the house at the top of the hill.

The household had begun to stir, the scullery and kitchens readying breakfast, Fannie helping Lady Agatha to dress for the day as Jack Fence attended to the master of the establishment. Elizabeth was already in the dining-room when Lady Agatha appeared.

"Good morning, Lady Agatha." The younger woman greeted the former owner.

"Good morning. You're up early."

"I couldn't sleep, I had the most distressing dreams."

"Nor could I," Agatha acknowledged.

The sound of the wheeled chair preceded Sir Giles into the dining-room, Jack negotiating the turn for his master and then moving to the buffet and the breakfast dishes.

"Eggs, sir?"

"And some sausage, I think. Good morning, ladies. I trust you slept well."

"Well, we didn't," Agatha informed him.

Giles Steadford smiled quizzically down the table towards his older cousin. "Don't tell me Our Friend saw fit to bother you."

Agatha gave him a withering look. "Giles, there may be a passel of gullible ninnyhammers in this establishment, but I assure you, I am not one of them. Nor, I must tell you, do I appreciate practical jokesters. Or my sleep being disturbed."

"I don't know what you're talking about," he replied with every semblance of innocence.

She regarded him with unconvinced eyes. "I suppose you know nothing of someone pacing about in the middle of the night."

"You suppose correctly. Nor, obviously, could I be the culprit," he told her.

Momentarily abashed, Agatha was quiet while Fannie brought a fresh pot of piping hot tea, refreshing their cups and placing the pot itself on a trivet next to the buttered and toasted bread.

"And you, Miss Wallace," Giles continued. "Were you awakened by ghostly pacing also?"

"It was not ghostly pacing," Agatha corrected with a great deal of asperity.

"I slept poorly," Elizabeth admitted, "but I heard no pacing."

"I hope," Agatha continued, "this conversation puts to rest the notion of an Abbey ghost."

"Oh, but it can't," Elizabeth put in quickly, earning

120

startled glances from both Giles and Agatha.

"I beg your pardon?" Agatha watched the girl carefully.

But it was Giles who replied. "I can thoroughly understand your reluctance to believe such a thing. I assure you, I am not far behind you. If it hadn't been for a strange dream I had, I wouldn't have given the matter a second thought myself."

"But it wasn't a dream," Elizabeth told him, earning another startled look. "You really did see him."

"I beg your pardon?" Giles said.

"For I've seen him, too," Elizabeth declared.

"Nonsense," Agatha said firmly.

"I wish it were," Elizabeth replied, her sincerity evident. "I assure you, I would much rather Sir Harry did not exist."

"Sir Harry?" Giles repeated the name, staring at her. "You mean you actually saw him, talked to him, too? It wasn't a dream?"

"It was no dream," Elizabeth replied.

"But it's Sir Henry, not Sir Harry," Giles countered.

Agatha looked from Elizabeth to Giles. "What are you two talking about?"

"He said his name was Sir Harry," Elizabeth told them. She looked towards Agatha then. "And he particularly wants you to see him, Lady Agatha."

Agatha Steadford-Smyth wore a very peculiar expression. "I don't know what either of you think you are doing," she said, watching them both.

"I know it sounds strange. Fanciful even," Elizabeth's words rushed together. "I didn't believe it myself at first, but you see, I've talked to him twice. And now that others have seen him, and he told me he'd talked to you—she turned towards Giles—"there's really no other explanation. He must be real."

"He told you he talked to me?" Giles asked, surprised.

"Yes, that's how I knew," Elizabeth said.

Giles looked from Elizabeth to Agatha. "You're quite sure you've never seen this Sir Harry or Sir Henry, are you?" Giles asked Agatha.

"Sir Harry Aldworth," Elizabeth added.

Lady Agatha's expression froze as Giles looked towards Elizabeth. "By George, that's what he said to me, too. Aldworth was the family name."

"How dare you?" Agatha said, her voice icy with rage that shocked both her observers.

"I don't understand," said Giles, "why you haven't seen him at some point."

Agatha's eyes were as cold and black as the darkest stormy night. Her voice was no warmer. "How dare you?" she repeated, anger making her words tremble a bit.

"I'm sorry?" Giles gaped at her. "Agatha, what's wrong?"

"What village gossiper have you been prattling with?" she demanded. "Both of you." She included the nurse in her anger.

"The workmen—," Elizabeth began and stopped, daunted by Agatha's expression.

"The workmen," Agatha repeated, the words falling like stones on their ears. Agatha Steadford-Smyth stood up, her glare raking across first Elizabeth and then Giles. "I would have expected better of you than to think you gossiped with workmen." Agatha threw down her napkin. "Please do me the favour of never, ever, daring to speak to me again."

Giles stared at the doorway as Agatha sailed through it, calling out sharply to Fannie as she left.

Elizabeth looked towards the major. "I don't understand—," she began, but her words were cut off by Harry's appearance at the foot of the table.

"My fault, I fear," Harry told the humans.

Giles stared at the apparition. "My God, man, you're real."

"I should have warned you, she might not be glad to hear my name," Harry told Elizabeth.

Elizabeth couldn't take her eyes from the Ghost. "What was that all about? Why was she so distressed?"

"Distressed?" Giles said. "She was angry, pure and simple."

"But, why?" Elizabeth persisted.

"Because I ruined her life," Harry told them both. "That's why I have to do penance to Steadfords. That's why I have to see that you two—"

"Please," Elizabeth interrupted, "Sir Harry, say no more. Please, don't."

"Don't what?" Giles asked.

Harry considered the young woman. "He'll have to know sooner or later," Harry said practically.

"I'll have to know what?" Giles interjected.

"Please—," Elizabeth repeated, her cheeks staining scarlet.

"Miss Wallace—," Giles began as a burst of noise came from the distant outside hallway. "What the devil is that?"

"Lady Agatha?" Elizabeth ventured.

The sound of many voices calling out and talking over each other echoed down the long hallway as Jack Fence appeared in the doorway.

"Jack, what the devil's going on?" Giles asked.

"I'm sorry, Sir Giles, but you have visitors."

"Not now, man," Giles complained.

"Yes, absolutely now," a lovely female voice overrode Giles's complaint.

Harry faded back through the dining-room wall as a slim blonde beauty sailed past Jack Fence and headed towards the head of the table.

"I've come to surprise you, dear heart," she said. And, so saying, she leaned down to deliver a soft kiss to his forehead. "Have you missed me as terribly as I've missed you?"

"Anne," Giles finally managed to say.

Lady Anne Hartley rewarded him with a merry peal of infectious laughter. "At least you've not forgotten my name, Giles, dear." She looked across the table, acknowledging the existence of the dark-haired young woman in a mouse-brown dress. "Hello," Anne said, smiling.

Elizabeth gazed bewildered into smiling turquoise eyes. Lady Anne's cheeks and lips were cherry-kissed, her perfect oval face held aloft by a graceful, patrician neck beneath which the very latest in fashionable clothing moulded a perfect figure.

"I am Anne Hartley, Giles's fiancé," the young beauty told Elizabeth. "Who might you be?"

Consternation registered in Elizabeth's eyes before she could cover it with a small smile. "I am Elizabeth Wallace," she replied.

"I'm sorry," Giles interrupted. "Anne, you quite startled me. This is Miss Wallace, my nurse."

"Your nurse?" Anne Hartley's brow rose a fraction. "Truly? Which sisters are you with, Miss Wallace?"

"None. She's a professional nurse," Giles answered for Elizabeth.

"I was not aware there were any such—females" Lady Anne said with every sign of sweetness. Only Elizabeth heard the barbed edge under her words.

"There are," Elizabeth said flatly.

"Not many, one would assume," Anne replied, smiling.

"Not as many as there will be in years to come," Elizabeth confirmed.

"Darling," Anne turned back to Giles, ignoring Elizabeth's presence. "I've brought friends with me and you must meet them. I've just been pining to see you, but I couldn't very well leave London before the Season was over. And then, Aunt Hester and I were invited to Lord Harleigh's for the summer and to the Prince's shooting box after that. I simply put my foot down yesterday and told them all I had to rush to your side. They wouldn't hear of letting me dash about the countryside alone, with just Auntie Hester, so here we all are, ready to make you feel ever so much better."

Anne finished her pretty speech with her hand possessively on Giles's shoulder. "You can hear all their noise. We'd best see them in the parlour before they devour it." Jack Fence appeared in the doorway and Lady Anne motioned to him. "Please inform the cook to ready a light repast for my friends, and help me take Sir Giles to the parlour," she commanded.

"I can come myself," Giles told her.

She stepped back from his side, gazing down at his chair. "What on earth is that contraption you're in?"

"It's a modification of a moving chair from Bath," Giles said. "Actually, it was Elizabeth—Miss Wallace's—idea. He looked towards Elizabeth's place, but she was gone. "Where did she go?"

"I have no idea, sweet. Come along and greet our guests," Anne told him prettily but quite firmly. "I shall attend to Miss Wallace, never fear."

"But where did she get to?" Giles complained. "I've not done my morning exercises yet."

"We'll give her a good talking to later, about her duties. Come along now," Anne said. "Everyone is waiting."

== 14 ==

"WHAT HAPPENED UP there?" Fannie asked for the tenth time since she and Lady Agatha had gotten back to the gatehouse.

"I don't intend to discuss it," Agatha said firmly. She pressed her lips firmly together and bent over her needlepoint frame.

Fannie watched her mistress work the coloured threads into flowered patterns, debating whether to pursue the subject further. She gauged the way Agatha was attacking her work and decided her questions could wait until later.

"I'll just see to starting up some soup," Fannie said.

"Do as you please. I'm not hungry."

"You will be sooner or later," Fannie informed Agatha tartly before she left the parlour.

In the gatehouse kitchen Fannie had no more than pulled out a large iron pot when she heard someone coming up the path through the rose garden.

Elizabeth Wallace tapped on the door as she opened it. "May I come in?"

"Do you know what happened up there?" Fannie asked without preamble.

"I'm not really sure," the nurse replied. She entered, closing the door and looking towards the entrance to the next room. "I came to apologise to Lady Agatha and to find out what we said that upset her so much."

"What were you talking about at breakfast?" Fannie asked the young woman. Her concern was very evident. "I don't think I've ever seen her more unnerved."

"We were speaking of the Ghost," Elizabeth began, stopping when she saw the abigail's expression.

"Well, she can't abide that subject, but I've never seen her take it this badly."

"Perhaps it was that we all saw him?" Elizabeth suggested.

"I still don't—," Fannie began and stopped. She looked at Elizabeth curiously. "Him?"

"Sir Harry. The Ghost," Elizabeth clarified.

Fannie blanched. "What did you say?"

"I said so many of us saw him. And Sir Giles and I even talked to him."

"Talked to him?" Fannie's voice was little more than a whisper. "What did you say the name was?"

"Sir Harry, or Sir Henry, we each heard it differently," Elizabeth said. "Actually, it was when we told Lady Agatha his full name that she became so upset. He said it was Sir Henry—or Sir Harry as he told me—Aldworth."

Fannie sat down hard on the nearest chair. "I don't believe you."

"What is it?" Elizabeth asked.

"You know. You have to know. Where did you hear his name?"

"Fannie, please. I don't know what you're talking about. I told you, the Ghost introduced himself. I know that sounds crazed, but he did. He truly did."

The serving woman shook her head in disbelief. "It's not possible."

"Possible or not, it's the simple truth."

Fannie stared at the young woman's sincere expression.

Elizabeth watched her. "What is this all about, Fannie? Why does that name affect you so? Who is he? Who was he?"

"Fannie?" Agatha called out from the front parlour.

"Coming," Fannie called back. Before she hurried out, she spoke in a low tone. "You'd best leave. She'll not be pleased to see you right now."

"But—"

Fannie shook her head. "Give it some time, girl. Give it some time."

"But who *is* he?" Elizabeth persisted.

"He's the man who ruined Aggie's life," Fannie said before she left the room.

Elizabeth stared after the woman. "He already told me that much," she said.

When Elizabeth returned to the Abbey she found Jack looking for her with word that she would not be needed today. Giles was driving out with his guests and would be gone until suppertime.

The old house reverberated with the overlapping conversations and laughter of Lady Anne's fashionable London friends.

"Did you hear what the Prince is putting poor Harriet through?" Leticia, Lady Hollingsworth asked her companions.

"Tell all, Letty, dear," Janet Redden said.

"You don't need to encourage her, pet," Lord Grantham drawled. He raised his quizzing glass to his pale eye, his thin, delicate body encased in a fashionable, perfectly tailored yellow satin, with wide, padded shoulders, frothy white cravat, and palest lavender pantaloons. "Letty can't abide secrets. She tells every single one she knows."

Letty laughed. "You are an odious boy, Granny, and I don't know why I bother to tell you anything at all. Just for that I may confide to everyone but you the latest *on-dit* about the Prince."

"Tell, tell," Susan, Lady Spencer urged. "I'm bored to tears with the country and things bucolic."

"That didn't take long," William, Count Leeds teased.

"Harriet is beside herself with consternation. It seems His Royal Highness has tired of pursuing Lady Hertford and has set his sights on our own dear Lady Bessborough."

"No," Lady Spencer leaned forwards. "Does Caroline know yet?"

"The Princess of Wales is always the last to know what her husband is doing," was Anne's opinion. "If, that is, she cares at all."

"He threw himself at Harriet's feet, truly," Leticia, Lady Hollingsworth giggled. "Can you feature it? He threw himself to his knees—"

"Not an easy task with all his weight," Lord Grantham opined.

"Can you just imagine the scene?" Letty asked the others. "Here he is, on his knees, clasping her 'round and kissing her neck with mad abandon and sobbing his love out to her as she struggles to get away."

"La, what happened then?" Susan asked her friend.

"It seems he went on vowing eternal devotion for hours and trying to get her to lie down."

"No!" William interjected. "Not even the Prince could make such an utter cake of himself."

"Well, he did," Letty affirmed.

"How did it all end?" Anne asked.

"How did Harriet keep from laughing out loud?" was Lord Grantham's question.

"She said she *would* have positively burst laughing, if her heart hadn't been breaking for the poor thing. She finally convinced him she loved her husband and would never become a man's mistress."

"Tell that to Lord Gower," William interrupted.

"Are they still lovers?" Anne asked.

"Yes," Letty answered for him. "In any event, she did stop him."

"And did he leave her in total dejection?" Susan asked.

"No." Letty giggled. "He stayed on trying her patience she said for two more hours, gossiping about all their friends' love affairs."

"Good grief, what a scene." William reached for his chased silver snuff box.

"What scene is that?" Giles asked from the doorway.

Lady Anne stood up, going to where he sat in the wheeled

chair. "There you are, darling. We've been waiting ages for you. Are you ready for our amble about the countryside? Are you sure you're quite up to it?"

"I'm fine," he informed them all. "My man has brought the coach."

"What fun we shall have," Susan, Lady Spencer said languidly.

Lord Grantham looked over at her knowingly and shared a small smile. "Susan is never so happy as when she can traverse the countryside and commune with Mother Nature," he told Giles.

"Come along," Anne said quickly. "Giles, dear, you must show our friends the extent of our lands."

"Not quite *ours* yet, dear Anne," William, Count Leeds, reminded the lovely blonde.

Lady Anne flashed William a brilliant smile. "I'll just call for Aunt Hester, dear Giles, and we can be on our way. She went to have a cold repast prepared for our journey."

"Are you planning on making a day of it?" Susan asked, her hopes sinking.

"No, dear. Just an afternoon of it."

"I really must have my nap before dinner," Susan told them all. "I truly can't function without it."

"Are you quite sure you can function *with* it, my dear?" Leticia asked in a syrupy tone.

"Yes, dear. I'm so much younger than you, you see," Susan told her questioner.

Giles Steadford kept silent, listening to his guests' conversation with only half an ear. His thoughts were with the Ghost—and with his cousin's abrupt departure.

Meanwhile, in the Abbey kitchens, Hetty Mapes was at war. The enemy was a skinny wisp of a woman whose thin grey hair curled into a hairstyle much too youthful for her years which did nothing to enhance the beauty of her angular face. Her prominent forehead and overlarge nose were not softened by her choice of hairstyle or by her expression, which at the moment was decidedly petulant.

"That is not how I said to prepare the ham slices," Hester Hartley told the cook.

"I've cooked ham, girl and woman, for over thirty-six years. And prepared cold nuncheons for more nobs than you've ever met," Hetty Mapes told her persecutor.

"I doubt that," Hester said sharply.

"Doubt all you like," the cook said graciously, "Truth is truth."

"Aunt Hester?" Lady Anne came down the servants' hall. "We're ready to leave."

"I suppose we shall have to make do with what your fiancé calls a staff while we are here," Hester said sniffing. "At least for the present."

"Nonsense," Lady Anne said, as if the cook and her minions were not in the room. "We shall make whatever changes are necessary, but they can wait until the morrow. Come along with what you've been able to put together from the larder here. We'll get things better organised soon enough."

Hester Hartley took the basket of ham, cheese, and bread from the cook with a satisfied expression. She even allowed herself a small, smug smile.

"Have one of the girls bring along the ale," Hester told the cook before she joined her niece. "I thought we'd enjoy a country drink."

They left the cook with her hands on her ample hips and a frown beetling her broad, perspiring brow.

"Are we all to be turned out without our wages?" June asked.

"Don't be daft, girl. Go along now and take that keg of ale to the coach before we've more grief from those two."

Once June was gone Martha looked towards Hetty. "That woman said Sir Giles is to marry her niece and they are to run the household."

"I'm not deaf, Martha. I heard."

"What's to become of us?" Martha asked.

Hetty wiped her perspiring brow. "Hand me the beater." Martha did as Hetty asked. "Well?"

"I've no idea," the cook said. "A few weeks ago, none would have convinced me that I would choose working for Sir Giles over anyone else. But then, I'd yet to meet Hester Hartley," she added grimly.

While Sir Giles and his guests toured the Abbey holdings, Sir Harry searched out Elizabeth Wallace. The Ghost found her once again in the spinney.

"You like it here," the Ghost said as he became visible a few feet away. He settled himself in a crook of the tree across from where she sat on a thick branching of gnarled roots, idly picking wood violets. When she didn't reply he continued. "I did not mean to get you both into trouble with Aggie."

"What happened between the two of you?"

"It's a long story," he replied. "Jack Fence has gone to ask Aggie to chaperone Lady Anne's visit."

"I doubt she'll do it. Besides, one would think they had enough chaperones already," Elizabeth said.

"That London crowd? Stuff and nonsense, girl. You needn't look so glum," he said. "After all, you've got some time to yourself now."

"And you've made quite a mistake, Sir Harry. Is it Harry or Henry?"

"Either. Actually my given name's Henry, but all call me Harry—called me Harry," he amended. "What do you mean, I've made a mistake?"

"You'd best be inside when Lady Anne arrives back."

"Why?" the Ghost asked.

"To help her do whatever it is you're supposed to do for the Steadfords."

Harry studied the young woman before him. "She's nothing to me."

"I thought you were supposed to help Sir Giles and his true love," the nurse countered.

"I am," he replied.

"You're not," Elizabeth told him.

"You're still upset with me," Sir Harry the Ghost told her. "I can tell."

"I am neither here nor there. You should concern yourself with Sir Giles and his true love, his fiancé, Lady Anne."

The Ghost leaned towards her. "That can't be so," he said with undeniable logic. "Only those who love Steadfords can see me, and you can see me. *Ergo*, you are his true love."

"You can spout your Latin all you please," she told the Ghost, "but the fact remains that he is engaged to Lady Anne. How do you know it isn't she whom you should be helping?"

Harry lapsed into silence, contemplating her words. He gazed up towards where a flock of birds were calling to each other, flying south in a jagged pattern.

"This has never happened before," he said.

"Well, it seems to be happening now," she told him.

He thought about it. "Not possible," he pronounced.

Elizabeth sighed. "I told you we weren't in love, but you wouldn't listen to me. Now, I really would like to be alone, if I may."

The Ghost hesitated. "I suppose I could leave," he offered.

"Thank you," the nurse said quietly.

Harry looked a bit glum himself. "I rather fancied having some company after all this time alone."

When she didn't reply Harry faded from view and soared upwards, invisible, allowing himself a few moments of riding on the freshening air currents, his thoughts flying higher than what was left of his almost weightless human self. While he floated, he pondered the possibility that he had been in error. It hardly seemed likely, but there it was.

He thought back over the little he had seen of the Londoners who had arrived at breakfast-time. There were four women and two men, all of them quite noisy and full of themselves. If this Lady Anne were Sir Giles's intended, it would probably mean even more of these interlopers arriving at the Abbey. The thought was not a pleasant one.

But duty was duty, Harry reminded himself. And he had never shirked his. Which meant he had best get back to the Abbey and present himself to Lady Anne. What he would do, if she saw him, was more than he could contemplate. He considered the unhappy Elizabeth Wallace moping in the spinney. She simply had to be in love with the major and that was all there was to it. Where Lady Anne fit into the puzzle Harry wasn't yet sure. But he had to find out.

15

HARRY ARRIVED BACK in the Abbey to find Fannie attempting to calm the cook. Much to his surprise, Lady Agatha herself was upstairs, giving June and Martha instructions on preparing the guest suites for the Londoners.

"Have you taken Lady Anne's things to the front guest suite?" Agatha asked the head maid.

"Yes, your ladyship. I'm sorry, I'd thought her to be put in the mistress's suite."

"That would be exceedingly improper, until they are married. There are connecting doors between the suites," Lady Agatha reminded the maid.

"Aggie," Harry said as he arrived in the upper hall. "I'm glad you decided to come back."

Frustrated by her lack of understanding, he lapsed into silence, content to follow her around as she prepared the rooms for their occupants. She was still working on the accommodations when the steady clip-clop of horses' hoofs heralded the return of Sir Giles and his guests.

The sounds of bored voices talking one over another traversed the stairwell.

"Martha, leave this room as it is," Agatha told the maid.

"But I haven't finished putting away Lady Anne's things."

"Leave the rest for later. She'll want her privacy as she changes and rests."

"Yes, your ladyship," Martha bobbed a swift curtsey and left the room. Agatha hesitated in the doorway, glancing back to survey their work, then closed the door right through Harry.

"That tickled," Harry told her but she heard nothing.

Glum, he sat down to wait for Lady Anne, telling himself there was no time like the present to straighten out a problem.

A thin, sharp-faced woman opened the door and entered the suite of rooms.

"Dash it all, but you're homely," Harry told her. "If you're to be his wife, I pity the lad."

"Anne?" the woman called behind herself and then came forwards into the sitting-room, pulling off her gloves. "She said this was to be your suite."

After a moment a blonde vision walked in behind the homely woman.

"Ah, that's better," Harry said, rubbing his ghostly hands together. "You are a picture, my dear."

Lady Anne glanced about the room. "It will do. For the present."

"Giles doesn't seem as attentive as I remember him to be," Hester informed her niece.

"He's been unwell," Anne reminded.

"Speaking of that, my dear—" Hester came closer. She began to unpin Anne's lustrous, thick hair. "Just how unwell is he?"

"I don't know, Hester. Ring for some tea, will you please?"

Hester went to do as her niece bade, while Anne walked into the larger of the two bedrooms which led off from the sitting-room. Harry followed Lady Anne, waiting until she turned towards him and then shimmering into full visibility. Or at least as full visibility as his amorphous body would allow. He gave Lady Anne a very grand, very low, bow.

"Sir Harry Aldworth, Bart., at your service, Lady Anne."

Anne Hartley stepped through him on her way to a cherrywood dresser where she picked up an ivory comb and turned back towards the sitting-room.

"I thought so," Harry said chortling. "You're either blind

as a bat, or you're not her." He floated along beside Lady Anne as she walked into the outer room. "You're not walking into walls," he told her gleefully. "I take that as a positive sign that you are not truly blind."

Anne handed the ivory comb to her aunt. "I think I'll wear the blue silk tonight, Hester. The one that matches my eyes."

"Giles will be bound to think you the most beautiful thing he's ever seen."

Harry the Ghost hovered near the doorway, taking a long look at Lady Anne. "He might just have his head turned looking at you. Better men than he have strayed down the primrose path because of a pretty face and figure."

"Bother Giles. He's easy to please. He's been so long away from polite Society he's not choosy. It's Granny I'm concerned about."

"You have him wrapped around your littlest finger and you know it," Hester told her wealthy niece.

"Having him there and keeping him there are two different things, unfortunately. He's sampled all over London. I want to keep him at my beck and call."

"How do you propose to do that now that Giles is back?"

Lady Anne shrugged. "All my friends manage to keep their lovers and their husbands apart."

Harry's form enlarged with rage. "Madam," he thundered at the woman who could not hear him. "You are despicable."

"Will Giles be able to walk again?" Hester asked her niece. "Or—to perform?"

"Father said his wounds could be permanent," Lady Anne told her aunt. "I must say, it will be a much easier situation calming Granny down about the whole venture, if Giles isn't—capable."

"It's too bad you can't simply marry Lord Grantham."

"I agree. But my father and his wife stand in our way, so that's that," Anne said practically.

"I shudder to think of you forced to winter all the way out here in the hinterlands."

"You shudder because you'll have to winter with me,

Aunt Hester. But never fear, we'll soon get Giles organised. He has other holdings, which I learned of as we rode today. We shall sell off whatever is necessary in order to set up a proper establishment in London. I should think this old monstrosity of a property will fetch a pretty penny—perhaps from Continentals or Americans or some such riff-raff. They love old ruins, I'm told."

"Old ruins, indeed," Harry said grimly. "We'll just see about your plans."

Lady Anne surveyed herself in the mirror Hester had brought her. "Yes, that will do quite nicely, Hester. Oh, and you'd best see to hiring the help we'll need to introduce me to the county. I intend to hold our engagement ball as soon as possible. Once all know of it, there'll be no backing out, even if he does find out about Granny."

"You're quite sure of all this?" Hester asked. "You were dead set against the betrothal when you were younger."

"Absolutely sure. Giles had very little competency when we were younger. Now that he's inherited the Steadford fortune, we'll deal quite well, I'm sure. After all, now he can afford me. And, with his infirmities, he won't be any problem for me."

"Problem!" Harry repeated in dark and dire tones. "I've heard more than a body ought to have to stand."

Elizabeth was in her room, changing for dinner when Harry appeared behind her. She saw him at once and uttered a little shriek.

"Sir Harry," she remonstrated, holding her robe tighter against her bosom. "You must not simply emerge in a lady's *boudoir*, in such a fashion."

"Hells bells, woman, this isn't the time for tedious formalities. This is a time for action!" the Ghost declaimed in ringing tones.

"You, sir, may call my sensitivity tedious formality, but I assure you, if you still had your proper body, you would understand my concerns."

"Now, don't go all female on me. We have work to do, so you'd best buck up," Harry told her plainly.

Elizabeth pulled her wrapper closer around herself, and turned to study the ghostly figure more closely. "What are you telling me?"

"I'm telling you that Lady Anne is a fortune hunter, plain and simple. She must be stopped before she ruins his life—and yours," Harry added.

"I assure you, I do not enter the equation," Elizabeth said.

"And I assure you, you never shall, unless we save him from this catastrophe."

"Sir Harry, you are being melodramatic," she chided.

"And you are being tedious." So saying his form evaporated from view, leaving Elizabeth more upset than she appeared.

Elizabeth Wallace descended to the lower floor with a slow and uncertain step. Hearing the muffled sounds of merriment from the parlour across from the dining hall, she lagged even slower. The green baise door beckoned across the wide hall. Elizabeth looked from the open parlour doorway to the closer servant's door. She hesitated for only a fraction of a moment, then headed for the green baise, escaping down the narrow servant's hall towards the kitchens at the end.

Sounds of conversation wafted towards Elizabeth from the open kitchen doorway, Fannie and Hetty Mapes sharing tea and conversation.

"I don't like it above half, I've got to tell you that flat, Fannie Burns. It's a wonder I'm still here this night after the way I was treated this morning," the cook was saying as Elizabeth walked into the wide, warm kitchen.

Hetty, seeing the newcomer, stopped speaking and turned back towards the open fire where pots of soup were bubbling.

Elizabeth's step slowed again. "I'm sorry," she said quietly. "If I'm intruding, please tell me and I'll depart."

Fannie gave her a brief, false smile. "Miss Wallace, they must be looking for you in the parlour."

"They've no need of me there. Nor, truth told, have I any wish to be there."

Fannie searched the young woman's face. "Whyever not?"

Elizabeth answered slowly. "I have little in common with the people in that room. I rather hoped for a friendly face and a cup of tea here with people more to my liking."

The abigail's expression softened. "And we're glad to have you, aren't we Hetty?" she asked to the cook's broad back. "Come sit at the table and I'll just find you a cup myself, if Hetty doesn't mind."

Since Hetty did not turn around, both took it to mean she had no objection to the nurse sharing a hot cuppa with them.

"I'm glad Lady Agatha came up to the Abbey," Elizabeth told Fannie quietly. "And a little surprised, actually."

"You could have knocked me over with a feather, I'll tell you that," Fannie replied as she brought two china cups to the table and served them both tea. "Hetty, you feel like a cuppa?"

"Not until after supper's served," the cook told the room at large.

Fannie stirred sugar into her tea and studied the younger woman across the table. "Lady Agatha was asked to oversee the household and the proprieties for Sir Giles while his fiancé is visiting. Has he mentioned how long those people are staying?" she asked.

"Not to me," the nurse replied.

The cook returned to sit at the table. "They don't look the type to be away from London for longer than they can help," she said flatly.

"Londoners," Fannie said the word in a pejorative tone.

"Dinner," Jack Fence said from the doorway. "They're ready." He saw the nurse. "Miss Wallace, Sir Giles has been asking for you."

Fannie gave the nurse an encouraging smile. "You'd best go on, girl."

Unwillingly, Elizabeth stood up. "Thank you for the tea."

Hetty Mapes regarded the nurse and, after a moment, nodded. She watched the pretty young woman leave. "She's nice, that one," Hetty told the others.

Fannie smiled a little. Jack Fence merely went back to his post.

In the dining-room, the small house party was assembling around the long, highly polished mahogany table as Elizabeth Wallace appeared in the doorway from the hall.

"There you are finally," Giles said.

"I'm sorry I'm late," Elizabeth replied quietly.

Lady Anne sank prettily to the chair at the major's left. "Nonsense, my dear. Giles simply works you too hard." Anne flashed Giles a brilliant smile. "The poor girl deserves some time to herself. But in the meantime, please, feel free to join us this evening, Miss— ah?"

"Wallace," Elizabeth supplied.

"Oh, yes, of course. How stupid of me to forget. Susan, Letty, gentlemen, this is Miss Wallace who will be joining us for dinner. She is Giles's nurse."

"How quaint," Susan said, eyeing the nurse carefully, taking in the dowdy, totally out of fashion, bottle-green dress, sensible hair and shoes.

"How surprising," Letty added, smiling a very wide, very insincere smile. "Come sit, Miss Wallace." She patted the seat beside her. The place where Elizabeth was accustomed to sitting had been taken by a tall, very handsome man who eyed the young nurse quite frankly through his quizzing glass.

"You must tell us about your unusual occupation," Letty continued and then smiled winningly up the table at her host. "And you, Giles, you naughty boy. I never knew what a rake you really were."

"A rake?" Giles questioned. Flattered more than he cared

to admit, he tried to look serious as he answered the red-haired beauty who was winking at him.

"Yes, a rake and well you know it. Leave it to you to find the only female private nurse in the whole of England who isn't a nun. My dear, you must give us all your particulars so that we may call upon you when next any of us is ill."

"I doubt you ever shall be," Elizabeth replied, a smile fixed in place upon her lips.

Letty hesitated, gauging Elizabeth for a long moment before she turned her attention to her tablemate and forgot the nurse existed.

"Miss Wallace—" Giles caught her attention. "Come sit."

Elizabeth walked unwillingly towards the head of the table and sat to Sir Giles's right, between her employer and a pleasant-looking blond man.

"David, Lord Grantham," Giles introduced. "Miss Elizabeth Wallace."

The blond man smiled, nodding slightly. "Charmed," he told Elizabeth.

"Your lordship," Elizabeth murmured, feeling extremely uncomfortable. "You're too kind."

"Nonsense," a male voice said from across the table.

Elizabeth looked towards Count Leeds as Anne spoke from her seat across the table at Giles's left.

"William, be good now."

"Annie, dear, I am always good." He spoke to Lady Anne who sat beside him, but his eyes never left Elizabeth's across the table. "As all the women who know me find out to their own satisfaction, sooner or later," he ended suggestively.

Elizabeth blushed and stared down at her plate.

"William," Giles interfered, "I'm positive you mean nothing amiss, but we are very far from London and such humour is not heard in these parts. I know you don't want to be misunderstood."

"Heavens, no," William drawled, his eyes smiling lazily into Elizabeth's. "I don't want to be misunderstood at all."

"Good," Giles said, nodding to Jack to commence serving

the first course as conversations eddied and flowed around the table.

Only Elizabeth was quiet. Excluded from the reminiscences of the others—the jokes and the past they shared—she added nothing to the conversation. Instead, she kept her head bent to her plate as the meal progressed and picked at her food, praying for dinner to be over so she could escape the room and the company.

Lady Anne monopolised Giles, keeping him bent towards her to hear every soft word. The others ignored Elizabeth as successfully as if she did not exist, and the meal continued interminable insofar as she was concerned.

At last, the final course was served and removed, and the men began to talk of brandy and cigars while the women were allowed to withdraw to the parlour. Elizabeth walked meekly behind Lady Anne, Lady Susan, and Lady Leticia until they reached the parlour doors where Lady Anne looked back at Elizabeth.

"That will be all for this evening, Miss Wallace. If we need you, we will ring."

Stung, Elizabeth bit back the quick words that came to her tongue and turned away. The tinkling of their laughter carried behind her up the stairwell as she climbed towards her bedroom.

They were lightheaded fools, and what they did or thought or said meant nothing to her, Elizabeth told herself firmly. The hot tears which burned behind her eyes came unwillingly, but she would not give in to them.

Pride goeth before a disastrous fall, she told herself firmly, but somehow the words gave no comfort at all.

$=16=$

THE NEXT FEW days Elizabeth was called to Sir Giles's rooms early each morning to help him with his exercises and then banished until dinnertime. She was told she could do as she liked, that Sir Giles would be busy with his fiancé and guests.

Elizabeth was treated very politely and kept at a distance, her meals made so miserable by Lady Anne's overly polite condescension, that she sent word after the first few days that she was unwell. She had a touch of fever and would keep to her rooms for her meals.

Lady Anne sent word back that she was terribly concerned, and, due to Sir Giles's delicate physical condition, it would be best for Miss Wallace not to come near the major until she was completely symptom-free.

Jack Fence found himself at Elizabeth's door, with instructions to learn whatever Elizabeth had been doing to exercise Sir Giles's legs. At first she demurred, sure that Lady Anne had sent the man.

"No, Miss Wallace," the valet told Elizabeth, "it was Sir Giles."

"Sir Giles?" Elizabeth repeated.

Jack Fence looked uncomfortable. "He said as how you were unwell and couldn't come to him, he wanted me to find the way of the exercises so that he could continue while you were indisposed. He doesn't want to lose time, he said to tell you."

"I see," Elizabeth replied quietly.

After she had instructed the valet in the exercises, Elizabeth sat in a rocking chair beside her bedroom window, looking out at the Abbey grounds. The first snows were whitening the landscape.

"I never figured you for a quitter," Harry said from the doorway.

Elizabeth looked up with a wan little smile. "I'm unwell, that's all," she said.

"Stuff and nonsense," he said bracingly. "She's filling his head you know."

"I realise that," Elizabeth told the Ghost.

"She's the one who kept at him about getting Jack Fence to learn the work. She told her aunt soon he won't be needing you here at all."

"And soon he won't," Elizabeth agreed.

"You must have more stomach for a fight than this, girl," Harry said. "You couldn't have picked such an occupation if you were lily-livered."

"Sir Harry, forgive me, but I don't think it's any of your business what Sir Giles does. Nor is it mine."

"Stuff and nonsense," he repeated. "She's planning a party for the whole county."

"I'm sure it will be quite the success of the Season."

"Yes, and she's planning on announcing their engagement at this little party, too." Harry floated nearer.

"I assumed she would."

"Is that all you've got to say?" Harry demanded. "Aren't you going to do anything about it?"

Elizabeth stared out at the snow-frosted oaks beyond her window. "There's nothing for me to do," she replied.

"Damn and blast, girl, there's always something that can be done. It's going to be a wonder if you weak-spirited moderns don't end up the downfall of England, not to mention damning me to Eternal Perdition."

"From what little you've told me, I rather think you've brought about your own downfall already, wouldn't you say?" Elizabeth asked the Ghost tartly.

"Don't be smart with your elders, girl," Harry ordered. "Besides, that's not the point," Harry said, sidestepping the issue. "You can't just walk away and let the likes of someone like that Londoner win out over you, now can you?" he demanded.

Elizabeth regarded the Ghost sombrely. "Gentlemen, such as you must once have been, seem to set great store in such things as winning out over someone or something else. It is a rather pugilistic view of the world in my opinion. We females, however, are constructed in some different parts than you males, Sir Harry."

"And well I know it," Harry told her darkly.

She ignored his words. "To my own way of thinking, someone I should have to wrest from someone else, if I were so inclined to do so, isn't worth the having."

"Very high-minded," Harry observed, "but it won't get you far in this world."

"I don't wish to go far. I am where I want to be."

"Yes, well, you won't be here for long if you don't do something about Lady Anne."

"There is nothing I can do," Elizabeth said in a rather dejected tone. "Even if I wanted to," she added quickly and turned away. After a moment she arose from the rocking chair and went to a walnut tallboy, fussing with her hairpins and combs.

"You may fool yourself, but you don't fool me," Harry told her plainly.

"I am not—" Elizabeth turned back towards the Ghost to defend herself, but he was gone.

Faint echoes of the Londoners' voices carried through the walls to colour Elizabeth's thoughts. Parts of her conversation with Sir Harry kept coming back to her, making her think about Sir Giles and Lady Anne.

Lady Anne wasn't right for Giles. She was much too frivolous and citified, but it was none of Elizabeth's business what he did. Except that he was her patient. He was beginning to have some control over the movement of his feet, which meant it might be possible that the damage to his muscles and nerves could be reversed.

Elizabeth Wallace had attended lectures by Charles Bell at the nursing hospice where she trained under the Sisters of Charity. His theories of the nervous system and its workings had been widely talked of and to have validity. If the major's muscles could be kept massaged and strong enough to respond when his nervous system called upon them, there was a chance he would be able to walk. That chance depended upon the muscles being able to carry out their duties. That would require the strength which had ebbed away as the major lay supine for the first months of his illness.

These past weeks Elizabeth had worked long and hard with Sir Giles to build strength back into his legs. Jack Fence, no matter how well meaning, could not have the knowledge of the human musculature that the nursing hospice had taught. It was important that the individual muscles were each exercised.

Surely Lady Anne would want her future husband to be whole, Elizabeth reasoned. And with that thought, she resolved on a course of action. She would ask to speak to Lady Anne and impress upon her the necessity for Giles's continued exercise, thus enlisting Anne's aid. After all, Elizabeth's concern was only for her patient's welfare, nothing more. She beheld her own reflexion in the mirror. Nothing more, she assured herself.

She was not in love with Giles. Sir Giles, she corrected herself quickly. She wasn't. But she turned away from the reflexion unwilling to acknowledge the conflicting emotions she beheld.

While Elizabeth wrestled with her feelings and her conscience, Lady Agatha was asking for an audience with her young cousin.

Surprised, Sir Giles told her emissary he was always at

Lady Agatha's disposal. Fannie hesitated, casting a look towards the other fashionables who were lounging about the morning parlour.

"Her ladyship would like to speak to you in private, Sir Giles."

The count unfolded himself from a wing chair by the fireplace. "I take it that's our cue to be off, my dears."

"William—thank you," Giles said as Fannie closed the parlour door. "My cousin and I have had a slight misunderstanding, and I should appreciate the chance to clear the air between us."

Lady Anne glanced towards her Aunt Hester but made no move to leave with the others. Hester cast a look towards Sir Giles before she stopped beside her niece.

"Could you help me a moment, dear?" Hester asked.

Anne smiled at her aunt. "I shall be up directly, Aunt." Lady Anne turned her turquoise eyes towards her fiancé. "I'd best stay with Giles for a few minutes."

A fleeting look of discomfort crossed Giles Steadford's countenance which Hester caught. Giles himself was answering Anne. "There's no need, Anne, if your aunt needs you."

"Yes, Anne," Hester said firmly, "please."

Lady Anne was not best pleased. She stood up, following her aunt out of the room and into the hall with rather poor grace.

Once outside, she glared at Hester. "Aunt, I wanted to hear what they were discussing."

"And he wanted you gone," Hester told her niece sharply. Remembering her dependency upon Lady Anne's parents, Hester smiled, softening her sharp tone. "Dear Anne, a man does not like to feel he is being managed. It's best if he feels he is in total charge at all times."

Anne almost stamped her pretty little foot. "I want to know what is going on," she said.

"And you will," Hester assured her. "I feel positive you will be able to elicit the information you need from dear

Giles without his even realising your curiosity."

Somewhat mollified, Anne accompanied her aunt along the hallway and away from the morning parlour. She even managed to nod sweetly towards Lady Agatha as they passed in the hall.

In the parlour, Giles awaited his older cousin. His curiosity was evident when his eyes met hers.

Lady Agatha seemed much more calm than she felt.

"Might I ask if Miss Wallace is available? This conversation concerns her as well," Lady Agatha informed her young cousin.

"Oh," Giles said. "Yes. Of course. I'll ring for her."

"I believe there's no need," Agatha told him. She went to the closed parlour door and opened it.

Fannie looked both startled and guilty as she beheld her employer. "I was just making sure that you weren't disturbed," she defended herself.

"Go find Miss Wallace," Lady Agatha instructed.

"Yes, your ladyship," Fannie said meekly. She hustled down the hall and up the stairwell. Agatha closed the parlour door and regarded Giles who was seated near the windows.

"I trust your guests have been made comfortable," Lady Agatha said.

Giles felt his impatience rise at her attempt for polite conversation. He bit back his curiosity and nodded. "I've heard no complaints," he fibbed. Lady Anne had treated them both to a long litany of the items that would need changing once their marriage was consummated. "Thank you," he continued, "for procuring the additional help."

"It wasn't easy," she told him baldly. "After the nonsense that has been bandied about concerning the Abbey and its fanciful apparition, we were required to search as far as Stoneybridge for the additional help."

"You were wonderfully successful," he told her.

"Thank you," Lady Agatha replied.

Both of them were rescued from having to find other

areas of talk by the arrival of Miss Wallace.

Elizabeth knocked once and entered to find both of them turned towards the doorway, awaiting her appearance.

"Good-day," Elizabeth said softly, closing the door behind her.

"Good-day," Giles said, finding himself suddenly lost in the dark depths of her cobalt blue eyes. "I trust you are feeling better?"

"I am well enough to perform my duties," Elizabeth told him quite firmly.

"I'm glad to hear it." Remembering Lady Agatha, his tone of voice became more formal. "Lady Agatha wanted to speak to both of us."

There was a brief silence in which Lady Agatha moved to perch on the edge of a green velvet chair. Elizabeth followed suit, sitting upon the nearest divan.

Lady Agatha regarded the plainly dressed girl for a silent moment, then turned towards her cousin.

"I must apologise for my abrupt departure upon our last meeting," Agatha said.

"There is no need," Giles began, only to be stopped by her ladyship's raised hand.

"Upon reflexion," Agatha told them, "I have come to the conclusion that neither of you was aware of the subject upon which you so crassly touched."

Lady Agatha did not add that it was her abigail who had insisted neither the nurse nor Giles was the type to gossip with locals.

"Agatha, I assure you," Giles said sincerely, "neither Miss Wallace nor myself had the slightest idea of what our conversation would mean to you. That is, of course, we ourselves were completely undone by the notion of a real, live ghost actually existing. We were no more prepared to believe such a thing than you are, I assure you," he ended as he had begun.

Agatha Steadford-Smyth took her time replying to Giles's disclosure. "But you are, now, convinced."

Giles hesitated, and in the moments of his hesitation Elizabeth answered. "I am, Lady Agatha."

"Yes, it's hard to dismiss," Giles told the former owner of the Abbey.

"I don't believe Lady Agatha's response was to the existence of the Ghost," Elizabeth said quietly, "as much as to who the Ghost is."

Agatha regarded the girl. "I find the entire situation impossible."

"So do we all," Elizabeth answered. "Including, I should say, Sir Harry himself."

Agatha's steady gaze faltered at mention of his name. She looked off towards Giles. "I should like to know precisely what you have learned about this so-called ghost."

"Do you know who he is?" Giles Steadford asked. "I mean was," he corrected.

Agatha answered slowly. "There was a certain personage my family and I were acquainted with whose name was the same."

"Sir Henry Aldworth," Giles said.

Agatha swallowed. "Yes." None spoke, each of them waiting for the other. Agatha broke the silence. "He was responsible for my father's death," she finally added.

"Oh, no." Elizabeth breathed the two words, her consternation showing as she looked towards Sir Giles.

"Agatha," Giles said, "please forgive us for bringing up such a painful memory." His expression sobered. "If this ghost is indeed some part of such a man, he is something to be reckoned with and not to be trusted."

"But he seems to be so benign," Elizabeth burst out. "I'm sorry, forgive me. But he says his being here is to help Steadfords, not hurt them."

"Help?" Agatha asked. She tried to hide her curiosity, but she could not prevent the lone word from slipping out.

Elizabeth spoke slowly. "Sir Harry says he is to atone to Steadfords." She saw Agatha's involuntary reaction at mention of his name.

"If this were true," Agatha replied, "why would I, for example, not have seen him?"

Elizabeth hesitated. "Perhaps because it would have been too painful for you."

Agatha raked Elizabeth with her eyes. "I beg your pardon?" she said coldly.

"You obviously cared for your father a very great deal, and it would be painful to come in contact with the personage who caused his death."

I suppose that is a possible explanation," Agatha agreed after a moment's hesitation. "If, indeed, this personage exists."

"Do you still doubt it?" Elizabeth asked.

"And well she should," Giles interjected. "I still have doubts myself. And you, Miss Wallace, if you are honest, you must admit to some doubts yourself."

Elizabeth remained quiet, unsure how to reply.

"In any event," Agatha said crisply, "I would like to put this episode behind us."

Of course," Giles said gratefully.

"Lady Anne has informed me," Agatha continued, "that she is eager to meet the county and would like to arrange a ball in honour of your arrival, if that meets with your approval."

Giles looked a bit doubtful, but he nodded. "If she would like it, I see no reason not to arrange such a party. If you will help?"

Of course," Agatha replied. "I can make a list of neighbours and notables you must invite. And arrange for the help. If we can, in the future, keep talk of a ghost to a minimum, it will help us to keep a full staff."

"I understand," Giles replied. He looked towards Elizabeth.

"As do I," Elizabeth said. "I have no wish to make others think me demented."

"Good," Agatha decreed. "I shall see to the arrangements for your festivities."

"Agatha," Giles stopped her as she was about to leave the small parlour. "May I also presume to ask you to remain in the household whilst my, whilst Lady Anne, is here?"

Agatha hid her surprise at his unwillingness to address Anne as his fiancée. "Of course. The proprieties will be observed."

"Thank you," he said as she departed the room.

Elizabeth started to follow but was stopped by a word from Sir Giles.

"Miss Wallace, I hope you are comfortable in your rooms and all," he continued.

"Yes, sir."

He hesitated. 'When you feel up to it, I would like to resume your ministrations regarding the exercise of my limbs."

Elizabeth rewarded him with a dazzling smile. "I am ready to begin immediately, Major."

He found himself smiling back, a sudden warmth spreading through him as he gazed into her happy expression. "Wonderful," he said sincerely.

= 17 =

THE ABBEY BALL was held on the first of November. The entire three storeys of the huge stone house were ablaze with candle and lamplight. Twenty extra rooms on the third floor had been readied for any guests who came from a great distance and might wish to stay over. These were in addition to the full complement of second-floor guest rooms and suites, and the extra servants' quarters which had been made up to house the retainers of the invited guests.

Agatha Steadford-Smyth went over the house with Fannie, checking their handiwork. Agatha was well pleased. "If we have need, we can put up thirty extra guests, plus their servants. Not including the London contingent." Agatha's opinion of Lady Anne's friends was conveyed by her disparaging tone and the manner in which she lumped them together in her thoughts and conversation. Privately she had told Fannie that all of them together weren't worth the salt of one good Dorset farmer.

Fannie agreed but said little since there was nothing she could do about their being at Steadford Abbey.

"I do feel for the girl, though," Fannie told her employer.

"Lord, I can't imagine why," Agatha replied. "She's of a piece with the rest of them."

"No, no, I don't mean Lady Anne. She's going to be a trial and a half for her husband and servants and should never leave London. That's a fact. *They* may like the way these prettified people look down their noses at the rest of us, but none else do. I was speaking of Miss Wallace."

"The nurse?" Agatha questioned her abigail.

Fannie nodded. "Do you remember telling me something was going on betwixt the two of them? Well, I think there is or should be, but neither of them knows it, more's the pity."

"Fannie Burns, you are making less sense than usual," Agatha said crisply.

Fannie sniffed at the rebuff. She sat across from Lady Agatha in the smallish sitting-room of the mistress's suite, holding a skein of yarn between her splayed fingers. Lady Agatha was rolling the yellow wool yarn into a symmetrical ball.

"Castigate me all you will, those two were made for each other, as you first observed."

"I did no such thing," Agatha defended.

"You did. I heard you myself."

"I said something was going on between them," Agatha clarified.

"Isn't that what I'm saying?" Fannie asked her. "He's a sensible sort of fellow. Not, mind you, the one I'd choose, but he's not as bad as he seemed at first."

"Thank goodness for that," Agatha said, "or we'd have lost the entire staff long before this."

"Yes. Well. Seen beside these London fops, he's a regular treasure. He won't spend the Abbey into the ground, nor will he neglect it as Nigel did." Fannie seemed unperturbed about casting blame upon Agatha's brother. Nor did Agatha demur.

"He's already been quite busy," Fannie continued, "seeing to the tenant farmers' needs and spending to improve the property and all."

"I see he's gained a fan," Agatha told Fannie dryly.

"I'm not saying he's perfect, but then again, what man is," Fannie asked rhetorically. She was rewarded by a sound very like a small snort from her employer. Fannie ignored such a lapse of manners and continued speaking. "Seen all in all, against others who could have ended up owning the Abbey, he's not, as I was saying, all that bad. Lady Anne, however, is. Mark me, she will ruin us all."

"Fannie, that's none of our business."

"Perhaps not. But Elizabeth Wallace is just the kind of good, sturdy girl a man like Giles needs to help run his estates and his households."

Lady Agatha allowed herself a small smile. "I hardly think any young girl, especially one as comely as Elizabeth Wallace, would appreciate being thought of as sturdy."

"Well, she is," Fannie defended.

"No doubt. But the gentleman in question is affianced to another."

"Probably a family arrangement," Fannie said darkly.

"Be that as it may, it is still a fact," Agatha reminded. "And that's all there is to that."

"Maybe," Fannie replied. "And maybe not," she ended enigmatically.

The first floor public rooms of the Abbey were thrown open, along with the wide double doors from the entrance hall to the huge front parlour and from the parlour to the ballroom beyond. In both the parlour and the ballroom, terrace doors were likewise open to the frosty November night.

Moonlight poured down upon the bare-branched trees that lined the Abbey road and the flagged stones of the terraces. Icy winds greeted the arriving guests as they descended from their carriages, their feet crunching across the brittle ground.

Inside the Abbey the stoked fireplaces, candles, lamps, and people had warmed the air to such an extent that the open terrace doors brought a welcome breath of coollness to the dancers in the ballroom.

Lady Anne stood in regal splendour between Sir Giles and Lady Agatha, being introduced along with Giles to the widowed Leticia Merriweather from the village, to the

Squire Lyme and his wife Eleanor and their twin daughters who were now sixteen and being presented to Society. The girls were fresh, wholesome-faced country redheads with plain, freckled faces and eyes of clear, innocent blue.

Lady Anne greeted the quartet of Lymes with wonderfully condescending grace. Her polished politeness and winning smile gave a first impression of genuine warmth as she met one set of arrivals after another. But when next she was addressed by one of the Lymes or another of the guests, her manner made it abundantly clear she had no recollection of who they were. Being so promptly forgotten or deliberately overlooked would nettle the most phlegmatic of souls and did nothing to endear her to the Abbey's neighbours or the county at large.

Margaret and Charlotte Summerville found themselves even more shabbily treated. Lady Anne took one look at Charlotte's luxurious sable hair and dark good looks and turned away to the next guests in line, ignoring the Spanish-complected beauty and her social-climbing mother. Giles, however, was more willing to spend time discussing the Abbey and his plans for it with the Summervilles.

Music filled the Abbey from the strings set up at the far end of the ballroom. As sedate minuets were performed, the Londoners allowed their boredom to surface.

"We seem to have fallen back into the last century," Lady Spencer told Lord Grantham. "I trust Anne won't decide to rusticate too long amidst such surroundings. It might take all the bloom off the rose," Susan ended, smiling suggestively.

Grantham smiled. "That's not our concern, is it, dear Susan."

"No?" Susan, Lady Spencer smiled a knowing smile. "I thought it might at least be yours, Granny."

He gauged his interlocutor. She was petite and curvy, with rounded good looks.

"Dear Susan," Grantham said with a suggestive smile.

Susan, Lady Spencer, rewarded him with a small, private glance of her own. When she spoke her tone was low, not to be overheard. "The hallway upstairs is ever so drafty isn't it? And you room is—what—the second door down from mine?"

"Is it?" He smiled. "I hadn't noticed." He watched her. "As of yet," he added.

"Susan," Anne came near her friend and her lover, "have you been forced to endure all our locals yet?"

"Not quite, sweet Anne, but if you are to live here, you simply must inform these people it is now the modern year of 1810, not 1710. The countryside does so lag behind London," Susan touched her fan to her lips, allowing herself a delicate, bored little yawn. She turned away from Lord Grantham, speaking smoothly and touching Anne's arm. "I'll go see to Giles for you, shall I? Then you can have a moment alone with Granny."

Anne beamed her thanks and turned towards her lover's bored eyes as Susan moved through the throng of country gentry.

"Susan is such a dear, close friend," Anne said.

Granny smiled lazily. "You'll never know how very much so," he agreed.

"I wanted to have a moment alone before the great announcement," Anne told her lover.

"Why?" Lord Grantham asked, earning a surprised and wary look from his *inamorata*.

"How can you ask why?" she demanded. Her tone carried enough urgency to make the people standing nearby look towards them. Anne and Granny both smiled, relaxing and joking for a moment as they moved towards a refreshment table. "I don't want to have you upset with me," Anne ended as they neared the table.

"But I'm not in the least upset, Anne."

"Nor should you ever be," she told him. "For there is no need for that. Or for jealousy."

"I can see that with my own eyes," he told her, earning a hard look from Lady Anne.

"You almost sound as if you take me for granted," she complained.

"No one in their right mind would ever take you for granted, dear Anne."

Interpreting his words as a compliment, Anne flashed her lover a brilliant smile, and, squeezing his hand, she left him to his own devices as she made her way back towards her fiancé.

Lord Grantham glanced around the room, dismissing all he saw, until he came to Charlotte Summerville. He met her gaze and smiled. When she returned his smile he walked towards her, his elegant figure clad in the finest sea-green taffeta, his cravat the most complex, his collar points the widest of all those assembled.

Lord Grantham reached Charlotte Summerville's side just as Elizabeth Wallace walked reluctantly into the ballroom, at each step telling herself she was going to turn back.

"Miss Wallace," Jack Fence spoke from near the doorway, "you do look a treat, if you don't mind my saying so."

She glanced down at the simple rose-coloured Empire-style silk gown she wore. "Thank you, Jack. Sir Giles sent word he wanted me to attend."

"And well he should."

Across the wide ballroom, Lady Anne had rejoined her Aunt Hester, Sir Giles, and Lady Agatha. Anne placed her hand possessively on Giles's satin-clad shoulder.

"Giles, dear, I think you should tell them."

Giles looked up at Anne, his brow furrowing into concentrated lines. "Tell them?"

"Great Jupiter, you can't let her do that to you," Harry thundered, destroying Giles's concentration.

Anne watched Giles's expression change as he gazed up past her towards the ceiling. "Darling Giles," she cooed as Giles stared at the Ghost who hovered near the ceiling high above Lady Anne' head. "What's wrong?"

"Nothing," he replied without much conviction.

"Don't let her do it," Harry said, only Giles hearing him.

"I can't help it," Giles said.

"You can't help what, dear?" Anne asked.

Giles looked back towards Anne. "What? Nothing . . . nothing at all."

Lady Anne turned towards Hester. "Dear Aunt, why don't you have someone silence the music so that Giles can make our announcement from here."

"Of course, dear," Hester said.

Hester Hartley started away from her niece but got no more than three steps away when the ground came up to meet her. Later, she could not explain how it had happened. None was directly in front of her, and she had not in her entire forty-two years ever stepped upon the hem of her own dress and cartwheeled across the floor. Nonetheless, that was precisely what happened.

Her head grazed the hardwood floor, leaving her momentarily stunned. Slowly the multiple figures she saw hovering over her resolved into individual concerned faces, the nurse Miss Wallace's amongst them. Whereupon Hester Hartley realised the spectacle she had made of herself and fainted dead away.

"Auntie!" Lady Anne cried out.

"Serves her right," Harry was saying over the din of voices as two servants came to lift Hester Hartley and carry her out of the ballroom.

"Sir Harry," Elizabeth remonstrated, then saw Agatha's quick look and Giles's warning one.

"The name is Luther, miss—Luther Lyme," the squire corrected as he bent to help with the fallen woman. "Not Harry."

"She'll be quite all right," Elizabeth continued to those assembled around her.

"She'll be quite all right," Squire Lyme repeated to the pretty blonde Lady Anne as he straightened up. "She's just a little overwrought. The excitement of the party and all, I'll warrant."

Lady Anne gave the country squire an incredulous look before turning back towards Giles. "Sweetheart, I still think it's time," she was saying as two servants carried her aunt from the room.

"Time?" Giles asked. "Don't you want to go after Hester to make sure she's all right?"

"No, I do not wish to go after Hester," Anne told him flatly. And then she sweetened her tone. "I think it's time," she repeated. She smiled encouragingly at her fiancé. When he made no move to speak, when he seemed unable even to understand her meaning, her expression became the tiniest bit petulant. "Our announcement," she reminded him.

"Pardon," a maid said from beside them. "You asked for champagne, sir." June carried a tray full of stemmed thin crystal goblets, each filled with bubbling French champagne.

"No, we did not," Lady Anne told the girl, irritated at the interruption.

"What a capital idea," Giles countered, taking two glasses as others came nearer to partake of the refreshment.

"I wonder about us, I must say, drinking champagne and fighting old Boney all at the same time," someone nearby said.

"We're civilised Englishmen," an answer came back. "We know how to separate our battles from the things which are worthwhile in their culture."

"Speaking of Boney," a country squire said to Giles, "you've been up against him, I hear. With Sir John Moore at Corunna, wasn't it?"

"Yes," Giles told the man, a bitter smile crossing his face. "We were there but the Fleet wasn't. Delayed by contrary winds."

"Had to fight for days, didn't you?" the man asked.

Elizabeth leaned nearer, Lady Agatha noting the nurses's preoccupation with the story of Giles's past.

Giles grimaced. "Soult wasn't about to let us break through."

"Giles?" Anne spoke through clenched teeth, though a small fixed smile was held firmly in place upon her perfect features as she turned him away from the squire. "This isn't the place for war stories, dear."

"Sorry," the squire said, a little put out.

"Don't let her get away with it, lad," Harry said, earning a quick glance upwards from Elizabeth.

Harry graced the chandelier over their heads, sitting among the brass chains that fastened the huge rack of candle sconces to the ceiling. "It's warm up here," he told them as he sat in thin air a few feet above the lighted candles, held in place by one ghostly hand.

"You must be careful," Giles said, earning a questioning look from Lady Anne.

"About what?" she asked.

Giles turned to stare at her. "I beg your pardon?"

"You told me to be careful," Anne reminded him.

"No, I—" He tried to ignore the Ghost floating above their heads. He looked towards Elizabeth, searching for a reasonable reply.

"Yes?" Anne regarded him.

"Nothing," he said finally.

"Nothing?" Anne questioned. She gave the nurse a brief glance, seeing Giles look towards her again. Miss Wallace seemed to find contemplation of the ceiling as rewarding as did Giles. Irritation fought with common sense for Anne's soul. She wanted to bash her fiancé's head and bring him to his senses, which seemed in danger of being overcome by the dark-haired beauty who now stood beside them.

"Perhaps," Anne said to Giles, "Miss Wallace should see to my poor aunt. After all," she flashed Elizabeth a brittle smile, "she is paid as a nurse in this establishment. For the moment."

"Of course—," Elizabeth began, glad of an excuse to leave the party.

"Nonsense," Giles interrupted. "You shall stay and enjoy yourself," he commanded. "Your aunt," Giles continued to Anne, "was merely a little lightheaded. There is nothing to concern yourself about." He sipped his champagne and turned slightly in his chair so that he could see Elizabeth. "You must stay. You are the only other one who sees him," Giles told her in an urgent whisper.

"Did you say something, Giles?" Lady Anne asked from the other side of his chair. She looked from him to Elizabeth and was rewarded by their guilty expressions. "What is going on between the two of you?" Anne asked them both suspiciously. Neither answered.

=18=

THE PARTY WHIRLED on around them as Anne contemplated Giles and Elizabeth.

"Is there something I should know about?" Anne asked.

"No," Elizabeth said quickly.

"Nothing at all," Giles agreed.

Distrustful and more irritated than ever, Anne whirled around, placing her champagne glass on the maid's tray. As Anne did so, the maid, June, felt herself pushed from behind.

In one and the same instant, Sir Harry floated downward towards the maid, Elizabeth Wallace let out a sharp little sigh, and Sir Giles said, "Don't."

"Don't what?" Agatha asked, her back to him, as June tripped and the entire contents of her overladen arms—silver tray, glasses, champagne, and all—tipped disastrously and dumped themselves across the bodice and lap of Lady Anne Hartley's exquisite silver satin gown.

"You fool!" Anne shrieked as her dress was doused with champagne and the glassware began to break at her feet. "How *dare* you?"

June blanched white with fear and backed away from the angry woman. "I didn't do nothing. I swear—"

"Get out of my sight this instant," Anne told the maid and was rewarded by the girl's wailing for mercy.

"June," Lady Agatha spoke calmly, "please be quiet. There's no real harm done."

"No real harm?" Anne repeated, affronted. "I never want

to see the clumsy oaf again."

Lady Agatha spoke quietly. "You are making a scene where others can hear, Anne."

"Do you think I care, after what she just did?" Anne replied.

"I would hope so," Agatha told her, "if you wish to keep the loyalty of the rest of your staff. June has been a good worker ever since she was first employed. Considering her youth, she has done very well indeed and is well thought of."

"By whom?" Anne demanded nastily.

"Anne—," Giles began but she interrupted.

"Giles, I'm sorry, but this is not something I will brook in my servants." Anne glared at June. "I not only want this person fired, I want the entire Abbey staff to go with her. I find them far beneath my requirements, and I shall hire all new." With that she gave Agatha an insincere smile. "Of course, I'm sure you have worked very hard putting the household staff together. Just as I'm sure you did all you were able, so please don't take my remarks personally. But, truly, none of this establishment is anywhere near up to London standards, and I will not abide such sloppiness in my future household."

"Lady Anne," Elizabeth stepped nearer. "It was not June's fault, I promise you."

"Really? What are you admitting, Miss Wallace?" Anne asked. "Did you perhaps engineer the entire incident?"

"I?" Elizabeth was stunned as were the others in the small group. "I was nowhere near either of you. I don't know how you have the cheek to even ask that."

"Cheek?" Anne repeated. "Please don't try to look so innocent, Miss Wallace. It just won't wash. You've had your sights set on the major since you were first hired. Don't bother to deny it. I know your type quite well. Perhaps you even engineered your very arrival in this household in the hopes of luring your poor crippled but eligible patient into your clutches."

"Anne!" Giles barked, shocked by her description of him

as much as by her accusations towards Elizabeth. "For God's sake, stop right now. You don't know what you're talking about."

"Don't try to defend the little baggage, Giles," Anne told her intended. "Men are always the last to see through women such as Miss Wallace."

Harry hovered just behind Giles, his tone gleeful. "Prick her pride and look where all the prettiness goes," the Ghost told Giles. "Now you can see what a mistake you're making with this one," Harry added for good measure.

"Be quiet," Giles commanded.

Anne thought he spoke to her. "Do not dare to defend her."

Elizabeth Wallace stiffened, returning Lady Anne back glare-for-glare. "I have no need of any defence but my own. And, if you were truly a person of the first consequence, you would not so demean yourself as to engage in hysterics before one and all. You, Lady Anne, are a spoiled little rich girl who can play such games to her heart's content. You may have need to, judging by your sour disposition. But I assure you, I do not indulge in such practices. Unlike yourself, I have no need to trap a man. Any man."

Only the sounds of the musicians at the far end of the ballroom intruded upon the silence that gripped the entire assembly. Then, Lord Grantham's low-pitched, sardonic laugh came to Anne's ears from somewhere nearby.

"What a marvellous entertainment we're being provided," he drawled. "And we were afraid we would be bored by country life, William."

Anne's cheeks burned with the sudden realisation that almost the entire room had heard the nurse's disparaging words. Anne Hartley turned to glare at her fiancé. Her face was the unbecoming red of a kitchen beet. Her stained dress was rather bedraggled looking as it dragged limply on the parquet floor.

"Giles Steadford, did you hear what this creature had the audacity to say to me? I demand you inform your servant that she is not allowed to speak to your future wife in this vein. Nor is she welcome to continue to stay under our roof."

Giles looked from Anne to Elizabeth and back. "She is not my servant," he said quietly.

"Are you going to tell her she cannot speak thus to me, or shall I have to defend myself?" Anne demanded.

"It would seem," Giles said reasonably, "she has already said all she intended to say."

"I want her out of this house!" Anne shouted in a very unladylike tone of voice.

Elizabeth's expression turned scornful as she stared back at Lady Anne. "Please do not excite yourself on my behalf, Lady Anne," Elizabeth said quietly. "I was just about to leave."

"Miss Wallace—," Giles began.

"Excuse me, please, Sir Giles," Elizabeth said. "I am grateful for your kind consideration, but I should not have accepted your most generous invitation to join this assembly in the first place. And I must be honest and tell you I have no wish whatsoever to remain in company such as"—Elizabeth's gaze penetrated Anne's angry eyes, but she bit off the words before she said Lady Anne's name—"such as this," she ended.

Elizabeth turned, her head held high, and started for the hall. Agatha hurried after the nurse, intercepting her in the hallway just outside. "Miss Wallace, please. Delay a moment."

The nurse stopped, allowing Agatha to reach her side.

"Miss Wallace, I am sure it is an imposition of the first degree, but it would be better if you stayed."

"Better?" Elizabeth queried. "For whom?"

Agatha considered the question. "For everyone, I would say, but most certainly for your employer, Sir Giles."

"I hardly think so. My remaining would force him into the uncomfortable position of mediator betwixt myself and his intended wife. I think it best I remove myself from the Ball and from the premises."

"The premises?" Agatha questioned.

"I intend to pack my belongings," Elizabeth explained. "There is nothing on earth which would keep me in the same household with that odious excuse for a female."

"Not even your patient?" Agatha asked, earning a startled look from the nurse. Agatha pressed her advantage. "Please give yourself time to think this entire situation through, my dear." Agatha spoke more warmly than Elizabeth had ever heard her. "Firstly, you would not want to give the impression that anything that half-witted Londoner said was true." Agatha smiled at Elizabeth's mixed expression.

"And secondly?" Elizabeth pursued.

"Secondly, the staff will appreciate your not leaving the scene of battle, as it were, since you are their champion, and so they all will know by morning, believe me. And, thirdly, because I should hate to have Lady Anne think she had bested one of us, even for a moment."

"One of us?" Elizabeth asked.

Agatha smiled. "All here feel you have become so."

Elizabeth returned Lady Agatha's smile. "You are very kind, Lady Agatha."

"Not all would agree with that assessment," the young nurse was told. "And I have not even brought up the more delicate subject of my cousin," Agatha continued. "His welfare surely should remain paramount, should it not? And there is none here to help him regain his health but you. If that girl does love Giles, the fact that you can help him recover should be of the utmost importance to her also."

Elizabeth conceded the truth of Lady Agatha's words and then surveyed the older woman's handsome face. "You said *if* she loves him."

"Yes, I did," Agatha confirmed.

Farther down the hall, Lady Anne swept out of the ballroom and to the grand stairwell. As she disappeared upstairs, the sounds of a late arrival carried down the wide hall. A newly hired footman, with ceremonial staff and properly sober syllables, intoned the names of the arrivals as he had those who had come before.

"The Earl and Countess of Angsley," the footman called.

Elizabeth's expression changed. Agatha followed the direction of Elizabeth's gaze. From where she stood she could just make out a very distinguished looking couple hesitating on the far threshold to the ballroom.

Lady Agatha recognised the earl and countess. "Giles did not mention he was expecting the earl," Agatha said. "Thank goodness they missed Lady Anne's scene," she said as she turned back towards Elizabeth. But Elizabeth was no longer beside her. "Miss Wallace," Agatha called out as she saw the nurse disappear through the green baise door to the kitchens. Agatha considered following but decided her duty lay with Giles and the arriving guests. She went to greet them.

Meanwhile, Lady Anne entered her rooms and gave her Aunt Hester a blistering version of the events that had transpired in the ballroom below.

"You must go back," Hester cried, aghast at the story her niece told. "You must change and return as if nothing had happened. Then you must insist Giles do his duty and announce your coming marriage."

"I don't want to see any of them, even Giles, ever again," Anne said petulantly.

"Nonsense," Hester said bracingly. "You are not going to throw away a fortune because of that little nurse, are you?"

"What?"

"Anne, if you leave, you will have cleared the field for that Miss Elizabeth Wallace-Nobody to gain her heart's desire and a king's ransom to boot—a fortune that should rightfully be yours." Hester saw Anne's conflicted expression and pressed her advantage. "You certainly don't want her to laugh up her sleeve at you, do you?"

Anne considered her alternatives, then smiled. "You're quite right."

Twenty minutes later Anne descended the grand stairwell once more and found that her aunt's advice had been sound.

"Lord Angsley, Lady Angsley, we are honoured," Lady Anne beamed a few moments later as she came to stand beside Giles's chair and once again take possessive hold of his shoulder.

She now wore a modish gown of the latest *à la Greque* style. Its straw-coloured silken folds clung to her slim figure suggestively, her small bosom made more alluring by the depth of the cut of the bodice and the height of the waist which was just beneath her breast.

"We had quite given up hope of your joining our little celebration," Anne told the countess, ignoring the questioning looks and quiet comments of the other guests.

"Darling Anne," Lady Angsley said, kissing Anne's cheek. "How good to see you, dear. We did indeed almost miss this lovely occasion. We are journeying to our Devonshire holdings, and I assured Alexander I could not ride one mile farther this night. We have come a prodigious distance already."

"Just to share our good news? How delightful," Anne cooed, as Lord Grantham passed nearby, Lady Spencer's arm linked with his as they headed towards the dance floor.

"Sweet Granny"—Anne overheard Susan's words—"do you think you could convince the musicians to attempt a quadrille?"

"I rather doubt they would know such a modern dance, Susan," Granny replied, "but I shall make a valiant attempt if it is your wish."

"It is."

"Your wish is my command," Lord Grantham was saying as they passed farther along the floor, the rest of their words lost from Anne's hearing.

"Well, not precisely, my dear," the Countess Angsley had been saying as Anne listened to her lover's conversation. "As I said, Alex and I are on our way to Devon. We've travelled over sixty miles in the space of two days, and I am quite depleted. We were going to press on for Stoneybridge when I remembered your gracious invitation, and since we were so near I insisted on breaking our journey for a bit and having the chance to see you."

"You must stay as long as you wish, mustn't they Giles," Lady Anne looked lovingly at the major. "We have the most comfortable accommodations for miles around."

"Thank you," Lady Agatha said with a tight smile. "It is gratifying that you approve of our humble endeavours."

Anne's gaze raked across Agatha's countenance, but her quick words of rebuff were never spoken.

"Dear Agatha," Lady Angsley was saying. "It's been much too long."

"Yes, it has Honoria," Agatha Steadford-Smyth replied. "I'm afraid I am not one for travel."

"That, my old friend, is the understatement of the year. Mama asked to be remembered when I told her we might pass a night with you. She said you owe her a rematch. Does that make sense to you?"

Agatha's smile was warm and wide. "Yes. She speaks of that deplorable game Whist, which I have never enjoyed except in your mother's company. How is her health?"

"Much better in recent months. And yours?"

"I remain as hale and hearty as ever," Agatha replied. "What of your children?"

A cloud crossed the countess's expression. Agatha looked from Honoria to her husband. Alexander was frowning.

"As well as can be expected, I suppose," Honoria answered finally.

"Are there health problems?" Agatha asked.

The Earl of Angsley glared at Lady Agatha. "Why do you say that?" he barked.

"Alexander," his wife remonstrated, "she meant no harm." Honoria smiled at Agatha. "We are, I fear, more tired than I realised. Do you think we might take leave of your guests and find a quiet room in which to recover our strength?"

"Of course," Anne said quickly, not allowing Agatha to

reply. "Lady Agatha would be glad to show you to your rooms. Wouldn't you, dear?" Anne ended sweetly.

Agatha regarded Anne Hartley. Then, without a word to the young woman, she returned her gaze to Honoria's. "Let me show you the way."

"Thank you, Agatha. I feel quite travel stained and done in. We shall have a lovely conversation in the morning, shall we?"

Anne answered, "I shall look forward to it," earning a puzzled look from the countess and then a smile.

"Of course, dear," Honoria told Lady Anne.

"Shall we?" Agatha asked, leading the way for the Angsleys to retire from the ballroom. As they left, Agatha graciously introduced them to locals who came near to meet the notable couple.

"Giles?" Anne queried as the Angsleys left. "Do you like my dress?"

Giles Steadford gave his fiancé's figure an appraising glance. When he answered he spoke in a very reserved tone of voice.

"Your appearance leaves nothing to be desired."

"Thank you," she said.

"Your actions are another matter," he continued. "I am appalled by your performance earlier."

Anne tried to smile. "But Giles, none of it was my fault."

"Even if that were true, your reactions were deplorable." Giles turned to summon Jack Fence.

"Giles?" Anne tried to get his attention.

"If you will excuse me, I am retiring for the night," Giles told her.

"But, our announcement—"

"Can wait," he told Anne plainly. "Jack, please help me from the room."

Jack Fence guided the wheeled chair slowly through the assembled throngs as Giles said his good-nights, urging the partygoers to continue their revelry.

Anne looked around the large room and motioned to her

Aunt Hester who had just returned.

"You should join your fiancé," Hester said as she neared Anne's side.

"I do not intend to leave yet. I have not danced with Granny."

"You'd best watch your step," Hester warned.

Anne smiled. "I always watch my steps, Aunt."

Lady Anne made her way through the crowded room towards the dance floor and Lord Grantham. Her aunt watched Anne's progress. And then followed, keeping a wary eye on her niece as she greeted the county people with a properly condescending civility.

= 19 =

WHEN SHE CAME out from the rooms she had quickly assigned to the earl and countess, Lady Agatha found Fannie in the upper hall.

"I've told Hetty what the earl requires for breakfast," said Fannie as she came towards Agatha. "Is there anything else we need to do?"

"No, not precisely," Agatha said. "I was talking earlier to Elizabeth Wallace, then she disappeared into the kitchens."

"Showing good taste, judging from what I've seen of that London crowd. I wouldn't want to hobnob with them either."

"Fannie—," Agatha warned.

"All right, all right. Should I find her for you?"

Agatha considered the question. "I suppose it's neither here nor there, at the moment."

Early-to-bed guests were already being shown up the grand staircase to their rooms as the party sounds continued below. Agatha smiled and nodded as the guests passed, then she retired to her own rooms, Fannie coming behind.

Down the hall, Elizabeth Wallace was leaning to light the fire in her small bedroom grate. She held her hands towards the blaze, letting its warmth grow before she began to undress. Her movements were listless, her thoughts far away. Unshed tears glimmered in her eyes.

The staff were up late clearing out the remains of the

party and had little rest the next morning. Arising earliest, the kitchen staff were bleary eyed and sleepy as they prepared breakfasts for the Abbey's residents and guests.

None was ready for the arrival in the kitchens, not long after the dawn itself, of Hester Hartley with messages to impart concerning the foibles of several of the Abbey guests.

"And," Hester continued to Hetty Mapes, "the earl requires a very special Chinese tea which you probably don't have—"

"I have it," Hetty replied. Into the ensuing silence she continued. "The earl's mother-in-law, *the Duchess of Langdon*," Hetty emphasised, "is an old friend of my former mistress, Lady Agatha. Lady Agatha and the dowager duchess introduced the earl to Lapsang Soochung tea, and we always have it on hand," she ended smugly. She was rewarded by the slight discomfort Hester Hartley allowed to show.

"And one thing more," Hester said, recovering her composure. "The nurse will no longer be eating with the family and guests."

Hetty Mapes looked from the skinny woman in front of her to Martha, across the kitchen at the open fire, where she was toasting the morning bread.

"I beg your pardon?" Hetty questioned.

"You heard me," Lady Anne's aunt replied. "Elizabeth Wallace will eat in her rooms or in the kitchen with the rest of the staff."

"Does the master know?" Hetty Mapes demanded.

"Of course he knows," Hester Hartley told the cook. She gave the servant a commanding gaze and then turned back towards the hall and the family-rooms beyond.

Hetty watched the woman's thin back as she flounced down the narrow corridor. "Did you hear that?" the cook demanded of her co-workers.

Martha turned from the fire. "She's a witch and so is her niece. I wouldn't put anything past her. Did you hear what she said to June in front of the entire staff? And the county, too."

"Well, what's to be done?" was what Hetty wanted to know.

"What's to be done about what?" Fannie Burns asked as she walked into the kitchen.

"Nothing you can help with," was Hetty's opinion. "Just those insufferable Hartleys and their airs."

Fannie made a face. "I've had more than I want to do with both of them. I don't know which is worse, the full-of-herself Lady Anne or the purse-faced Hester."

Martha's laugh escaped before she could stuff it back inside, earning her a smile from Fannie and a glower from Hetty Mapes.

"Don't encourage the girl," Hetty said to Fannie. "Martha's altogether too flighty already."

"What about June and what happened last night?" Martha asked pertly. "None of us, including you, Hetty Mapes, is long for this establishment once those two take over."

"Don't we all know it," the cook agreed.

"I'd best get Lady Agatha's tea up to her," Fannie said.

"We're all that sorry about Miss Wallace," Hetty told Lady Agatha's abigail.

"Sorry?" Fannie frowned. "Why? What's wrong with her?"

"I can't imagine she feels quite right, having been yelled at before all last night."

Fannie shrugged. "She is a strong girl."

"That's as may be, but there aren't many who would accept that sort of treatment, let alone being relegated to the servants' table after all this time."

"Elizabeth Wallace is a sensible girl and she—" Fannie stopped in midsentence. "Hetty?" she asked finally. "What did you say?"

"You heard me right, and it's Sir Giles who's approved such goings on," the cook added with a dark look. "I knew he wasn't a right one the minute he arrived."

"He didn't," Fannie said. But she sounded unsure enough to elicit a knowing look from her old friend.

"He did," Hetty assured.

Fannie shook her head. "Who's to tell her?"

"From what pickle-face had to say, I assume she took it upon herself," the cook declared.

Lady Agatha's tea tray was ready. Fannie picked it up, but her thoughts were elsewhere as she climbed the stairs towards her mistress. Once delivered of the tray, Fannie found that Lady Agatha had her own reactions to the news from the kitchens.

"You must go to her," Agatha declared.

She earned a dubious look from her serving woman. "But why?"

"To tell her she must not leave, of course. What else?"

Fannie regarded Agatha. "Is she planning on leaving?"

"Wouldn't you?" Lady Agatha countered.

Fannie thought about it, then left Agatha's rooms and hurried back down the upper hall to Elizabeth Wallace's door.

"Yes?" A muffled voice answered after Fannie's second rap. The door opened, and Elizabeth Wallace was standing before Lady Agatha's abigail.

"May I come in?" Fannie asked.

Elizabeth hesitated. Then she stepped back, letting Fannie enter.

The abigail glanced about the small, plain room and then turned towards the nurse, coming to the point. "Lady Agatha sent me to see how you were feeling this morning."

Elizabeth made an attempt to smile. "Please thank her for me. I am tolerably well, thank you."

"And planning on leaving," Fannie said, seeing the open trunk near the clothespress.

"I am unwelcome."

"Not to any that matter," Fannie answered promptly, earning a grateful look from Elizabeth.

"Thank you, Fannie, but my situation here is untenable now."

"Because Lady Anne is against you and wants you gone?

177

Or because she doesn't want you at table?"

Elizabeth Wallace surprised the serving woman by smiling, a very real, very warm smile. "Lady Anne means little to me. That is to say, she means next to nothing to me. Nor do her pronouncements."

"Then why leave?" Fannie asked.

"It's a very complicated story," Elizabeth said.

"Does it concern Sir Giles?"

Elizabeth considered the question, and then sighed. "It concerns him perhaps more than I, at first, realised."

"Then stay," Fannie urged, "and fight for him."

"For him?" Elizabeth questioned, her brow rising.

"For what's good for him. And for the Abbey," Fannie replied.

"It won't wash, Fannie."

"Why not? What else is wrong?"

"As I said, it's a long story."

"Which begins?" Fannie prompted.

"Which begins," Elizabeth said and stopped, unsure what to say next.

"Let me make it a little easier for you," Fannie said. "Your hesitation and your decision have something to do with the Earl of Angsley, do they not?"

Elizabeth's surprise was evident.

"Do you deny it?" Fannie asked.

"How did you know?" Elizabeth responded.

"I didn't. But Lady Agatha has very acute perceptions, and I have a few views and ideas of my own. Lady Agatha mentioned your sudden departure when the Angsleys arrived." Fannie watched Elizabeth's reaction. "You wouldn't leave your patient because of his own nonsense, or you'd have left the day after you came. My guess is your decision to depart is one part due to Lady Anne and her threats and three parts due to the arrival of the Angsleys." Fannie gauged the younger woman. "I think you need to talk about it."

Elizabeth considered the abigail's words, then just shook her head. "No. It can't help."

"You never know," Fannie said reasonably. "You worked for them and they fired you, did they?" she asked kindly.

"No," Elizabeth replied.

Fannie took her time. "Girl, you can tell me the truth."

"I am," Elizabeth said.

"Then answer me honestly. Your problem with the Angsleys had to do with your work, yes or no?"

"Yes," Elizabeth told Lady Agatha's servant. "It had to do with my work."

"They were not happy with it," Fannie added.

"They were not happy with it," Elizabeth agreed.

"They gave you bad references," Fannie said.

"They gave me no references," Elizabeth replied.

Fannie shook her head, appalled at the lack of feeling in some of the nobility. "Miss Wallace, they had no idea of what fate they were consigning you to. They are so far removed from our stations in life, they do not understand. You must find it in your heart to forgive them."

"I have tried to forgive them for many long years past," Elizabeth told her questioner. "And I have asked for their forgiveness."

Fannie took in the nurse's words. "Were you then responsible for one of their own passing on? Or so they thought?"

"No."

"But you were threatened with the possibility," Fannie added. At Elizabeth's expression Fannie's own turned grim. "You were threatened."

Elizabeth found her eyes filling with unwelcome tears. "I'm sorry." She turned away. "Please forgive me, but your kindness has very nearly undone me."

"Elizabeth, I hope you don't mind my calling you by your name, but I feel very kindly towards you. And I know Lady Agatha does also. It's just that when you have been through so very much grief and discomfort with the major, it is very hard to understand how passing guests such as the Angsleys could convince you to give up all your work and leave like this without a backwards glance."

"I do not leave without a backwards glance," Elizabeth replied quietly.

"But you are leaving."

"Yes."

"And it does have something to do with the earl's arrival." Fannie watched the younger woman. "Why do the Angsleys affect you so much?"

Elizabeth stared down at her own hands. "Because they are my parents."

The rest of the day passed quietly. Most of the guests slept late and were served a midday nuncheon in their rooms.

Fannie reported her amazing news to Lady Agatha, who thought back over the countess's responses to her queries about the children Lady Agatha had not seen since they were small.

"Fannie, tell the countess we will take tea together," was Agatha's only response to her abigail's information.

"And?" Fannie asked.

"And," Agatha replied, "we shall see what we shall see."

"What about Miss Wallace."

Agatha considered the question. "Tell Homer and the rest of the staff that there are to be no carriages available to Miss Wallace until tomorrow morning. Then we shall leave the decision to her. In the meantime, we have work to do, Fannie."

"Are you going to speak to her parents?"

"No," Agatha responded.

Fannie was surprised. "You won't tell them?"

"It's not my place. Nor do I think they, or Elizabeth, would be best pleased if I interfered."

"I hope you know what you're about," Fannie told her employer.

"So do I, Fannie. So do I," Agatha answered.

= 20 =

THE EVENING AFTER the Abbey Ball, an early supper was served by Martha and Jack, June having been banished to the farthest reaches of the scullery, away from any chance of encounter with Lady Anne or her Aunt Hester.

Sir Giles and Lady Agatha presided over the table, where Lady Anne and her London friends kept up a continual conversation with the Earl and Countess of Angsley.

All the other guests had departed for home earlier in the day despite the November snow which covered the Abbey road with a light frosting of white. During the early evening hours more snow fell outside. The newly enlarged Abbey staff kept fires lit and burning in the dining hall, the main parlour, the library, and each of the occupied bedroom suites.

"It's been years since I've been to the Abbey," Honoria Wallace, Countess of Angsley, told her host and his cousin as she sat beside Sir Giles at the fifteen-foot-long mahogany table.

At the opposite end Honoria's husband, Alexander, picked at his food and listened with half an ear to Lady Anne who sat at his left, trying to interest the tall, distinguished looking man in her conversation.

"Don't you agree, your lordship?" Anne was asking.

She was rewarded with a blank look as the earl reached for his lorgnette and surveyed the blonde beauty beside him. "I beg your pardon?" he said.

"I was saying the buttered crab was remarkably good. It reminds me of the Duchess of Portland's assembly this Season past. I believe that was the last time I had the pleasure of your conversation," Anne finished prettily.

The Earl of Angsley stared the woman down. "Quite," he replied, ending the conversation. He dropped his lorgnette and returned his attention to his plate, ignoring Lady Anne's presence as she glanced across the table towards William, Count Leeds, and flashed him a brilliant smile.

"Is everything satisfactory, Billy?" she asked.

The count sketched as good a bow as he could give Anne from his seated position. "Where you are, dear Anne, all else fades from view but your beauty."

Lady Anne smiled and glanced up the table towards Giles who was deep in conversation with Lady Angsley. Lady Anne lost her smile when she could not gain Giles's attention. Turning her attention to Count Leeds, Anne was surprised when she heard Giles call her name.

"Yes?" she said, flashing Giles a brilliant smile. She had not seen him all day and had assumed the worst—that Elizabeth Wallace was crying upon his shoulder, attempting to ensure her tenure whilst pretending to be invaluable.

"Where is Miss Wallace," he asked.

Anne felt her friends' eyes, as well as those of the Angsleys and Lady Agatha, turn towards her.

"I'm sure I wouldn't know, nor would I have any reason to ask," Anne told Giles.

"Then I'll find out for myself," Giles said. Whereupon he turned towards the man who stood near the buffet. "Jack, please tell Miss Wallace we are waiting dinner for her," Giles told the valet.

"Giles," Anne remonstrated, "such a gesture is entirely uncalled for. We have already begun to serve."

"None but the first removes," Giles responded. He looked towards the valet. "Go on. Something must be wrong or she would long since have been down."

"Who is this Miss Wallace?" the countess asked.

"A servant," Lady Anne responded.

"An employee," Giles corrected, "and a damned important one."

Anne glared down the length of the table at Giles. "Not, however, important enough to cause swearing at the dinner table nor to ruin a perfectly good dinner. Not to mention that you shall be keeping the earl and the countess waiting."

"There must be a reason she's not here," Giles said, ignoring the rest of Lady Anne's words.

"Of course there is," Anne replied tartly.

Lord Grantham gave her a sardonic smile. "Perhaps you will explain it to us, Anne, dear," Grantham said.

"Miss Wallace is not at table," Anne said, "because she is a servant and is not invited." Seeing her Aunt Hester's expression, Anne leavened her words with a small laugh. She looked around the table towards her London friends and the Angsleys. "Giles has been rusticating in the country for so long he has assuaged his loneliness by taking servants to the table."

There were the beginnings of a few small smiles around the table until Giles spoke. "Elizabeth is not a servant," he said. "She is my employee, and she has taken every meal with the family since she arrived."

Anne glared at him from the opposite end of the table. "More's the pity."

Giles stared at Anne. "Since Miss Wallace is, as you say, in the habit of dining at table, how would she know not to join us this evening?"

"I presume she had the good manners to realise her place," Lady Anne said crisply.

"Her place is here," Sir Giles rejoined.

"How terribly modern and democratic of you," Lady Spencer said.

"What the deuce are you nattering on about?" the Earl of Angsley demanded. "Are we to eat our dinners or not?"

"We shall continue as soon as Miss Wallace arrives," Giles replied.

"No!" Anne cried. "If you must have it all out in the open, Giles, I sent word to the girl that she would not be welcome at table, just in case your treatment of her had gone to the poor girl's head."

"His treatment of a servant?" the countess asked.

Anne forced herself to smile. "It seems Giles has become quite attached to his nurse."

Honoria Wallace blanched white. "His . . . nurse?"

Giles was livid. He stared down the table at Lady Anne. "You told Elizabeth she wasn't invited to my table?" he asked Anne incredulously. "How dare you issue orders in my household and to my staff?"

"The staff was told they were your orders," Lady Agatha said quietly from her seat at Sir Giles's right. She earned a nasty look from Lady Anne. Agatha returned it with a polite, but distant smile.

Honoria, Countess of Angsley, caught her host's angry eye. "Did you say Elizabeth Wallace?"

"My nurse," Giles clarified. He did not see the mix of expressions in the countess's face, but Agatha did.

Agatha watched her old friend. "Honoria? Is something wrong?"

The Earl of Angsley answered for his wife. "My wife is perishing from hunger, as are we all. Giles, are we going to eat our dinners or what?"

"We shall eat, your lordship," Giles replied. "Timothy, see that the earl's goblet is refilled." Giles looked down the table. "I am sure you all will be able to survive on your first course and your wine until Miss Wallace arrives and the next course is served."

Agatha was still looking across the table at the countess. "Are you feeling quite well?" she asked.

"I'm not sure," the countess replied quietly.

"Honoria?" the earl looked towards his wife. "Is something wrong?"

His wife gave the earl her undivided attention. "We are waiting for Sir Giles's nurse, Alexander—a Miss Wallace."

The earl stared at his wife, then looked towards his host, his expression turning as cold as the icy weather outside the Abbey walls.

"I am appalled," the earl said. As he spoke he stood up.

"Please, your lordship," Lady Anne began, but the object of her words ignored her.

"Honoria," the earl said to his wife, "we are leaving immediately."

"Your lordship," Giles began, "I assure you, it will only be a matter of moments—"

"It seems," Lord Grantham told Giles, "his lordship is not of a mind to wait even a few moments."

"Granny," Anne warned him before she turned her attention back towards the earl. "Please, Lord Angsley, I assure you there is no slight intended. After all," Anne continued, "Giles has been alone out here so long. He has simply become attached to the members of his household for lack of more appropriate company." She aimed the last of her words at Giles, trying to lighten the mood around the table. "For all I know, he will one day ask the stable man to table."

"If I so choose, I will," Giles informed Anne, her London friends, his aunt, and the Angsleys.

The Earl of Angsley stood up. "We must leave, Honoria. This very moment."

"No," Anne cried out. "Please, your lordship," she implored the earl and his wife, "your ladyship, please do not allow Giles's bad manners to infect your view of our company. He means no disrespect, I assure you."

Honoria saw her husband's expression and stood up. Their stiff-faced facades stopped Anne's words.

They were so obviously insulted Anne looked up the table towards her Aunt Hester, wordlessly imploring the older woman.

Hester saw Anne's distress and moved her chair back, coming to her feet. "Countess—your lordship, please— there is no reason to cut short your dinner, or your sojourn because of an inferior type of person. Sir Giles certainly has not intended to insult you—" The thin woman turned her narrow face towards her host.

Giles ignored Hester but could not very well ignore her words. "Obviously, no insult has been intended," he said.

The Earl of Angsley cast a fulminating look across the length of the table, towards his host. "Sir," he said in ringing terms. "You cannot think I will presume such a pass has come about without your knowledge."

"I beg your pardon?" Giles said.

"Alex, dear," Honoria interrupted. "Truly, I do not think they realise—"

Giles looked behind the earl and countess to the doorway where Elizabeth Wallace now stood. Giles smiled. "At last," he said. "You see, I told you there was no reason—"

"Giles," Lady Agatha told her cousin, "be quiet."

Shocked at Agatha's quiet rebuff, Giles hesitated. In the moments of his hesitation the earl and the countess saw Elizabeth in the doorway.

"My God," the earl said. "I knew it would one day happen, I told you."

"Elizabeth—," Honoria began.

Elizabeth Wallace came forwards. "Mother," she acknowledged, much to the amazement of the others in the room. Except Lady Agatha, who watched Elizabeth closely as she greeted her parents.

"Honoria," the earl said in a cold tone, "I am leaving these premises at once." So saying, he turned his back on the room and stalked from it without a backwards glance towards his daughter.

Quick tears stung Elizabeth's eyes, and Honoria found her own green eyes filling as she gazed at her daughter's unhappy expression. "It's been so long. You look too thin, Elizabeth." Her mother sniffed back her tears, keeping her own unhappiness to herself. "I'd best go after your father. He's very upset."

The dining-room was silent after the earl and countess departed—until Agatha called to Elizabeth to join her at the table.

Giles stared at his nurse as she came nearer and sat down. "I'm sorry, I had no idea," he said.

"Nor did any others," Lord Grantham informed them both, smiling at Elizabeth more warmly than he had in the past.

"Nothing has changed," Elizabeth insisted.

"Everything has changed, my dear," William, Count Leeds, drawled. "Trust me, your position in this household has just vastly improved."

"Why should that be so?" Elizabeth asked.

"You are not that dense," Hester Hartley informed the earl's daughter.

"I am a nurse," Elizabeth said. "And an employee of Sir Giles until he no longer requires my services."

Giles said nothing. He looked down at his tea and called for a hot cup, keeping his thoughts to himself.

"Well, Giles?" William demanded.

"Well what?" Giles answered finally.

"What do you think of this turn of events? How many men can say they are nursed by an earl's daughter?"

Giles looked from William to Lord Grantham. "I have no idea."

Lord Grantham exclaimed, smiling at Elizabeth, "I would have said you were much too pretty to be both well-born and rich also."

"Granny!" Anne exclaimed, cut to the quick.

Grantham smiled at Anne. "Darling Anne, you are very obviously both pretty and well-born, but let us be frank. You are not rich."

"Nor am I," Elizabeth informed the room. "I earn my own way in life. My father feels I am demeaning myself by attempting to follow a professional life and has cut me off without a cent."

"Demeaning?" Giles roused from his silent moodiness.

"Yes, demeaning," the earl's angry voice came from the doorway.

The others looked towards him. Elizabeth was surprised her father was still in the hall.

"Alexander, dear—" Honoria's voice came from beyond her husband. "Please—not in front of the others."

"I do not intend to discuss my family's business before this company. However, since you are all here, and since you have been privy to this exchange, let me say very clearly that my daughter is following a course which is not only unnecessary but against my wishes. She has broken her mother's heart by putting herself in such a vulnerable position and pursuing a career."

"My dear Alexander, the world is rapidly changing around us and as it does, so do the roles women may choose to play. Others have pursued a career, some to great merit."

"Blue-stockings," Alexander Wallace pronounced.

Giles stared past the others towards the tall man in the doorway. "How can you say what Elizabeth is doing is unnecessary when it is more than most ever accomplish? Thanks to your daughter I am beginning to regain the use of my limbs."

"If you are recovering, it has nothing to do with my daughter."

"But it does," Giles countered. "She is better than any others who have cared for me. She has pushed me to do more than I could have or would have without her. She has brought back some feeling and movement to my limbs."

"To your limbs?" the earl repeated.

"My legs were useless before she began to exercise and massage them."

"Your legs!" the earl exclaimed. "You are telling me my daughter handles your limbs? My daughter—an unmarried woman—and you dare tell me of your legs?"

"Yes." Giles nearly shouted at the man. "My legs—and my mind and my heart."

Anne spoke from the foot of the table. "Giles, please, don't say such things. And don't upset yourself so. It is not good for your health and it is bound to be misinterpreted."

Giles was not listening to Lady Anne's warnings. "Elizabeth is helping people. When have any of us been able to say the same?" He glowered at the assembled group of Londoners. "Well? Answer me! Tell me why she should not be allowed to do with her life what she pleases."

"Because she's a woman," the earl nearly shouted.

"That's not a good enough reason, Lord Angsley."

"Sir, I can see that you hold with the most modern of views. Which, I must say, shows an intolerable lack of breeding upon your part. I insist you say no more. You are an invalid, and, as such, I cannot call you out upon the field of battle, but by God, sir, I tell you straight out. You are no gentleman."

"And you are no father," Giles returned as the earl left the dining-room.

There was a deathly silence in the dining-room until Giles roused himself and rang for Jack Fence.

"We are ready to be served," Giles told his man.

"Giles," Anne protested. "Surely, you are not going to allow this."

"Allow what?" he asked.

"My niece speaks for us all," Hester Hartley told the major. And, so saying, she stood up. "She is much too polite and gently bred to spell out the problem."

Giles scowled at the woman. "Well, one of you had best make yourself plainer than that."

"That fact is, old boy," Lord Grantham said quietly, "we now face a rather ticklish proposition."

"Which is?" Giles demanded.

"Not putting too fine a point on it," Grantham continued, "if we eat with the daughter, we will be snubbing the earl."

Elizabeth started to rise from her chair, but Giles commanded her to sit. "No, Miss Wallace, I insist. You are still in my employ?"

The nurse hesitated and then sat back, her eyes on her plate while Giles Steadford regarded his guests.

"Now then," Giles said to the others, "I shall say this only once. This is my home, my table, and my food. Any who do not wish to eat with Miss Wallace are free to leave."

"Giles," Anne protested, "please reconsider what you are saying."

"Why?" he demanded.

"Because this—woman—is not fit to appear in polite Society with proper and gently bred ladies."

"That is quite the outside of enough," Giles interrupted. "I will not listen to such calumny. Nor will I have Miss Wallace subjected to it."

"Interrupt all you like, but it's the truth," Anne said in ringing accents. "I cannot ask my guests to so lower themselves."

"Sir Giles—," Elizabeth began.

"No," Giles told her. But he was looking down the table at Anne. "I insist you apologise to Miss Wallace for such rude behaviour."

"I?" Anne stared at him, then stood up at her place, following her aunt's example. "I shall not apologise for the truth. And if you insist upon her staying, I shall go," she threatened.

Giles regarded Lady Anne coolly. "I shall tell the kitchen to send a tray to your rooms."

Anne shook with barely contained rage, her colour heightened as she stood at the foot of the table, defying her fiancé in front of her oldest friends.

"Giles, I am not joking," Anne said. "I shall leave not only this table and this room but this house," she warned, "if you do not reconsider your position. And mine."

"If you are planning on leaving for London, I think you should wait until morning. At this time of year, it is dangerous to be travelling late in the evening," Giles told her mildly.

Insulted, Anne glared first at Giles and then at the cause of her humiliation. "Susan, Letty, Janet—," she called out, waiting for her friends to stand up before she turned from the table. With Hester leading the way, the Londoners left the room. William, Count Leeds, looked back rather regretfully as the roast sirloin passed him by on its way to the head of the table.

At the doorway Anne turned, unable to resist a parting shot. "I have never been so insulted in my entire life," she told the small group at the table. "But then I can see I was not aware of what was really happening in this establishment."

"Miss Hartley," Agatha interrupted. "You'd best explain your meaning clearly. I won't stand for innuendos about what I allow under my roof. Under Steadford Abbey's roof," she corrected herself. "I am here as chaperone. If you have something to say, please say it plainly."

"Anne," Hester called to her niece, arguing softly against Anne's saying any more. Hester led the younger woman away after looking disdainfully towards Lady Agatha.

Lady Agatha reached to pat Elizabeth Wallace's hand as Giles motioned to the footman to put the platter of roast beef on the table beside him.

"You have lost your guests," Elizabeth said quietly.

Giles smiled at her, including Agatha in his gaze and his words. "The only ones I care about remain," he told them both.

Agatha gave the young man an approving look. "I must say you are one of the few of your sex who seems to grow better upon acquaintance. You even seem to have a portion of common sense."

Giles smiled at his cousin, amazed at how lighthearted he was suddenly feeling. "I shall take that as a compliment and treasure it."

"You should," Agatha replied, her own dark eyes twinkling. "It may be the only one you ever receive from me."

Giles laughed. "I can readily believe that."

Elizabeth looked from Lady Agatha to Sir Giles, tears sparkling in her eyes and on her lashes. "How can you both appear so calm, as if nothing happened?"

"I am so very sorry," Giles said quickly. "I wasn't thinking of how upsetting this entire scene must have been for you."

Elizabeth fought back the tears. "I have caused problems between you and your fiancé."

"And good riddance," Fannie said from the doorway and earned a quick disapproving look from her mistress. Fannie came forwards carrying a decanter of wine. "You should hear what they've been telling the staff. It's a wonder Sir Giles had a dinner served tonight for all the help who are packing to leave."

"Fannie," Giles said, "you must tell them they have nothing to fear from that quarter. No matter what else, I shall never allow my people to be treated badly."

"It's not our concern," Agatha said primly, giving Fannie another warning look.

"But it is," Giles insisted. "The staff are very loyal to you, Agatha, and always will be. What you and Fannie say can do a great deal of good. Fannie," he continued, "have you eaten yet?"

"I beg your pardon?" Fannie was startled. "No."

"Good, come join us, then," Giles said. Agatha glanced at Giles as he continued. "You share your meals with Lady Agatha at the gatehouse, and you have always shared her meals here at the Abbey. There is no reason you should not continue to do so."

Fannie looked towards her employer. When Agatha said nothing against the idea, Fannie smiled. "There's certainly enough places set," she told them all as she sat down.

= 21 =

GILES SAT IN the library near the fire with a glass of port. He held a book in his lap but had grown tired of trying to read it. Lady Anne and the other Londoners were closeted within their rooms, already packing to leave.

Giles looked up when Agatha and Fannie joined him. "Have they gone? Her parents," he asked as Jack Fence poured them each a tiny glass of sherry.

"Yes," Agatha replied. "The earl would not even agree to wait for morning. Honoria said she tried to convince him to reconsider, but he was determined to be off."

"They won't get far in this snow," was Giles's opinion.

"I imagine you're quite right," Agatha replied.

"The poor girl," Fannie said. "He never spoke to her before he left. It's no wonder she couldn't eat her supper."

Agatha agreed. "I knew something about that girl looked familiar," she said after another minute.

"You know her family quite well?" Giles asked. His curiosity was apparent as he leaned forwards, taking in Agatha's every word.

"I knew her grandmother best, her father's mother. She was a sharp-tongued woman, but honest. I think Elizabeth must take after her Grandmother Wallace. I haven't seen the family in years. I don't think I'd seen young Elizabeth but twice in her entire life and both times when she was a child." Agatha thought about it. "I never connected her to Alexander."

"Wallace is a common enough name," Fannie said.

"True." Agatha finished her sherry and stood up. "It's also true that it's getting late. We'd best say good-night."

Giles nodded. "I wonder what made her decide to leave her family and become a nurse. Originally I assumed she needed to work, for her sustenance."

"There are various kinds of sustenance," Agatha said mildly.

"I'm not sure I understand what you mean," Giles told his cousin.

"Then I think you should ask Elizabeth about her reasons," Agatha said as they said their good-nights.

"It's truly none of my business," Giles countered.

"Isn't it?" Agatha asked him.

Giles watched the two women leave. After a few moments Jack Fence appeared in the doorway.

"Sir?"

"I'm ready," Giles told the valet.

Jack went along to the servants' hall, calling to Tim that the master was ready to go upstairs.

Giles wheeled his chair to the bottom of the stairwell, moving easily through the widened doorway. Jack and Tim lifted him from the chair, making a seat for him with their interlocked hands. Grasping each man with one arm around their shoulders, the men carried him up the wide stairs.

They reached the top of the stairs a little out of breath. Giles stared down the hall towards Elizabeth's door.

"Sir?" Jack saw the direction of Giles's gaze. "Do you wish something else?"

"What?" Giles thought about knocking on Elizabeth's door, asking if she was all right. But he would be subjecting her to an audience of Jack and Tim. "No, I'm ready for bed," Giles decided.

Jack and Tim carried Giles into his sitting-room and on into the bedroom. Tim left as Jack helped his master undress.

At the far end of the hall, behind her closed bedroom

door, Elizabeth was crying into her pillows, more upset than she wanted to admit. Her interview with her mother had been brief and ended when her father stormed into the room, demanding that his wife not talk to the girl until she had come to her senses and come home. It took Elizabeth long hours before she drifted off into an uneasy sleep filled with dreams of her father and of Anne Hartley.

In the front guest suite Hester was helping her niece undress, still arguing about Anne's determination to pack for London and leave at first light.

"I will not put up with such insults," Anne insisted.

"Dear Anne, of course you are upset. Anyone would be. But you have a solemn duty to bring this sad sinner, Sir Giles, to his senses before he ruins his entire life. You cannot leave him to such a female. You must make him see the error of his ways."

"I can't very well stop him," Anne said petulantly.

"Yes you can. You will simply have to put your foot down," Hester replied.

"I did earlier and you saw what happened."

"Anne, dear, you must learn to handle men with honey, not vinegar. Then all will be well. Firstly, you must rid this household of that Wallace girl, but you must do it in such a way as to make Giles think it his own idea."

"I'm not positive I want to bother," Anne told her aunt.

"Of course you do, darling. You're simply overwrought. But you cannot allow a fit of the dismals to ruin all your hopes and plans. After all," Hester reminded, "all of London has been whispering of you and a certain gentleman who shall remain nameless. We can't have your reputation ruined by a dissolved engagement, now can we? It would look as if it were he and not you who begged off."

"I don't care," Anne said pettishly, but that was not true and she knew it. "I want to be alone."

Hester thought about saying more and then decided to let her words of wisdom wait until the morning.

"Good-night," Hester told her niece. "I shall wake you with hot chocolate." Hester closed Anne's bedroom door and walked quietly across the small sitting-room towards her own smaller bedroom.

Anne was sometimes difficult to manage, but managed she would be, Hester told herself. Anne would marry Giles, no matter what else transpired. Fortunes such as that of the Steadfords did not hang about waiting for young ladies to pluck them, not even young ladies as pretty as Anne. Hester Hartley had been a poor relation her entire life long. She knew the value of ensuring that Anne made a good marriage. In the beginning Hester had not been enthused about the match, but now that he had inherited the Steadford holdings, they would be very comfortable indeed, she and Anne. Hester felt sure she could train her young niece in the ways to get around her husband and thus ensure her own and her aunt's futures.

Sir Giles himself was in his own large bed, just about to drift off to sleep. His eyes were falling closed when he heard the pacing.

"What the devil—," Giles said, coming fully awake as he stared towards the open sitting-room door. Sir Harry stood in the half-light from the waning fire, peering in towards Giles.

"Still awake, I see," the Ghost asked.

"I was almost asleep," Giles told him.

"I don't see why you should sleep when I can't rest," Sir Harry told the human. Giles Steadford stared at the apparition, earning a grimace. "Why are you staring?"

"Forgive me, but it is still hard for me to get quite used to the fact of you," Giles explained.

"Well, don't fly into a pelter about it," Harry said. "I haven't the patience at the moment, after what you humans have put me through lately."

"What we've put *you* through?" Giles asked incredulously.

"Banging and thrashing about for weeks on end and then bringing that sad group of devilish bad ton to overrun the house. I don't know what I am to do with you," Harry complained.

"I'm afraid you've quite lost me," Giles said.

"Yes, and that seems rather too easy to do," Harry informed the young major. "I warn, you're building towards a proper Cheltenham tragedy here if you don't watch what you're about."

"I don't know what you're referring to," Giles said again.

"Don't be such a coxcomb," Harry complained. "Can't you see the girl's in love with you?"

Giles considered the Ghost's words. "Are you saying I've treated her badly?"

"Badly? Damn and blast, man, you've been a rogue and a half, and well you know it."

Sir Giles tried not to stare so obviously at the Ghost, who was now making himself comfortable on top of the nearest bedpost.

"Isn't that rather uncomfortable?" Giles asked.

"Actually, no." Sir Harry contemplated the human. "I hope you're going to make this all come out right."

"Sir Harry, I must insist that if you are going to remain at the Abbey, you refrain from interfering in my private life. I should like your word on it."

"I suppose you bloody well would, but you won't get it," Harry told Giles.

"I'm afraid I must insist most strongly," the major said even more firmly. "Or else."

"Or else what?" Sir Harry asked, curious.

Sir Giles thought about it. "I'm not really sure, but I assume there must be remedies against haunting."

"You wouldn't," Sir Harry said. "You couldn't," he added. "You'll not be rid of me until I've gotten you well and proper married. If even then," he added. "I'm not sure whether you're the end of my duties or not."

"Your duty is to see me married?" Giles asked, incredulous.

"I know, it seemed quite impossible to me, too, given your disposition."

Sir Giles digested the Ghost's words. "But, why me?"

"You're a Steadford of Steadford Abbey," Sir Harry said as if the words explained everything.

"And?" Giles prompted.

"I have a debt to pay to the bloody Steadfords of Steadford Abbey," Harry added, more glum than angry. "I must ensure you find your true loves."

"You had rather an easy job of it with me," Giles said.

"I can't see how you figure," Harry told the man plainly. "I've had an excessively difficult time getting either of you even to see me, let alone hear me, not to mention listen to me."

Giles was looking up at the Ghost with an incredulous expression. "You mean she can see you?"

"Of course. Anyone who loves a Steadford can see me."

"By my honour," Giles exclaimed. "I had no idea."

"Which is why you need my help," Harry said.

"I hardly see how. After all we've been engaged since we were children."

It was Sir Harry's turn to stare. Which he did, outright, at the human who lay in the bed below. "Engaged since you were children? Who the blue devil are you talking about?"

"I'm talking about Anne, of course. Who else?" Giles said, surprised.

"Elizabeth. The woman you're in love with."

"Elizabeth?" Giles repeated her name. "You're crazed. That's nonsense," he sputtered.

Harry gave the human a long-suffering look. "I told you it wasn't easy," he said as he faded from view.

"Wait—" Giles called out, but the Ghost was gone.

It was a very long time before Giles managed to fall asleep.

Morning brought a very contrite Anne to the breakfast table. She was all sweetness and smiles, the more so as she saw Giles's deeply preoccupied expression.

"Shall we put yesterday behind us, then, Giles?"

Giles Steadford regarded his fiancé. "Miss Wallace must be welcome at table."

"Of course, dear Giles, whatever you decide."

Giles received her words with surprise. "I must say you seem quite reconciled this morning to an idea you were quite set against last evening."

"I have had a chance to think about it," Anne told him. "I feel very strongly that as long as Miss Wallace is needed, she shall do whatever you wish, as a matter of course." She smiled prettily and was rewarded with a brief smile from the major and a quick one from her Aunt Hester across the table.

At that moment, Elizabeth Wallace herself made her appearance in the dining-room. Lady Anne kept her smile in place as Elizabeth came forwards.

"Good morning, Miss Wallace, I trust you slept well," Anne said sweetly.

Elizabeth regarded Anne from behind tired eyes. Dark smudges beneath her lashes told of her lack of rest. "Thank you," she replied quietly.

"Let me help you," Anne said, taking a plate. "The eggs are exceptionally good this morning." Lady Anne handed over the plate. "I am amazed we've never met, since I know your parents quite well."

"I've not lived with my parents since I began my training."

"So you were never brought out?" Anne asked.

"I was a little too busy," Elizabeth replied quietly.

"Anne, dear." Hester spoke as she stood up. "You don't want to sound as if you are quizzing Lady Elizabeth." She flashed a quick smile to the others. "Excuse me, I almost forgot that I meant to mention a special receipt to the cook for our dinner."

She left the three younger people behind, nodding to Lady Agatha as they crossed paths in the hall. Agatha waited at the doorway for Fannie. As she waited, she watched Hester Hartley go through the green baise door across the hall. Fannie came out the very same door a moment later.

"I take it," Agatha said, "Hester had business with the staff which she did not want to discuss with either of us."

Fannie grimaced. "She said she had a very special receipt she wanted to tell to Hetty."

Agatha replied dryly, "I'm sure she is busy spreading morning cheer in the kitchens. Come along now."

Fannie was just behind her mistress as they entered the dining-room. Seeing Lady Anne at the table, Fannie slowed.

"Good morning, Agatha, Fannie," Sir Giles said.

Agatha responded to his greeting and nodded towards the two young women. "Fannie?" she added as she moved towards the buffet and lifted the silver cover from a dish of sausages.

"Fannie, please, I've had a place set for you," Sir Giles said.

Behind Fannie the sounds of London voices came down the hall. The abigail hesitated still and looked for guidance from Lady Agatha who simply sat down at the table and began to eat. "You'll like the eggs," Agatha told Fannie after a moment.

Fannie moved forwards, picking up a plate as Lord Grantham and the others entered the room, calling out cautious greetings and discussing their imminent departures.

"We've quite overstayed our welcome, I fear," Lady Spencer told Anne. Smiling up the table at Sir Giles, Susan continued, "And I for one must press on to Kent to meet my husband and the family."

Conversation about Prinny's health and the old King's latest mental aberrations eddied about the room as Fannie sat down between Lady Agatha and Miss Wallace, eating her food quietly, ignored by the visitors.

In the kitchen Hetty Mapes was not so lucky. Rather than being ignored by Hester Hartley, the cook was regaled with instructions about Lady Anne's culinary likes and dislikes.

"Yes, but Sir Giles particularly likes his meats plain as plain," the cook told the interloper.

"He'll soon learn to like these sauces," Hester replied.

"If you're here long enough," Hetty said in a low tone.

Hester smiled wide, her plain face no prettier with the expression. "Oh, I shall be here long enough to instruct you. I make my home with Lady Anne and will continue to do so after her marriage to Sir Giles. Of course there will be many changes that will take place in this establishment then, I can assure you."

"You can count on it," Hetty Mapes replied in a dour tone.

The cook went back to her work, ignoring the presence of the town woman who began to search through the pantries.

"Should I help her find what she's looking for?" Martha asked Hetty.

"She's not requested help," Hetty pointed out. "But you might go after her and make sure she's not stealing."

"Hetty." Martha's eyes widened. "Would she do that?"

"I put nothing past the lot of them," Hetty informed her helper. "Nor will I be docked for what's gone missing while they're in and out of everything."

A worried Martha hung about the pantry door, trying to watch the woman who was picking up and examining each of the stores shelved there.

22

AN HOUR LATER, young Tim came bursting into the kitchen from the outside yard. "Hetty, they're back!"

"Keep your tongue in your head, young man, and your voice down. There's no need to shout," the cook told the young helper.

"What is all this noise about?" Hester appeared from within the pantry. "Who is back?" she questioned.

She earned a quick glance from Tim. "It's the nobs. The groom is riding up the hill now," he informed her.

"The earl is back?" Hester was thrilled. She turned on her heel, lifting her heavy black skirt a bit as she hurried along to tell Lady Anne the good news. "They've reconsidered," she was saying as she left the kitchen.

"Reconsidered what?" Tim asked the cook.

"Whether to serve Hester Hartley for dinner or feed her to the pigs," Hetty Mapes replied.

"Huh?" Tim asked, scratching the back of his head and staring at the woman.

"Never you mind, Timothy. It's best in this world to mind one's own business at times. And this is one of those times."

But the Earl of Angsley was not returning. The groom was ushered into the front parlour where he waited only a few minutes before Jack Fence came to accompany the young man up the stairs. They walked into the master's suite where Elizabeth Wallace was conducting Sir Giles's morning exercises. The young man stared at the wheeled contraption beside Sir Giles's chair.

Sir Giles regarded the youth. "You were sent with word for Miss Wallace and myself?"

"Sir, my mistress says to tell you his lordship has suffered some sort of lapse."

"What are you saying," Elizabeth asked, leaving her patient's side and taking an involuntary step towards the groom. "What's happened? An accident on the road?"

"No, Lady Elizabeth. It's more a stroke-like, my mistress says. He's calling your name, she said to tell you. All worried he seems, and she can't make him understand you're not there."

"Where is he?" Giles asked.

"We got as far as Stoneybridge last night, sir. They've put up at the public inn for overnight, but now we can't move him, the doctor says."

"I must go to him," Elizabeth told Sir Giles.

"Yes, of course. Jack?" the major called out.

"Sir?" Jack hurried back into the sitting-room.

"Go down and have the gig readied immediately for Miss Wallace." Giles continued speaking as the valet left the room. "Your parents are welcome here, Elizabeth. If your father is too unwell to travel, please don't hesitate to bring him back to the Abbey."

"Thank you." She favoured Giles with a sincere look of appreciation before she turned towards the groom. "I'll get my pelisse and be with you directly." She fled the room, running to get her wrap.

The groom watched her and then looked towards the man who sat before him, his legs uncovered to the knees, his feet in a basin of hot water. The groom's eyes drifted back to the wheeled chair which sat beside Sir Giles.

"A wonderful invention," Giles said, seeing the direction of the youth's gaze.

The groom stared into Giles's dark eyes. "If you say so, sir."

* * *

Within ten minutes Timothy was driving Elizabeth Wallace down the Abbey hill in the Abbey gig. They followed the groom's horse as he raced back to Stoneybridge Inn to tell the countess her daughter was on the way.

Elizabeth arrived in the inn yard within a few minutes of the groom. Tim shook his head, unsure why they hadn't overset the gig going so fast and furious along the rutted and icy road.

Urging young Tim ever faster, Elizabeth hadn't seemed to notice the bouncing they got. She held on to the side of the light carriage, the cold wind whipping through the hair that escaped her plain chip bonnet, and kept calling to him to hurry faster.

When they arrived, she jumped down before Tim could climb down to help her. She ran across the cold mud and patches of ice in the inn yard, racing like a young hoyden through the low doorway and into the two-storey white-washed building.

In the best front room upstairs, Honoria Wallace sat beside her ailing husband, wringing her hands. She watched the doctor minister to the earl, not hearing the quick footsteps outside until the door opened and Elizabeth came rushing through it.

"Elizabeth. At last." Her mother stood up.

Elizabeth hugged her mother and then turned towards the bed, her glance taking in her father's pale brow. "How is he, Dr. Sayles?"

"He's had quite a setback, Miss Wallace," the doctor said, eyeing her steadily. "He keeps calling for you. I understand the earl is your father."

"I shall explain about my family later, Doctor. I did not keep my birth a secret on purpose," Elizabeth told the man who had helped her career ever since she had arrived in Dorset. "It just never came up."

"As you say," Dr. Sayles answered. "We shall discuss the topic later."

Elizabeth approached her father's bedside and looked down at his closed eyes and fevered brow for a long moment before accepting the chair the doctor had brought around the bed.

She leaned towards the earl's ear. "I'm here, Papa."

The Earl of Angsley stirred in his fitful sleep. "Elizabeth?"

"I'm here."

"Elizabeth," he repeated weakly.

"Shhh . . . there's no need to talk," she said. She took his hand and squeezed it gently. "Everything is going to be all right, Papa. Just rest now."

Sounds from the doorway brought the doctor to open it wider. The innkeeper stood outside, his round and reddened face a study of worried aggravation.

"It's not my food," the innkeeper defended in a loud voice. "There's nothing wrong with my inn nor my food."

"My good man, none said there was," Dr. Sayles replied.

"That's as may be, but I don't want any to be saying that they took ill at Lewis Shumley's inn, and that's a fact. I run a good clean establishment and none can say otherwise." The man looked past the doctor to the young woman who sat beside the bed and the woman who was turned towards the doorway. "None can say otherwise," the man repeated.

"Please leave us," said the countess to the innkeeper.

Unwillingly, he let her shut the door in his face as he continued to protest his innocence.

The countess looked from her daughter to the doctor. "We cannot stay here," she said.

"Can he travel as far as the Abbey?" Elizabeth asked.

Dr. Sayles considered the alternatives. "I imagine that is the best choice we can make at this point, and the closest. The coach must travel as sedately as possible. He should not be jostled about any more than absolutely necessary."

"I understand, Doctor," Honoria said.

"Countess, you are blessed in having a daughter who is skilled in the medical arts. She will be able to ensure the earl as much comfort as possible during the journey back."

"And you, Doctor?"

"I shall come to the Abbey in the morning. If I am needed

in the night, Miss Wall—your daughter, can send for me."

Honoria Wallace, Countess of Angsley, looked towards her daughter. "I suppose the sooner we leave, the better," she said.

"Yes," the doctor agreed. "I'll go round up your men and arrange the coach."

When the doctor left the small room, Honoria came nearer the bed. "He shall hate it, going back there. When he wakes, he shall be very displeased."

"He may hate it, Mother, but he will be alive."

Honoria sighed. "Oh dear," she said, "just think what he will say when he wakes to find you nursing him."

"Mother, I don't want to contemplate the scene he shall make."

"You must forgive him, dear. He cannot help the way he is."

"Nor can I, Mama."

"More's the pity for you both," her mother pronounced as they readied the earl for his journey.

The trip back to the Abbey took the better part of two hours. The large black coach with the earl's crest emblazoned on the doors picked its slow way along the ice-flecked dirt road. Behind the earl's coach, the Abbey gig brought most of the Angsleys' belongings, the interior of the coach having been stripped of all save soft blankets and pillows for the earl.

Elizabeth sat on a small stool, holding her father steady in the coach seat. Her mother sat opposite, dozing as much as she could while they travelled.

The groom who had brought news of the earl's illness was sent ahead to let the Abbey know they were arriving and of the help they would need in taking the earl to his rooms.

At the Abbey, Lord Grantham drew Lady Anne aside in the small blue parlour. Unseen, Sir Harry lurked nearby, eavesdropping on their every word.

"Darling," he spoke softly, "I can't make heads nor tails of what I'm hearing. Is the earl on his way back to the Abbey?"

The Ghost grimaced. "As usual, I'm the last to know."

"Yes," Anne was telling Granny, "a groom came ahead to have his rooms readied."

"And he has been taken ill?" Grantham continued.

"It would seem so. The countess sent for the odious Elizabeth." Anne spoke her true feeling softly, not to be overheard.

"Odious, is she?" Harry asked the woman who could not hear him. "I'll show you odious, madam."

Anne tripped, her hand reaching out to Grantham for support. She found herself stopped in front of the large gilded hall mirror that flanked the grandfather clock.

"Now that," Harry told the young woman as she glanced in the mirror, "that is what odious looks like, Lady Anne."

"Are you feeling quite well?" Granny asked, alarmed for his own health.

"Yes. I can't imagine how I tripped." She glanced back at the floor behind them. "This entire house needs to be torn down to the ground and rebuilt."

"I'd like to see you try," Sir Harry challenged the oblivious female.

Lord Grantham was still obviously concerned about his health. "What precisely is wrong with the earl? Why is he allowing them to bring him back? He was at such pains to be gone."

"I'm not quite sure," Anne replied, "nor do I much care, unless this means he will be reconciled with his daughter and remove her from these premises. Granny? What's wrong? You look quite overset."

"He's upset," Harry put in. "Imagine what you've just done to me. She can't leave now, I haven't gotten them together yet."

"Dearest Anne," Granny said, "I've been discussing this

entire subject with William, and we feel it necessary to push off even earlier than we thought."

"How soon?" Anne asked, crestfallen at the thought of being left alone at the Abbey with her fiancé.

"Preferably before the earl arrives back."

"Good riddance," Harry said to the empty air. "Best news I've had all decade."

Anne moved quickly to intercept Grantham as he started towards the door. "I don't understand what the sudden urgency is."

Harry pulled a face. "Great Beazabub, don't encourage him to stay."

"Anne, the Influenza is deadly, and it is the only illness I know of which comes on one suddenly. The earl was in the best of health as late as last night, for God's sake. I do not wish to be ill on the morrow or dead soon thereafter."

"We don't know he's that ill, and it could be something much less dangerous," Anne said.

"It'll be enough to keep him here until I've done my duty, I promise you that," Harry said as he rose to float along just above their heads.

Granny smiled down at her. "I never was much of a gambler. In fact I abhor the sport. I don't like to lose, you see. Therefore I would rather take my chances on the road to town than in a sick household."

"And what am I to do?" Anne demanded. "Even if there is no danger to my health, I shall be trapped out here alone for the entire winter."

"Not if I can help it," Harry murmured above them. He turned over, floating on his back and disappearing into the ceiling.

"Darling, you've not been listening to your fiancé. You're going to be out here for much longer than the winter. Giles plans on spending the year 'round at the Abbey. He's said so at least a dozen times that I've heard myself. You'd best learn to like country living."

Anne's consternation slowed her stride. Her hand went

to the arm of his expensively tailored blue satin jacket. "But what is to become of us, you and I? I shall never see you."

"You will soon be bouncing babies on your lap, no doubt."

"If I don't die of the Influenza first," she retorted. "Not I, I assure you. I intend to suffer no such fate. Neither the Influenza nor the babies."

"Men expect to be graced with heirs, my dear child."

Anne watched his face carefully. "You've no wish for an heir," she reminded him. "You've said so many times over."

"As a younger son, I have no dynastic duties," Lord Grantham said. "And as a man I would rather spend my time and my competence pursuing my own pleasures whilst I am here, rather than storing up riches for a progeny who would probably deplore me in any event. I should make the most awfullest of fathers, I'll warrant. I am much too spoiled, you see. I want my mistress's undivided attentions."

"Granny—" Anne watched his eyes. "Would you marry me?"

"Anne, dear," he drawled with a wide, lazy smile, "this is so sudden."

"I am as serious as death," she told him. And waited.

"Lord, what a way in which to phrase it," Grantham replied. He looked longingly towards the stairwell. "This isn't precisely the time to discuss—"

"Bosh," Anne interrupted him. "I must have an answer now. Before you have galloped off and I am left here, miles and miles from London and everything and everyone I love."

"And what of Giles?" Granny asked.

Anne dismissed Giles with a wave of her hand. "I hardly know him, and he certainly has shown no great interest in our union. He shall honour his word," she added quickly. "He would never do less. He is a gentleman."

Lord Grantham felt the gentle sting of her words. "Are you implying I am somewhat less so?" he asked.

Anne pressed his arm seductively, her turquoise eyes regarding him through half-closed lashes. "You and I are much too close to be less than honest with each other, Granny. And we suit each other, right down to the ground."

He hesitated, thinking about it. "I've not thought of marrying anyone," he confided. "I've never seen the charm of the matrimonial state."

Anne smiled. "I can think of several," she said. "And I would be the very best wife you could find. For I already know . . . what you like."

"You are the most intemperate flirt," Lord Grantham told her. But he smiled.

Just as he was about to say more, they were interrupted by the arrival of Leticia and William, descending the stairs and calling out to them.

"Granny, Susan has sent us to find out what you have heard. She is afraid to leave her rooms."

Anne grimaced. "We were in the midst of a very important conversation," she told them both.

William stared at her. "In the middle of the hall?" he asked, aghast.

"Nevertheless," Anne persisted.

"Anne, dear," Granny interrupted her, "you'd best speak to Giles, hadn't you?" At her questioning look, he continued. "If you're leaving, that is."

"Leaving?" Leticia gauged Anne's expression.

"By Jove," William interjected, "then it is bloody dangerous around here, isn't it? What do you know that you're not telling?"

Anne laughed. "Many things. Many things, indeed."

She started past the others towards the stairs. "You look quite happy for someone who's afraid for her health," Letty remarked as Anne passed close.

Anne did not reply and Letty spoke again, this time raising her voice a bit as Anne started up the stairwell. "Is Giles joining our little party?"

"No," Anne responded, "he's quite content to rusticate forever."

Leticia turned back towards William and Granny. "Now

what can have happened here?" she asked.

Lady Anne Hartley found Sir Giles in his sitting-room, discussing the arrangements for the guest suite that would house the ill Lord Angsley.

"Giles we must speak," Anne told him. "I am very worried about the earl returning to the Abbey."

"I doubt the doctor would have allowed him to travel if it weren't the only way."

Anne shook her head. "I'm not speaking of his health, I'm speaking of ours. The rest of us." At Giles's frown she continued. "You may be willing to sacrifice your own health, but you can hardly expect others to do the same. You have no idea what is wrong with the man."

Before Giles could reply, Sir Harry appeared beside Anne. "Don't you dare tell her anything," the Ghost commanded.

Giles hesitated.

"What are you looking at?" Anne asked, glancing past her shoulder towards where Giles seemed to be staring. All she saw was an empty chair and the wall beyond.

"Nothing," Giles told her.

"Thank you very much," Harry replied.

"Well, I can't very well tell the truth," Giles told Harry.

Anne's hand went to her mouth. "I knew it, you've not been honest with us."

Giles hesitated and then spoke slowly. "Perhaps it would be best for you to protect yourself by leaving the Abbey."

"And do not think I shall hesitate," Anne told him in no uncertain terms. "I must tell you I want nothing more than to leave this countryside. I am not made of the cut of cloth that is needed to be a country wife, Giles. I'm sorry, but I must withdraw from our arrangement."

Harry grinned behind her. "You see?" he said to Giles. "I told you so."

Giles could not take his eyes from the woman who had very nearly become his wife. "I think you've made a wise decision," he told her.

"Well!" Anne's perfectly pointed chin rose in the air. "If that's all you have to say on the subject, I can see how very right I am. We do not suit in the slightest."

"I agree," he said quietly.

Anne's irritation grew. "You need not be quite so agreeable, Sir Giles. I bid you good-day," she said, sweeping from the room in high dudgeon.

"Just like a woman," Sir Harry groused. "Don't give her what she wants and she complains. Give her what she wants and she gets upset. There's no pleasing the fair sex."

Giles found himself smiling. His spirits lifted for the first time since Lady Anne had arrived. "By Jupiter, I can't imagine what I should have done if she had not changed her mind about me."

"You would only have been unhappy for the rest of your natural life. I, on the other hand, should have been doomed for the length of eternity," Sir Harry told the human.

The departures of his London guests interrupted Sir Giles's conversation with the Ghost. Giles went through the formalities of leavetaking, amused by the hurry in which the London dandies and their female travelling companions conducted their good-byes. Determined to be quickly away, they did not linger to discuss the situation but urged the few servants they had with them to work faster.

New snow was falling as the two carriages pulled away from the Abbey steps and headed towards the London road.

"They didn't even stop to ask about Lady Anne's defection," Sir Harry observed as Giles looked out the wide front window of the master's suite watching the departing coaches.

"She's probably told them of all my faults by now."

Sir Harry regarded the major. "Shouldn't you be doing your exercises?"

Giles found himself grinning. "Were you ever in the Army, Sir Harry?"

"How did you know?" Sir Harry asked. He looked pleased.

"You have a tendency to order others about," the Ghost was told. "I recognise it since I've had to fight it in myself. You would do well to follow my suit and try to curb that habit."

"I don't see why," Harry defended. "I can talk all I want, and only you and Elizabeth can hear me. Since she's used to you and you're used to the chain of command, I haven't a problem."

"I'd say you have a large one," Giles corrected.

Sir Harry, inordinately proud of his unassailable logic, frowned. "Have I overlooked something?"

"Yes," Giles told the Ghost. "You haven't managed to make Elizabeth notice I exist except as a patient."

Harry beamed. "Ah ha, then you *do* like her."

"Of course I like her," Giles said, surprising himself more than Sir Harry. He thought about what he had just said. "That is, I have always liked her."

"Ha," Harry said succinctly.

"It's true," Giles defended himself.

"When she first arrived you treated her so shabbily it's a wonderment she stayed."

The earl's arrival interrupted their conversation. As Jack, with Homer's help, brought the wheeled chair up the stairs, Giles looked towards the Ghost.

"Do you think Elizabeth will stay now?" Giles asked. "If she is reconciled with her father, may she not leave with her family?"

"She'd not leave a patient before he is well," Harry replied.

Giles looked down at his own legs. "Truth to tell, I can move them a bit now." He demonstrated what he meant, raising first one leg and then the other before looking back at the Ghost. "She might assume I can do without her."

"Then you'd best be telling her you can't," Sir Harry said flatly. "You've gotten out of the wrong engagement. Now you don't want to lose the right one, do you?"

"Sir Giles?" Jack and Homer came into the room, the Ghost fading from view.

"I'm ready," he said, helping them hand him into the wheeled chair.

"You're a bit better, sir," Jack told his master. "You can almost stand by yourself, I'll warrant." He lost his smile when he saw the major's sober expression. Unsure why this news wasn't greeted with more enthusiasm, Jack Fence kept a prudent silence.

"I want to see Elizabeth—Miss Wallace," Giles corrected himself.

"The earl's coach is just arriving, sir," Jack reported.

$=23=$

GILES STEADFORD ENLISTED his cousin Agatha's help in keeping Honoria Wallace occupied and out of her husband's sickroom.

The countess meant well, but her constant worried questions and wringing of hands cast a pall over the room which Elizabeth told her mother quite firmly was not to be permitted.

"Patients need rest and quiet," Elizabeth repeated as she thrust her mother towards the waiting Agatha.

Giles took a moment to peruse Elizabeth's tired visage. "I would say that nurses need their rest, too."

She smiled, the tiny tired lines around her mouth and eyes disappearing for a moment. "I'll try to remember."

"Will you join us for tea?" he asked.

"I'll try," she promised.

"Capital," Giles said. "We shall be telling ghost stories."

Elizabeth's tired eyes widened in surprise. "And Lady Agatha?"

Giles grinned. "Come to tea in an hour and you shall find out," he promised as Elizabeth went back to her father's bedside.

Fannie served teacakes and blackberry jam, along with Chinese teas and a special cherry brandy cordial in the sitting-room of Lady Agatha's suite.

"I thought it would be cosier up here," Agatha told Honoria Wallace and the major. "And you are just across the hall if Elizabeth needs your help." She went on to reassure the countess. "Now, what shall we talk about?"

"I vote for ghosts," Giles said smiling.

Honoria was properly dismayed by the conversational topic Giles had brought up, but her consternation was nothing next to Lady Agatha's.

"Truly, Giles, you must not talk of such things," she remonstrated.

"Even if one doesn't believe, if one thinks the subject is all suggestion and dreams, it still makes wonderful tea conversation." Giles smiled.

"Pray don't keep repeating this nonsense," Lady Agatha implored her cousin. "There's enough talk in the village as it is. Soon you'll not be able to find any left who are willing to work at the Abbey."

"But he's a friendly ghost," Giles countered.

Honoria Wallace attempted a small smile. "I realise you are trying to lift my spirits, Giles, but I cannot find even one small laugh inside me at this subject. Or any others, truly, until I know my husband is safe."

"Wouldn't you like to see a ghost?" Giles asked.

"You can't possibly believe in ghosts," the countess replied as her daughter walked into Agatha's tiny, tidy sitting-room.

"Of course not," Fannie said. "Who in their right minds would?"

"Those who have seen one, I suppose," Elizabeth answered as she gratefully accepted a cup of tea from Fannie.

"Are you serious?" her mother asked.

"You can't be serious," Fannie was saying at the same time. "You've not seen a ghost."

"But I have," Elizabeth admitted. "Lady Agatha knows."

Fannie and Honoria both turned to stare at Agatha Steadford-Smyth who looked exceedingly uncomfortable.

"These children have been funning you. There are no ghosts," she said emphatically.

"Not even ones named Henry Daniel George Aldworth, Bart.?" Giles teased.

Agatha tensed and gave Fannie a quick warning glance. Fannie looked stunned and was just barely shaking her head.

"Agatha?" Giles asked, losing his smile.

"Are you all right, Agatha?" Honoria asked. "You're not coming down with something, too, are you?" She sounded worried.

"I'm fine," Agatha replied quietly. She stood up. "I think I shall take a little nap before I change for the evening."

Giles was concerned. "I hope I did not upset you, Agatha."

"How could you not?" Fannie asked sharply.

"Fannie—don't." Agatha silenced her abigail. "If you'll excuse us."

Fannie followed Lady Agatha into the next room as Honoria looked from Giles to her daughter. "Have I missed the point here?" she asked.

"It's not our business, Mama," Elizabeth said quietly. "Let me take you to your room and get you to rest a little."

"What about your father?" Honoria asked.

"He is sleeping quite comfortably now."

"And his heart?" Sir Giles asked.

Elizabeth looked towards the major and smiled. "He seems to be over the worst of it. In fact, he seems quite well, considering." She turned back towards her mother. "I am now worried about your getting a bit of rest."

"If you will lie down, too," Honoria countered.

Elizabeth agreed to spend a quiet hour resting with her mother in Elizabeth's own room. They walked together across the hall.

Jack, seeing them leave, came to the doorway. "Would you like to go back to your rooms, sir?"

Giles nodded. As he waited for Jack to cross the room he noticed movement near the windows. Harry stood wrapped in the green brocaded drapes, looking dejected.

"I'm sorry, I didn't see you there," Giles told Harry.

"I beg your pardon, sir?" Jack answered. He glanced towards the drapes. "There must be a draft, sir. I'll check the window."

Giles stopped him. "Don't bother. The window is fine."

"Sir?"

"I want to exercise," Giles stated, with great purpose in his voice.

In the Earl of Angsley's suite all was quiet but the sound of the earl's own snoring. The drapes were drawn against the pale wintry sun and the snowflakes which flattened themselves against the windowpanes.

Sir Harry perched on the edge of a bedside chair, staring at the pale patrician face that lay against the embroidered pillowcases. Something—perhaps the sense of being watched—brought Lord Angsley awake. He blinked and blinked again as his eyes adjusted to the dim light.

Staring down at him was a shadowy form that almost floated in the air. "What—" Alexander Wallace stared at the vision. "Where am I? Honoria?"

"Keep your voice down," Harry commanded.

"You're Death," the earl whispered, his eyes widening.

"I am not," Harry said rather crossly. "Next you'll say I'm an Avenging Angel."

"Angel . . . ," Alexander repeated and he was rewarded by an astonished expression from the vision above him.

"You heard me," Harry said. "That is something to be considered. If you can hear me, you must be part of the answer." Harry's tone changed. "You must listen to me," he declaimed in his best Avenging Angel accents.

"What is it you want?" the earl finally managed to croak.

"I want to save you from Eternal Damnation," Sir Harry told the man. "You have one chance alone to make right all the wrong you've done."

"All the wrong?" Alexander Wallace tried to sit up, but the apparition hovered closer and the earl fell back against the pillows. "What wrong?"

"You must save your daughter's life," the Ghost intoned, rather pleased with how serious he sounded.

"I've tried," Alexander sputtered. "She won't listen to me."

"You must insist she marry the owner of Steadford Abbey," the Ghost told Elizabeth's father.

"What did you say? By gad, I'd rather have her marry a Red Indian than continue this gallivanting around the countryside as she has been. But she won't listen to me. She never has. She's an unnatural girl, that one, too strong by half."

Sir Harry considered the man's words. "Then you must stay here and keep her at the Abbey until she marries Sir Giles. You will never be a grandfather if you daughter does not marry the owner of the Abbey," he said in funereal tones.

"Never. She's my only child." Alexander Wallace closed his eyes. "I must be dreaming."

"You will be doomed forever," Harry promised, watching to see how well his ruse was working.

Alexander Wallace wouldn't open his eyes. "I'm dreaming," he said again.

Harry grimaced. "You humans are all alike—scared of everything. I don't know what I'm to do with the lot of you."

Alexander Wallace opened his eyes again, cautiously gazing upwards. He looked straight through Harry and saw nothing. The earl's heartbeats returned to normal. He sat up on his elbows, peering about the room to make sure he was alone, then sighed as he leaned back against the pillows. "I'm at the Abbey. They brought me back to the Abbey . . . ."

"Marry the heir . . . ." The three words echoed in the air above him.

He stared at the empty space, then closed his eyes again. He told himself he was trying to remember the shape of the apparition which had floated over him. He told himself he was not hiding from whatever it was. That whatever it was did not exist.

Still, he kept his eyes closed and soon drifted back off to sleep.

Elizabeth was leaning over her father when he awoke.

Honoria stood on the other side of the bed, watching fretfully.

"Elizabeth—"

"Yes, Father, I'm here."

"I'm not well, girl. I'm not well at all."

"You'll be fine, Father."

"No," he said, "I'm seeing things, hearing things. I tell you, I may not have long."

Honoria leaned towards her husband. "Oh, Alex, don't say that."

Alexander Wallace grasped his daughter's hand more tightly. "I don't think I can leave this place for quite a while," he said. "As much as I might want to," he added.

"Sir Giles says you may stay as long as you wish or need," Elizabeth reassured her father.

"It may be quite a while," the earl said again.

"There is nothing to worry about," she responded.

He closed his eyes. "Good. Maybe it will all work out," he said.

"All work out?" Elizabeth repeated.

"I want to talk to your mother," Alexander Wallace said.

"I'm right here, dear," Honoria told him.

Elizabeth felt her father let go of her hand. "I'll leave you your privacy," she told them, walking out of the bedroom as her mother leaned to kiss the earl's brow and tell him all was well.

== 24 ==

GILES STEADFORD CAME out of his room and started down the length of the Long Gallery. Snow still fell outside, a white blanket surrounding the ancient stone walls and drifting into crevices and cracks. The snow gave a feeling of being safely cocooned from the outside world. Held protected within sturdy castle walls.

"Giles!" Elizabeth's startled voice came from behind him.

Major Sir Giles Steadford turned. Leaning a bit heavily on a sturdy malacca cane, Sir Giles stood on his own at the opposite end of the Long Gallery.

Elizabeth stared at him as he came back towards the head of the stairs where she stood.

"I was hoping to surprise you in a few weeks by walking into a room as if there were nothing to it. You have caught me out ahead of time."

"I can't believe it," Elizabeth breathed the words.

"Isn't this what you've been working towards?" he teased.

"Yes, but—" Her eyes glowed. "Oh Giles, this is wonderful."

"I agree," he said as he stopped beside her. "This is a view I have never before had of you."

She looked up into his dark eyes, unsure of his meaning. "I beg your pardon?"

"Looking down upon your head. "I've always been looking up at you," he reminded her. He took in the thick, lustrous hair the colour of chestnuts and sable, the dark cobalt of her large eyes, the smooth porcelain of her brow. "I want to kiss you," he told her softly.

Elizabeth's breath caught in her throat. "You do?" she whispered.

"I do," he affirmed, leaning closer.

"I see," she said. Her breath was caught in her throat, making her heart stutter its beats.

Giles leaned even closer. "I wonder what we should do about this situation. . . ."

"I have been told—," she began, his face bare inches from her own.

"Yes?" he asked.

"—it is usually best—"

"Yes?" he prompted, his eyes on her lips.

"—to follow one's instincts in these matters."

And so Giles did, bracing himself against the thick oak railings as he brought her into his arms and took possession of her lips, his own heart leaping as he felt her respond. His arms wrapped more firmly around her, drawing her as close as he could.

"I must say, I've never seen quite this form of therapy before," Agatha informed them tartly. "At least not for the strengthening of weakened limbs."

Giles looked up, startled, as Elizabeth buried her face against his chest, her cheek touching the soft velvet corduroy of his waistcoat.

"I assure you, this treatment works wonders, Cousin Agatha," Giles told the older woman, his smile wide and full of love.

"I would suggest you speak to Elizabeth's father before pursuing this particular course of treatment any further."

Giles reached to tip Elizabeth's chin upwards. "Would you think me crazed if I said I think I must have loved you since the day you made me accept that blasted Bath chair?"

Elizabeth smiled. "I think old Sir Harry has been working his magic. And I think it best we get you back to that chair for a bit. You don't want to overdo."

"Are you already bossing me about?" Giles asked.

Elizabeth grinned. "Haven't I always?" She looked back

towards Agatha. "Do you think we can manage him back to his chair?"

Lady Agatha came forwards to help. "I've yet to see the man I couldn't manage."

She hesitated to leave them alone in his suite, but decided it was rather late for the normal amenities. Walking back into the hall Agatha headed down the Long Gallery, then walked, slowly, towards the rows of family portraits, stopping near where Giles and Elizabeth had stood a short while before.

Feeling rather foolish, Agatha looked towards the windows high above. She saw nothing but the white flakes piling up against the mullioned windows.

"Are you here?" she asked softly.

Sir Harry appeared near the end of the Gallery. "Aggie, can you see me?"

Fannie Burns came down the hall from the green baise door at the back of the house. "Oh, there you are. I've got together all the household accounts you said must be gone over." Fannie came closer. "What are you doing?"

"Nothing," Agatha replied.

"There are altogether too many people in this house," Sir Harry complained.

"I thought I heard you speaking to someone," Fannie said.

"Do you see anyone here to speak to?" Agatha asked.

"No."

"Then your question is answered."

Fannie thought of teasing Agatha about maybe talking to ghosties, but decided against it. Her mistress didn't seem in the mood to be teased.

"Are you ready to change for dinner?" Fannie asked instead.

"Yes." Agatha came towards her abigail. "I'm coming."

Sir Harry floated nearer. "Aggie, you can't see me yet, can you, girl?" He stopped where he was. "Or hear me," he added glumly. "Why is it the only one I want to have know I'm here doesn't even believe I exist?"

Sir Harry watched Lady Agatha walk away, following Fannie towards her bedchamber.

"It's almost your birthday, Aggie, girl," he said softly.

Fannie disappeared through the doorway but Agatha hesitated. She looked back down the hall, directly at where Harry stood, and there was a quizzical expression on her face.

"Is it you?" Agatha whispered. "Could it be you?"

As she stared down the empty hallway, she caught sight of a shimmering form near the head of the stairs. She blinked and it was gone.

"Is something wrong?" Fannie's voice came from inside the suite of rooms.

"No," Agatha said as she walked inside.

Down the hall Sir Harry was smiling happily. "She saw me," he told the empty hall. "She saw me. I know she did," he said as he danced a ghostly little jig straight through the wall. "She spoke to me, by Jupiter. Ah, but we're making progress, Aggie, my dear. We truly are! Just you wait and see."